Series by Julie Johnstone

Scottish Medieval Romance Books:

Highlanders Through Time Series
Sinful Scot, Book 1
Sexy Scot, Book 2
Seductive Scot, Book 3
Scandalous Scot, Book 4

Highlander Vows: Entangled Hearts Series
When a Laird Loves a Lady, Book 1
Wicked Highland Wishes, Book 2
Christmas in the Scot's Arms, Book 3
When a Highlander Loses His Heart, Book 4
How a Scot Surrenders to a Lady, Book 5
When a Warrior Woos a Lass, Book 6
When a Scot Gives His Heart, Book 7
When a Highlander Weds a Hellion, Book 8
How to Heal a Highland Heart, Book 9
The Heart of a Highlander, Book 10

Renegade Scots Series
Outlaw King, Book 1
Highland Defender, Book 2
Highland Avenger, Book 3

Regency Romance Books:

Scottish Scoundrels: Ensnared Hearts Series
Lady Guinevere and the Rogue with a Brogue, Book 1
Lady Lilias and the Devil in Plaid, Book 2
Lady Constantine and the Sins of Lord Kilgore, Book 3
Lady Frederica and the Scot Who Would Not, Book 4

Lady Frederica and the Scot Who Would Not

Scottish Scoundrels: Ensnared Hearts, Book 4

by
Julie Johnstone

The best way to stay in touch is to subscribe to my newsletter. Go to https://juliejohnstoneauthor.com and subscribe in the box at the top of the page that says Newsletter. If you don't hear from me once a month, please check your spam filter and set up your email to allow my messages through to you so you don't miss the opportunity to win great prizes or hear about appearances.

If you're interested in when my books go on sale, or want to be one of the first to know about my new releases, please follow me on BookBub! You'll get quick book notifications every time there's a new pre-order, book on sale, or new release. You can follow me on BookBub here: www.bookbub.com/authors/julie-johnstone

Dedication and Thanks

I know I thank my editor every single time I write a book, but this book was a beast, and without Danielle's patience and guidance this novel may have never been finished. I cannot express my gratitude enough for her skill, and I am ever thankful for our ongoing collaboration.

I also have to give thanks to Louisa Cornell who edits all things Regency for me! Louisa keeps me on my toes and makes sure none of my pesky American speak pops into my stories.

And I want to thank the ladies in my readers group aka the Wenches, who inspired me to keep going on the novel when things got really tough by simply asking when it was going to be done and telling me how much they were looking forward to reading it!

Lastly, I want to thank my mom who is always, always a constant source of encouragement. Even when I think I can't, my mom is sure that I can!

Prologue

1835
London, England

*D*oom was sitting heavy on Gabriel Beckford's shoulders. He'd awoken with it an hour or so earlier on the cot in his club, the Orcus Society. The plaguing feeling wouldn't go away, and he'd been lying there staring at the shadows dancing on the walls, trying to discern what was causing it. No luck so far. He likely should just get up and go home to his new house and his new wife, but he didn't move.

He knew why, and it shamed him that he was avoiding Georgette. Though they had been wed six months, it still didn't feel real. In a sense, it wasn't. They loved each other, yes, but as friends—the closest of friends. They had the kind of friendship, the kind of *family*, that had been forged on the dangerous streets of London as orphans. Gabe had always had his younger sister, Blythe, but Georgette and their other friend, Hawk, had no one else. The four of them had made a blood vow in the dirty, rat-infested basement of the orphanage to be one another's family.

That vow had seen them all through years of danger. That vow had kept them alive. And now that vow had been destroyed by Hawk. He had obliterated their bond with one unthinkable act.

Gabe swallowed back the disgust that came every time

he thought of Hawk forcing himself on Georgette and ravishing her. Gabe had wanted to kill Hawk when Georgette had come to him, crying, shaken, and terrified because she'd discovered a couple of months prior that she was with child. She was starting to show and didn't know what to do. Hell, he still wanted to kill Hawk, but Georgette had made him promise not to touch the bastard and begged Gabe never to tell a soul that they'd wed for anything but love. She didn't want anyone to know what Hawk had done because she didn't want her unborn child to ever know. How could Gabe go against that wish? He couldn't. Besides, he felt partly responsible for what had happened to Georgette. Hadn't he known Hawk better than anyone? Gabe should have known, should have protected Georgette.

Finally forcing himself up, Gabe tugged his shirt over his head and searched the dark office for his boots. His mind turned, and the nagging feeling that something terrible was about to happen increased while his thoughts ricocheted from that worry to the recent past. How had he not seen that Hawk was capable of such a thing? Gabe had not seen it because he'd been working during the day and fighting in matches at night to earn money to buy this club. He'd not had time to see it, and that was a failure on his part. Yet another failure to protect someone he'd vowed to take care of. It was the second largest failure of his life. The first had been when he'd failed his mother. She'd died in the dingy room they let because she'd gotten sick from having no heat or food or warm clothing. He'd failed to provide for her, and it didn't matter that he'd only been eight. That was old enough.

Gabe's jaw clenched as he shoved on his boots and made his way out of his office and through the quiet halls of his new club. He approached the door to the alley, now guarded at all hours since Hawk had taken to causing trouble for Gabe since he'd wed Georgette. Hawk had sent men to break into Gabe's club twice, once starting a fire and the other time stealing the cash on hand from the night's earnings.

Fury filled Gabe's chest. Hawk wanted to be with Georgette, and somehow the man had conveniently twisted it to be Gabe's fault that he was not, rather than placing the blame where it belonged: on Hawk's own base shoulders. Now Hawk spent his time punishing Gabe for "stealing" Georgette from him.

Being infuriated was useless. But it didn't change the fact that he was just that. Hawk had tipped over some edge of reason, and there didn't seem to be any coming back from it. Maybe it had been all the hard years on the street. God knew the things they'd endured living hand to mouth as orphans. The begging. The shame. Being looked down upon and, worse, being treated as if they were invisible. Gabe had channeled his anger into boxing, but Hawk didn't have quick feet or fists. Instead, he had channeled his anger into illegal trading. They made money in two very different ways, but Gabe hadn't judged Hawk. No, he judged all the people who had turned a blind eye to the problem of children living alone on the streets.

Gabe paused in front of Bear, whom he'd known for years now. "Did you see Blythe home personally?" Gabe asked.

He didn't truly think Hawk would ever try to harm his sister. For one thing, Hawk didn't blame Blythe for losing Georgette. He blamed Gabe. For another thing, Blythe had saved Hawk's life two years earlier, and for everything good within him that Hawk had lost, he still seemed to be upholding the street code of a life debt. Blythe had saved him, so he would never hurt her. Still, Gabe wasn't willing to risk it.

"Exactly as you asked," the man said.

Gabe clapped Bear on the shoulder. "Thank you. I'll be back. I'm going to check on the warehouse."

He normally was the last person to ensure everything was secured at the warehouse after closing every night, but he'd fallen asleep before doing so tonight. Maybe that's what was clawing at his mind. The warehouse made him a tidy profit each month and was the first thing he'd bought. He stored excess supplies for not only his club there but many of the clubs in Covent Garden paid him a fee to store theirs, as well.

Bear cocked an eyebrow. "You spend an awful lot of time here and at the warehouse for a newly wedded man."

Gabe didn't like lying to everyone, especially his sister, but he'd promised Georgette, so he just shrugged. "Georgette understands."

Bear didn't look convinced, but he nodded. "I still can hardly believe you're wed." Bear said the same thing daily and gave Gabe that same probing look. The man knew something wasn't quite right, but he wouldn't ask. "I never saw that coming."

Neither had Gabe. "It surprised us both," he said, offering the same response as always, then turned and headed out the door. He paused in his fast-paced trek to the warehouse and glanced around the quiet back street of Covent Garden, searching for anything out of the ordinary, but all he saw were dark streets and burning oil lamps.

What was bothering him tonight? He thought about the people closest to him. The list no longer included Hawk, so only Blythe and Georgette remained. He considered other men friends, but he only allowed them on the outer edges of his life. None of them knew the truth about who Gabe was. None of them knew that he and Blythe had come to London from Scotland when they were eight and seven, respectively. None of them knew his mother had brought them here to find work after his dad had died, but all she'd found was poverty and then death. None of them knew he'd once eaten thrown-out food when there was nothing else to eat. How he'd huddled with his sister on their cot in the dead of winter in the freezing orphanage with only one blanket, which he'd insisted Blythe use. How the orphanage had lost its funding three years after they'd landed there, and so Blythe, Gabe, Georgette, and Hawk had all taken to living on the streets rather than risk being split up. They'd made an abandoned building their home, and they'd all learned to beg and con, eventually each of them finding something they could do.

Gabe was good with his fists and fast on his feet. Blythe was a genius with numbers. Georgette had the sweet disposition and a face that lured people to Gabe's fights, and Hawk made sure people knew about the fights. It had been good for a time. When had it gone wrong? A year and a half ago when Gabe had bought the club?

Hawk had wanted in, but his idea for the club and Gabe's idea for it had not been the same. Gabe wanted to entertain the nobs, and then someday, he could partner with them to open even more doors—respectable doors— that would get his sister out of Covent Garden. Hawk had wanted to take all the nobs' money and ruin them for the way he'd always felt they looked down on him, on all of them. Gabe knew his worth, though. He didn't need to destroy people to feel equal to them. It had been the first breach in their friendship.

Gabe squeezed his eyes shut for a minute and inhaled a

long deep breath. His lungs burned from the cold as he tried to settle his disquiet, but it wouldn't hush. He started toward the warehouse again, slowly going through his list of responsibilities. The club was closed for the night. Bear was on guard. Blythe had been seen safely home. Georgette would be home, asleep in her room.

Her room… Hell, that was it! The babe's cradle. It had been mistakenly delivered to the warehouse, and Georgette had asked him to bring it home tonight. She'd threatened to retrieve it herself yesterday, her anxiety growing with each passing day. Not everything was ready for the babe's arrival yet, and that arrival was fast approaching.

He eyed the warehouse in the distance, then looked over his shoulder at the club. He considered going back to ask Bear to help him retrieve the giant box prior to doing his evening checks, but he decided against it. Bear needed to stay on guard. It was late, and Gabe could slide the damn thing along if he had to. His house was in spitting distance of the warehouse anyway.

He turned back toward the warehouse and noticed two figures marching toward it.

Two figures with long hair…

He squinted, certain he could not be seeing what he thought he was. But there they were—Georgette with Blythe not ten feet behind her.

"What the devil?" he bellowed, already knowing the answer. Georgette had given up on his doing what she'd asked and had decided to fetch the cradle herself. She apparently had recruited Blythe to aid her, as well.

Blythe stopped in her pursuit of Georgette and started toward Gabe, but Georgette kept striding toward the warehouse—or striding as much as a woman eight months gone with child could. It was more of a waddle.

"Georgette!" Gabe shouted as she reached the warehouse door. He heard keys jangling, and knew she must have taken his extra set out of his office at home.

"Don't you 'Georgette' me!" she shouted back at him without stopping what she was doing. "I can't sleep knowing the cradle isn't ready!"

"I planned to bring it home momentarily," he replied, rushing after her even as Blythe still came his way.

Georgette slung open the warehouse door, then turned, taking a few steps toward him. "Then hurry your arse up before—"

A *boom* blasted the calm of the night, and the ground beneath Gabe's feet began to shake. Before his mind registered what was happening, Georgette seemed to fly through the air toward him as the warehouse behind her burst into orange flames. Blythe's screams echoed around him, and Gabe's heart stopped, then started again at a full gallop. He raced toward Georgette, passing his sister along the way. Georgette was lying facedown in the street surrounded by debris and moaning.

The feeling of doom that had been with Gabe since he'd awoken dropped him to his knees beside her. He turned her over, worry snaking through him at the blood trickling from her mouth and nose. He began to scan her body for injuries, then stilled with a curse frozen in his throat. A piece of thick wood was buried deep in her chest. Her eyes were glassy, but she was mumbling something to him.

"Go get help," he called to Blythe. Then he leaned in, his body shaking violently, and said, "It's going to be all right."

She grasped him by the arm as she coughed, blood spewing from her mouth. "Remember your vow to me, Gabe," she struggled to say. "You won't kill him."

"Shh," he cooed instead of answering and cupped her face with his hand as waves of guilt and grief washed over him. Her gown was soaked in blood, and the only color on her face was the brown of the eyes that clung to his.

"Thought I loved him," she said, her voice a threadbare whisper.

Gabe frowned. "What?"

"I...thought I loved him," she repeated. "Gave myself to him because I thought I loved him."

Her words rendered him speechless.

Her hand dropped from his to the street, her breathing growing more labored. "Sorry. So sorry. Saw him kill...a man over a quarrel for money, and...knew I could never be with him again. Then...then he forced me." Her eyes fluttered shut, then opened once more and locked on Gabe. "I was scared," she whispered. "Needed protection from him...for me and the babe. Hoped one day..." She coughed up more blood. "Hoped one day maybe I could let him into the babe's life. He used to be good."

She'd lied to him. He couldn't hate her. He couldn't even be angry with her. She'd been desperate, and she'd been afraid to tell him the whole truth. Now he understood how Hawk could have twisted things in his mind and blamed Gabe, even if it still wasn't reality.

"Gabe... Gabe... I'm cold."

He gathered her to his chest and held her tightly as she began to shudder.

"Gabe... Keep your promise to me."

Her desperation sliced through him and cut into his thick hatred of Hawk, who must have done this. When her nails dug into his arm, he pulled back and met her frantic gaze. "I'll keep it," he vowed, hugging her close again. "Go in peace."

Her body gave another shudder, and a cool burst of breath wafted against his cheek. Gabe froze, afraid to look at her and equally afraid not to. He knew that whooshing sound. His mother had made that same sound. That was death, claiming its next victim. He pulled back once more and their eyes met for a brief moment before hers fluttered closed.

Behind him, footsteps thudded in rapid succession. Gabe laid Georgette on the ground, only now noticing the heat from the flames of the warehouse. He stood on weak legs and turned to see an onslaught of people coming at him from his club and the surrounding houses and businesses. Orders were being shouted, and Bear was suddenly there, along with the local doctor and three other men who hurried to take Georgette to the doctor's office. Gabe followed in a daze, moving through the stream of people dashing this way and that to try to contain the fire. Blythe appeared out of the darkness as Gabe trailed behind the men carrying Georgette's still body. She took one look at Gabe and swept her gaze back to Georgette. Her mouth slipped open, her only show of shock, and then she walked slowly toward him, put her arm around his shoulders, and they moved as one behind the men, through the thick smoke billowing from the warehouse.

Not long later, Gabe stood with Blythe at his side and watched helplessly as the doctor worked first on Georgette, pronounced her dead, and then tried and failed to save the babe. He saw the doctor talking to him, heard Blythe answer the man when Gabe failed to, but it was as if he were floating above, looking down on the scene, drowning in the guilt and rage that he couldn't contain. His throat burned with the need to bellow, and when he opened his mouth, an inhuman sound poured out of him. The grief he'd held in for years—for the loss of his father, then his mother, then Hawk as a friend, and now Georgette—burst forth, scraping his throat raw.

Near dawn, Gabe left the doctor's office and somehow made his way back to his office. He ordered everyone out of the club, but Blythe refused to go. His sister. The only other person left whose loss could cut him to the quick. It was too late to push her away, but he'd be damned before he'd let anyone else close again.

"Gabe, what are you doing?"

He couldn't recall ever having heard his sister sound so worried. "Waiting," he said, knowing deep in his bones that Hawk would come.

"For what?" Blythe whispered, kneeling suddenly and glancing up at him. "She's not coming back, Gabe. I'm sorry. I know you loved her."

He sat still, his heart thudding, his mind processing what his sister was saying. She thought he'd just lost the woman he loved. And he did love Georgette, just not as Blythe believed. He'd let her keep believing it, though. He'd not betray his promise to Georgette, even in her death. His vow was his honor, and that honor was what separated him from Hawk.

"Gabe, please." Blythe squeezed his knee. "Let me go get the vicar."

"Soon," Gabe promised. "Go now. Hawk will come, and I don't want you here when he does."

Her eyes went wide. "How do you know Hawk did this?"

"I simply know."

Hawk had known Gabe's pattern of going to the warehouse every night. He'd surely intended to kill Gabe in that explosion. Georgette should have been home, asleep. But that damn cradle…

Gabe's throat burned and tightened with her loss, the loss of her child, the knowledge that he'd failed to protect her just as he hadn't protected his mother. He grasped his sister's hand as she turned from him. She looked back at him sharply, eyebrows raised in question. "You're all I have left," he said. "I won't fail you."

Blythe's eyes filled with tears that she brushed quickly away. Beckfords did not cry. Crying was a luxury they could ill afford. "Someday, Gabe…" Her words drifted to silence, but he knew what she'd intended to say.

Someday he'd meet someone else, love someone else. He'd never found someone like that in the first place, and he didn't want to. "Have one of the men see you home," was all he said in response.

⊰ ⚜ ⊱

Gabe didn't know how long he sat there staring out the window after Blythe had left, but when the door behind him creaked open, he blinked, realizing the sun was fully in the sky.

Standing just in the doorway was Hawk, his face twisted in loathing and covered in soot. So he'd been at the fire, just as Gabe had suspected. Fury filled him as he rose from his seat.

"You killed her," Hawk said.

Gabe's mind registered the wretchedness, the broken-ness in Hawk's voice, but ice filled his heart, freezing any sparks of sympathy, even as the burning desire to kill Hawk heated his blood. But he'd made a vow, and he would only break it if Hawk tried to kill him. He moved toward Hawk and came to stop in front of him, nothing but a sliver of air between them. *"You* killed her," Gabe said. "You blew up my warehouse, thinking to kill me."

Hawk grabbed Gabe by the shirt, twisting the material into his fists. "I loved her. I loved her, and you took her from me." The veins in his forehead protruded, and his voice shook.

Gabe shoved Hawk away, sending him reeling backward toward the door and slamming him into it. Hawk slid to the ground in a half-crouched position, holding his head in his hands as if it might fall from his neck. "I loved her," he said, looking down.

Gabe stared at his old friend, rejecting the compassion that tried to come. "You *killed* her," he said. "She loved you, but you drove her away with the blackness in you. She came to me for help. I didn't take her from you; she ran from you."

Hawk jerked his head up, rose, and bellowed, "No! No! You killed her!" He kicked over the chair in front of him as he strode toward Gabe and stopped when they were a hairsbreadth apart. "I could have worked things out with her, made her understand I had to kill that man, but you, *you* intervened." His nostrils flared, and Gabe could hear the man grinding his teeth. "You took her from me and now she's dead." He stared at Gabe misery etched on his face. "She wasn't supposed to be there. *You were.*"

Hawk's jaw flexed and released, flexed and released. Gabe curled his hands into fists to keep from putting them around Hawk's neck and squeezing the life out of him. "You killed her, and you killed whatever love she held for you the day you murdered someone in front of her and then ravished her when she no longer wanted anything to do with you."

"She loved me still," Hawk insisted. "She would have

come back around. But you couldn't just let us be. You always have had to be the damned savior, the hero, the one we were all supposed to count on. You took her from me, and it's your fault she's dead."

"You're out of your head." Gabe turned away, the desire to kill Hawk so strong that he was shaking from it. He needed distance, but Hawk grabbed Gabe by the forearm. Gabe swung back toward him, their gazes clashing.

"Someday, Beck, you'll meet a lady, and you'll want to make her yours. And when you do, I'm going reappear in your life and take her from you, as you've taken Georgette from me. Then you'll suffer the rest of your life as I'm suffering." Hawk offered Gabe a twisted smile. "Brothers to the end, Beck. That's what we are. Brothers to the bloody, bitter end."

Chapter One

1839
London, England

$\mathscr{I}$t was a plain black curricle, some nondescript carriage with a pair of matching horses and two oil lamps hooked to the front to guide the way in the dark night. But the lady inside, sitting under the folding hood, let out a low whistle as she pulled the carriage close to the mews, giving it away for what it was—a curricle to a new life.

Lady Frederica Darlington sprang up from her hiding place by the trees that lined the side of her parent's now quiet and dark townhome, and dashed through the moonlit shadows toward the carriage. Yellow-orange light illuminated Blythe Beckford's face as Freddy drew near.

The woman cocked her eyebrows, swept her gaze over Freddy, and shook her head. "I should've realized a nob like you wouldn't know the proper attire for danger unless it slapped you in the arse."

A nob like her? As if she had ever been like other women of the *ton*.

"If I fit in with the *ton*, I wouldn't be here," Freddy said, taking in the men's pantaloons Blythe was wearing, which molded to her curves like kid gloves. Freddy wished she could have gotten her hands on a pair of those.

"I suppose that's true," Blythe said. "Get in." Blythe was

a savvy survivor of the most dangerous streets in London, and Freddy had learned rather quickly that women of the rookeries, where Blythe was from, didn't mince words, which suited Freddy perfectly. She was blunt herself, and no amount of being told she ought to temper her words, her tone, and her opinions by Mama, sisters, or governesses had ever changed her, much to everyone's disappointment. She was a yellow duck in a pond where all ladies were supposed to be white geese.

Freddy scrambled into the curricle and ducked under the hood to sit on the narrow bench beside Blythe—a feat made difficult by her impractical gown with its layers of silk skirts.

"What ridiculousness drove you to choose a gown for tonight?"

"The ridiculousness known as practicality," Freddy responded, not bothering to curb her sarcasm as she settled beside Blythe on the seat.

"Did I ruffle your petticoats?" Blythe said and then chuckled.

Freddy straightened up. "Not at all."

Though in truth, Blythe had managed to unknowingly find Freddy's sore spot—her confidence. It had been trodden on for years by people she loved, and some she didn't. 'Freddy you ought not to...' they'd tell her. There were so many things she naturally did that everyone said she ought not to do that to finish the sentence would take her all night. She'd tried to change, but it was impossible, and if she couldn't change herself, then she had to change where she lived. It's the only way she would ever belong. People in Covent Garden seemed to actually appreciate independent, unusual natures like hers, so that's where she would live.

"Explain yourself," Blythe said.

"I used to 'borrow' my brother Huntley's trousers." Freddy shoved her skirts out of her way as she attempted to find a comfortable position. "But he's moved out, and that left only the male servants, and it's impossible to 'borrow' any of their clothing."

"Why?" Blythe demanded, as if she could not for the life of her imagine anything she wished to do being impossible. Of course, she couldn't. She'd grown up with freedom, unlike Freddy.

"It's not as easy as you might think to sneak into a servant's room and take his trousers."

Blythe snorted. "Nobs are so very unresourceful." She waved a hand at her pantaloons. "I pilfered these from one of my brother's errand boys. Dorian is twelve summers and thin as a piece of parchment."

"I've told you at least a hundred times before that I am not a nob," Freddy said with a grimace.

"You're wearing silk on a mission into Covent Garden in the middle of the night to help a Cyprian flee her monstrous benefactor. That makes you a nob, even if you are a rather odd one." Blythe clicked her tongue and set the horses into motion. "And a rather naive one, too. There's great danger in Covent Garden. And you—" Blythe shook her head. "You intend to leave your cosseted world for mine?" She paused a moment, likely to make her point. "You won't survive a day."

"I've survived six months working secret missions with you," Freddy pointed out, feeling rather smug about how well she'd gotten along in the rookery aiding Blythe in helping women who wished to escape prostitution. And with that thought, Freddy yanked the hood of her cloak up to shield her face from view. Though few people were out this time of night in Mayfair, she still needed to be careful. When she left this life, it would cause a scandal, but she couldn't leave until she could take care of herself and her elder sister Vivian was good and wed. She'd promised not to ruin Viv's chance at securing the match she wished to make.

Blythe maneuvered the curricle around a hole in the road before saying, "You're awfully confident for someone who's spent all her life in the bosom of safety and luxury."

"I'm confident," Freddy said, patting Blythe's arm, "because I have procured such an excellent teacher."

"I don't know how I let you talk me into this hare-brained bargain. You don't even behave like a proper lady ought to."

"You know I know how, though!" Freddy said, indignant. "It just doesn't come naturally to me. And I did not talk you into it! I was the one that pointed out to you my own lack of proper decorum! Then you fairly drooled like a dog when I told you my idea."

"Don't call me a dog."

"Oh, for heaven's sake. I did not mean it literally. I think you lovely and you know it." Blythe had a flawless complexion and flaming-red hair. She was truly exquisite. "I would not have made the offer to teach you to be a lady otherwise."

"I assumed you offered because we would both get something from the bargain."

"Well, of course, that's why I made it. But my world is different from yours." Freddy sighed. "See, it's like this. You can teach me how to be savvy on the streets and how to be a bookkeeper so I can be dutifully employed and have means to live, and then I should be able to get along in Covent Garden, yes?"

Blythe gave her a sideways glace of mirth. "I think it'll be bumpier than that for you, but yes, you should be able to survive."

Freddy grinned. "Well, in my world, while I can teach you to be a lady—and they will likely overlook your being a commoner, since you can bring a large dowry to a marriage—they would never give you a passing glance if you were not pretty, no matter how much of a 'lady' we make you into. Personally, I like you the way you are. I cannot see why you wish to wed a lord, anyway."

"And I can't see why you wish to flee your comfortable life in Mayfair for one in Covent Garden," Blythe replied. "Nor do I understand why you wore silk instead of a serviceable gown, at the very least. You can't be haughty and survive in *my* world."

"I'm offended," Freddy said, jerking her gown from under her bottom and finally becoming comfortable. "I'm far from haughty, and you know it."

"Humph."

"I hate when you do that."

"Do what?" Blythe asked, sounding all innocent.

"Humph me. I hate it when you humph me."

"Humphing is a way of life in Covent Garden, *nobbie*, so you might as well become accustomed to it."

"Duly noted," Freddy said, though the exchange caused a brief moment of panic. What if she secured her future in Covent Garden only to find she didn't fit in there, either?

Dash the thought. She shoved it away.

"Vivian surprised me by returning to the bedchamber before I could change into a serviceable gown. I had to jump under my coverlet in the gown I'd worn to supper, slippers and all. I was sure Viv would notice, but she didn't. She was so busy droning on about the man she wishes to wed—Lord Asterly—that she was oblivious to the large lump my slippers made under my coverlet."

"What does your sister coming into your bedchamber have to do with your being unable to change?" Blythe asked as she steered the carriage toward Covent Garden.

"We share a bedchamber, first of all. And second—" Freddy paused to grab the railing on the side of the carriage as they hit a bump. "—Ever since Viv decided she's in love with Lord Perfectly Boring, she's become quite the nuisance."

"How?"

"She's now a strict rule follower, whereas before she followed them only loosely. She even threatened to tell our parents if I didn't cease my *improper* behavior—her words not mine—until after she's good and wed. She made me vow it. She says a scandal surrounding me would taint her unfairly, and Lord Asterly's family has their noses turned up so high, I'm surprised the lot of them don't drown when it rains."

Freddy's stomach tightened, thinking upon her sister while shadowy trees and rows of townhomes blurred by. Vivian's attitude was just the latest in a string of changes. Her eldest sister, Guinevere, had wed and now had children, and her dear friends Lilias and Constantine had also wed and started families. Those four had tolerated Freddy's differences more than anyone, though she knew well that her boisterousness and bluntness embarrassed them sometimes. Yet, when they had started their secret society, the Society of Ladies Against Rogues, it had seemed Freddy might have found a small place in her world where she belonged. But SLAR was all but defunct now, the other women too busy for missions, leaving Freddy alone and lonely. They had all changed, though each of them had suited the *ton* much better than Freddy ever had hope to.

"Your sister said that nose thing about the family of the man she wants to wed?" Blythe asked, breaking the silence.

"No, I said that part. Anyway, if I'd tried to put on a sensible gown, Vivian would have questioned why I was doing so and then tattled on me. I didn't dare attempt to change after she fell asleep for fear of waking her up."

Blythe nodded. "Did you have a chance to look at the reports I gave you?" she asked, changing the subject as the carriage rattled over a bridge.

"Oh, yes, I finished them. There's a shortage in the rent column by thirty-five pounds, and your brother really needs to find a better supplier of whisky. The one he currently uses is swindling him. I did some research, and he's paying precisely twenty-five pounds too much a month."

"I know," Blythe said, her tone heavy with humor.

"You know?" Freddy frowned. "Whyever did you give me that report to look over if you already knew your brother was being fleeced? That took me several hours!"

"Is that all?"

The strangest feeling blossomed in Freddy at the amazement in Blythe's voice. It took her a moment to puzzle out what the fullness in her chest was—pride. She was proud that Blythe was amazed at her mathematical abilities, and if she did say so herself, her detection skills were not bad at all, either. She realized, sitting there in the carriage as they bumped down the road, she'd never truly felt accomplished. Awkward, yes. Accomplished, no.

Freddy had to suck in her lips to keep from grinning like an idiot. "I'm fairly good with numbers, as I mentioned." Actually, she could see numbers and how they worked together clearly and easily in her head, but she suspected Blythe might think she was boasting if she said so. "Why did you give me those reports to look through if you already knew that?"

"Don't be thickskulled. It was a test to see if you're ready to take over my job at the Orcus Society."

A thrill shot through Freddy at the thought of being gainfully employed at the well-known gaming club. "Did you speak with your brother, then?"

"No, not yet. I was too busy ensuring he'd be occupied tonight so we could aid Belle without his knowing. If Gabe finds out about our work helping Cyprians, he'll put a stop to it. He hovers over me and frets over my safety worse than any mother."

"I doubt that," Freddy said, thinking of her own over-bearing mother.

"Tonight actually worked out perfectly. Gabe has challenged Lord Brooke to a fight after he heard news that Brooke had beaten Belle, so *both* men will be occupied."

"That does work out nicely," Freddy murmured, fighting her disappointment that Blythe hadn't spoken to her brother yet on Freddy's behalf. There'd be no job there if Mr. Beckford did not approve. He was half owner of the club, and though Guinevere was wed to his silent partner, the Duke of Carrington, Mr. Beckford made the decisions about whom to hire. Guinevere had told Freddy as much when she'd inquired rather slyly about it after Blythe had proposed Freddy assume the role of bookkeeper so that Blythe could concentrate on learning to act like a lady.

Freddy had to get Mr. Beckford on her side, because she feared Guinevere would try to stop her from leaving the *ton* by persuading Carrington to tell Mr. Beckford not to offer Freddy employment. Guinevere seemed to care more than she used to about causing scandal now that she had her own children.

"I'll speak to him," Blythe said, her tone reassuring. "I had to make certain you could do the job after just a month of instruction. If you didn't notice and question why the figure for whisky was so high, then you didn't possess the sense to be a bookkeeper. The job is more than just being good with numbers. It's curiosity, an ability to puzzle things out, and you can't be afraid to face Gabe."

"I'm not afraid of your brother," Freddy said. A recollection of the man she'd met under most unusual circumstances popped into her head. Mr. Beckford may have been known as the King of the Underworld, a title that she suspected he had claimed to instill fear in his competitors, but he had compassion.

"Really?" Blythe sounded amazed. "Most people are."

"I'm not most people." She wasn't trying to be smug; it was the simple truth. She was different, to the consternation of almost everyone she knew. She didn't possess an appropriate amount of fear, according to Mama, but Freddy didn't think she needed to fear Mr. Beckford. She'd seen the compassion in his eyes when they'd met six months ago and he'd been staring down at her after she'd awoken in a strange place, then asked her if she was all right. He hadn't known her at all, but he'd been concerned. She'd heard it in his voice again when he'd promised her that he'd find the men who had knocked her in the head, stolen her carriage, and left her on the street in the rookery for all sorts of terrible things to happen to her.

He'd been angry. Of course, some of his anger had been directed at her. He'd lectured her on coming to the rookery on a mission and told her she had no business there, even after she'd explained to him about SLAR. That, in fact, seemed to vex him more.

"That's true enough," Blythe said. "I grant you're rather

unique, but don't assume that you know my brother. You met him face-to-face only once, and watching him a few times in the cellar boxing ring of the Orcus Society does not mean you know him. You didn't even speak to him those other times, and he didn't know you were there."

Freddy narrowed her eyes. "What are you trying to tell me?"

"He'll drill you if you raise a suspicion, such as someone swindling him."

"I would think he should, so as not to falsely accuse someone."

"I've seen him make a grown man piss his trousers when Gabe was quizzing him."

And Freddy had seen Blythe's brother knock a man flat on his back with a single, dizzyingly fast, well-placed punch. In fact, she'd seen him knock three men on their backs with a single hit. One to the eye, one to the jaw, and the other to the nose. She'd been in the cellar of the Orcus Society on three occasions now. Each time Blythe had sneaked her down there and disguised her, she'd said it was for lessons on rookery men. One about pickpockets, one about gamblers, and one about men who imbibed too much.

What Freddy had really learned, though, was that she loved to watch Blythe's brother fight. He moved with the grace of a swan, but he fought like a wolf. She remembered staring at him and studying him. He was fascinating. His eyes narrowed in concentration when he fought, his square jaw tensed, and the muscles of his arms coiled. And he had a habit of smirking as he playfully waved his opponents toward him, then smashed his fists into their faces. He was a man of contradictions. He clearly enjoyed fighting, as if it were a game, but he also fought to win as if it were life or death.

Freddy touched the locket she always wore, the one that had been ripped off her neck the night she'd met Mr. Beckford. He'd ensured her locket had been returned to her, but he'd not sent a single word or note of friendly correspondence. Of course, he hadn't. The man had likely never given her a passing thought after sending the locket to her. After all, she didn't lure men to her. She chased them away with her unladylike behavior, as Mama had long told her. A pox on men. Who needed one, anyway?

Yet, she would have possibly thought a man such as Mr. Beckford, born and bred on the savage streets of London, might have been different, might have been more tolerant of a unique sort of woman. Not that she cared. She did not. Still, she did wonder what sort of woman a man like Mr. Beckford was drawn to. For knowledge's sake alone, of course. A woman could never be too knowledgeable. So she asked, "Why has your brother never wed?"

"Holy hell. Don't tell me you're soft on my brother."

Heat seared Freddy's cheeks. She was not soft on him. She didn't want a man. She'd dismissed the notion she would ever find one who appreciated who she was after her disastrous first Season. Men fled her. She'd been labeled Frightful Frederica, for heaven's sake. But instead of speaking of things that pained her, she said, "Don't say *hell*. It's considered vulgar. And according to those in the *ton*, a lady is never vulgar."

"That's ridiculous," Blythe said.

"Yes," Freddy agreed, "but it's the world you want to join."

"I said *piss* not long ago, and you didn't remark on that."

Freddy pursed her lips. "I meant to."

"But you got distracted by thoughts of my brother."

Blythe's tone was one part mocking and another part surly.

"Not on him, specifically," Freddy lied, embarrassed and appalled to realize she had.

"I thought you said you didn't have any interest in love or marrying," Blythe accused. "I'd have never agreed to this bargain if I thought you might get all moony over Gabe."

"I don't, and I'm not. Enough talk of me. Why do you wish to wed a lord?"

They had entered Covent Garden. Oil lamps illuminated the streets, and music and merry laughter seemed to float on the breeze, no doubt from one of the many taverns or brothels. Blythe sighed as she turned down Broad Street, where Belle lived in the house Lord Brooke kept her.

Blythe stopped the curricle in front of the largest townhome on the street and said, "Because. The only way for Gabe to be accepted into Society is if one of us marries into Society."

"He wants that?" Freddy asked, disappointed. She would not have imagined Mr. Beckford the sort of man to care whether the *ton* opened their doors to him or not.

"No," Blythe said. "He doesn't care. I do. I want him to be welcomed into fancy homes with stiff-lipped servants and make deals with gentlemen who would never hold a pistol to his head or blow up a warehouse they thought him in. And since he won't ever wed again, not even to secure a less dangerous future, I will."

Before Freddy could respond, Blythe jumped down from the curricle, the Hessians she was wearing smacking into a puddle and sending water splashing up around the boots. It took Freddy longer to descend with her cumbersome skirts, and by the time she was standing face-to-face with Blythe, the woman was shaking her head.

"I'll secure you some breeches for next time," she said.

"If we need to run, you're going to be in trouble."

Freddy nodded, but her mind was still on what Blythe had said about the pistol and the warehouse. "Did those things really happen to your brother?"

"Yes." Blythe secured the horses and turned to her. "You ready? I can't say how long the fight will last, so we need to hurry."

Blythe started to take a step toward the large, looming house, but Freddy put a hand to her elbow.

Blythe turned back, her large eyes seeming even bigger in the night. "Second thoughts?"

"No. Of course not." She was here because Belle had insisted Freddy was the only one she truly trusted. Belle wanted to leave Lord Brooke because he was cruel, but she did not want to leave this way of life, no matter how much Freddy had tried to persuade her to do so.

"You gonna stand and stare at me all night, or are you gonna tell me why you grabbed me?" Blythe asked.

"Why won't your brother ever wed again?"

"Why do you care?" Blythe narrowed her eyes.

Freddy didn't know, but the question had popped into her head and she'd asked it. It was one of the things Mama despised most about her. "Because it seems to me you should not have to sacrifice yourself."

"Maybe I don't consider it a sacrifice." Freddy opened her mouth to ask about that, but Blythe put up a hand to silence her. "I'm not going to stand here on the street and spill the secrets of my heart to you, Freddy. So don't ask again. And as for Gabe, well, he was wed before to Georgette, whom we grew up in the orphanage with. She died, and he still loves her desperately."

Freddy plucked at a loose thread at the cuff of her gown while trying to keep the question bubbling to the surface of her mind silenced, but it burst out anyway. "What was Georgette like?" Freddy wanted to pinch herself when Blythe's gaze narrowed further.

"Forget him, Freddy."

This time heat swept Freddy's whole body. "I never said—"

"You didn't have to," Blythe interrupted. "Most women fawn over Gabe and fall all over themselves to get him to notice them, and he's never paid one of them a passing glance. And it's been four years since Georgette's death. He lives like a damned priest. And to answer your previous question, she was reserved, delicate, and sweet."

All the things Freddy wasn't. She did try to be nice, but her blunt speech often made her seem unthinking. An unbidden memory of Blythe's brother came to her. His speech had slipped to a rough burr when he'd vowed to find who had stolen her carriage. "You know, I noted that your brother sounded as if he had a slight Scot's accent the night he aided me when my carriage was stolen…"

Blythe's eyes grew impossibly wide, and Freddy watched as the normally unflappable woman's jaw slipped open. "Did it now? Well that's a bit of shocking news. I've not heard that Scot's burr from Gabe in years. He mostly buried it the day he buried our mama. He only ever let it out around Georgette and me, but when she died, it was as if a part of him—the part that let people really know him—died, too. I've not heard his burr since then."

"How did he come to have a burr at all, though?" Freddy asked, curious.

Blythe made an impatient sound, but then took a deep breath, and said, "We came from Scotland. Our parents were Scots, and when our da died, our mama brought us here to find work, but she died not long after. Gabe had a heavier accent than me. I suppose because he was a year older."

"Well that explains why you have an accent and why your brother represses it, but why do you?"

"Gabe trained me to speak in cultured English tones. He said the life he had planned for me required it, and honestly, my burr just seemed to fade more and more with the years." Blythe grinned. "I do slip from time to time, eh?"

Freddy nodded, distracted by the memory of Mr. Beckford's burr. It had tightened her stomach, but it was his calloused fingers gently threading into her hair as he'd checked her skull for bumps or cracks left by the ruffians that had unfurled a heat between her thighs and left her aching. He hadn't seemed offended by her personality. Then again, he hadn't been around her for very long.

Still, she had thought, possibly, by the sort of burning look in his eyes and the way he'd touched her, that he might desire her. It had been fairly thrilling, given the way he looked, and she was fairly certain she'd never inspired desire in a man before. In fact, it had been so thrilling that she had thought of him since—and not as a proper lady of the *ton* should. She had wondered if he would be the sort of man who would be willing to ease her ache and introduce her to passion, but clearly the mutual desire had been in her imagination. Pity that. Just because she didn't need a husband didn't mean she never wanted to experience carnal pleasure.

Blythe pointed a finger in Freddy's face. "I recognize that lustful look."

Freddy blanched, and Blythe snorted, then said, "Forget him, Freddy. There's no competing with the ghost of Georgette. Now, come on." Her clipped tone and rapidly departing figure left no room to argue or question. They were just to the door of the townhome, Freddy raising her hand to knock, when the door flung open. Belle stumbled out and collided with Freddy. They went down hard, in a tangle of arms and legs, and Belle reacted like a cat faced with the prospect of being dipped in water.

She went wild, clawing at Freddy in an effort to scramble off her. She yowled so loudly that Freddy clenched her teeth as she growled at the woman to calm down, a plea that mingled with Blythe's barked order for the woman to "cease her bawling." Between Freddy pushing at the woman's shoulders and Blythe grabbing the woman's arms, they managed to get her off Freddy, but it was just in time to see what had made the woman run out the door in terror. A giant man raced toward them with a bleeding forehead and rage in his eyes.

Chapter Two

Gabe danced around his opponent in the boxing ring, drawing out the fight with that conceited arse Lord Brooke. The patrons of Gabe's club, who'd wagered on the fight, pressed closer as he delivered another hit to Brooke's face—a nice, powerful right hook that sent the man reeling. The cheers erupted around them, making the damp air in the cellar of the Orcus Society a degree warmer with all the hot breath blowing out simultaneously.

Deep, rowdy voices vibrated Gabe's eardrum, and after a moment, the merriness of the crowed morphed to jeering. Men didn't much tolerate losers, and that's what Brooke was at this moment, whether he was one of the richest nobs in London or not.

For one breath, Gabe considered ending the fight now and getting back upstairs to the gaming rooms. He liked to oversee things most nights, but when Brooke finally managed to come fully upright and glared as if he wanted to kill Gabe, he knew the man wasn't properly remorseful yet for hitting Belle. Thankfully, Gabe had every confidence in the men who worked for him to watch things upstairs in his stead, so he had time to ensure this bastard never laid hands on a woman again in Covent Garden.

Brooke swiped the back of his hand across his face, smearing a red streak of blood over skin so pale it reminded Gabe of fish flesh, then he came at Gabe like any man would who'd foolishly let his anger take control of his head. Unthinking, he charged straight at Gabe, damn fists not raised high enough to protect Brooke's long, aristocratic nose. Gabe took advantage. He shot out his arm and broke Brooke's nose for him. Bone crunched, and the man's eyes widened at the same moment the vessels burst and a river of red poured from his nostrils.

Gabe grabbed the man by his expensive linen shirt, no longer spotless white, and yanked him close. "I heard you hit Belle in Lovelett Theatre last night. Cracked her lip."

"She deserved it," Brooke said, trying to shove away, but Gabe gripped the man tighter, thinking of his own mother now. If she'd not died on that filthy cot in the dirty room they'd lived in long ago, she might have become desperate enough to sell her body like Belle, to put up with a so-called benefactor who hit her.

A hush had fallen over the cellar, and the even breathing of twenty men waiting to hear what would be said next hissed in the room. "No woman deserves to be hit, Brooke. And when you're in Covent Garden, you're in the place I call home. If I ever hear you've hit a woman in my home again, I'll find you, even if I have to come to Mayfair to do so. And you won't be able to use your arms and legs when I'm done with you."

"Mr. Beckford! Mr. Beckford!" came the screech of a woman.

The high-pitched sound of frantic terror cut across the room with the precision of a bullet and pierced Gabe's singular attention. He jerked his gaze to the stairs while shoving Brooke away from him. A woman wound her way down the stairs, and when she came fully into view, Gabe recognized Belle Whitehall by her long hair the color of a moonbeam. The men parted to let her pass as she moved off the last step, then paused, her hand coming to her disheveled hair before it fluttered to her face. Her cheeks turned red as she stood there, alternately patting at her hair and tugging at her dress, which was torn at the front to partially expose her breast and right shoulder, which had a dark purplish-yellow bruise on it. She had a fresh cut on her lip and wild eyes. Whatever had happened to her had only just occurred, and since Brooke had been in the ring with him, he knew it wasn't the man directly, but he wouldn't put it past Brooke to have given orders to deal with Belle.

Gabe started toward her in long strides, but he wasn't halfway to her when she screamed. He glanced over his shoulder to find Brooke fast approaching behind him. Belle's fearful sobs filled the silence and made Gabe's jaw clench in reaction to her distress. He stepped toward the man and delivered a punch straight to his jaw that knocked him down and out.

Gabe let out a shrill whistle. Immediately, Lark and Norris, two of the club guardsmen, materialized. He pointed at Brooke. "Detain him until I return."

He didn't wait to ensure they obeyed his command. He didn't need to. He didn't trust many men, but the ones he did, he trusted implicitly to follow his orders. He had his hand on the railing of the stairwell before he remembered he'd taken off his shirt before the fight. He turned, and a patron was holding it out to him. "Nice work, Beckford."

"Thanks," he replied, taking the shirt and turning back toward the stairs to find Belle gone.

He wasn't overly worried she'd flee into the night. Bear manned the only entrance into and out of this club, and Bear may have allowed her entrance, but he wouldn't let her out given the state she was in. His doorman had a protective nature longer than the Thames River, which was one of the main reasons Gabe had hired him in the first place.

He pounded up the stairs as he yanked on his shirt and set himself into a semblance of order, but he slowed as he turned the handle of the door to the gaming hell. The noise of the club, as well as the light from the chandeliers, washed over him. He stepped into the hall that contained only two men engaged in what appeared to be a serious conversation, and Gabe tipped his head to them as a swish of red skirts at the end of the hall caught his eye. That had to be Belle. She'd had red on.

"Beckford!" one of the men cried. Gabe frowned, irritated not to immediately be able to put a name to the face of a man who apparently knew him and more than slightly annoyed that he was going to be detained for a moment. There were a few rules he lived by that he would swear had helped him rise from homeless street orphan to a man who owned three clubs and a stake in a shipping empire, and the first rule, the main rule, was to treat every person he met as if they were important, because they were. People mattered. He could recall the burn of shame he'd once felt when dismissed by others just as clearly as he could recall the taste of the scone he'd eaten for breakfast that morning.

"I apologize," Gabe said, casting a glance over his shoulder in the direction Belle had been headed. He faced the man who now stood before him. He was tall, nearly eye to eye with Gabe, and though Gabe was sure he didn't know the man, something about him did strike him as familiar. "I was departing, but I'd love to—"

"Meet me?" the man said with a friendly chuckle. "My eldest sister Guinevere is wed to your partner, Carrington. I think I may have been the last in the family to know the duke was in business with you."

"Yes," Gabe said, his mind touching briefly on the fact that Carrington had recently decided to tell Guinevere's whole family of their partnership. He also knew that Carrington intended to let it out to the *ton* as general knowledge soon. His old friend had said that in staying a silent partner, he was supporting the ridiculous idea that men of Society should not work to earn a living. Gabe agreed.

He had to find Belle, and yet, he lingered for a moment, thinking of Lady Frederica, whom he'd worked hard to forget. And that was after only one face-to-face meeting with the unusual chit. He pushed the ridiculous impulse aside. He couldn't stop himself from dreaming about her, but he could damn well stop himself from asking how she was and if she'd been getting up to anymore trouble. It was none of his concern. *She* was not his concern. "Pleasure to meet you, Lord Huntley."

"Huntley will do. You must call on me sometime."

"At Mayfair?" Gabe blurted out like a fool. He wasn't a blurter—ever. What the devil was wrong with him?

Huntley's brows dipped together. "No, I don't live there anymore. I'm on Clairbourne Street. Have you been to my parents' home with Carrington?"

"No." He'd been there because he'd followed Lady Frederica the night he'd met her, but he couldn't say that. Nor could he reveal that his attraction to Huntley's sister had been instantaneous and ferocious. It had, in fact, unsettled him. He couldn't ever let a woman close, and it wasn't just the vow Hawk had made four years earlier that stopped Gabe. It was Gabe himself. Letting people too close brought pain when you lost them, and he damn sure didn't need to see a chit home who'd managed to intrigue him after one brief encounter. So instead, he'd had his coachman do so. But he'd no more than returned to his own home, where Blythe had cared for the lady's injuries, when the nagging need to ensure she had made it home safely had begun. And try as he might to ignore it, it had grown until it was all he could think about.

It was just a habit to keep people safe, nothing more. And after his talk with her about not returning to the rookery, he'd been left with a hefty dose of doubt that she'd heed him. She was headstrong, that one. He could see it in the set of her jaw, the tilt of her chin, and the determination in her eyes. So he'd gone to the address he'd overheard her give his coachman, and he'd watched her house. Not just that one night, either. Oh no. He'd been there a dozen times. One had to be thorough, or so he'd told himself, until he finally admitted he was lusting after a chit he had no business lusting after.

"I believe Carrington mentioned in passing that your family lives there," Gabe said.

"Ah. Well—"

"I really have somewhere I need to be. I am sorry."

"Yes, yes." A nod came from the man. "Don't let me hold you up."

Gabe offered a smile, then strode toward the back-alley entrance, relieved to see Bear standing in front of the door at the end of the shadowy hall, arms crossed over his broad chest, and looking down at Belle, who stood before him. Her pleading to leave the club floated to him as he closed the distance between them. The woman was frantic to flee Brooke and to persuade Bear to return with her to the townhome Brooke provided for her.

"Bear won't leave his post," Gabe said, interrupting her. She sounded like she was getting wound up for a long story.

She swiveled toward him, swaying as if she might fall,

and Gabe caught her by the elbow to steady her but quickly released her when she flinched. That had been unthinking. He knew not to touch a woman who'd suffered abuse at the hands of a man. His first experience with that had been Georgette, but there'd been many abused women since, unfortunately, that he'd tried to aid.

Gabe took in Belle's injuries. A busted lip was the least of them. She was missing a tooth and another was chipped. "Did Brooke do this earlier or last night?" He motioned to her face.

"Some last night and some right before he left to fight you. He said this is what would h-h-happen if I ever tried to leave him."

The desire to return to Brooke and treat him with the courtesy the man had treated Belle curled Gabe's hands into fists. "Were you planning on leaving him?"

"Yes, and he got word. Your sister came to help me," the woman said, tears filling her eyes.

"My sister?" Inside, it felt as if all his muscles had coiled into a tight ball. "Where's Blythe?" He was simultaneously proud of his sister's huge heart and angry at her impetuous nature. He'd told her time and again not to take risks.

"That's what I was trying to tell him," Belle said, pointing at Bear. "Your sister and Lady Frederica are at Brooke's townhome."

He frowned. "Lady Frederica?" Her image came to him. She was a plucky, tiny thing with a mass of unruly chestnut hair that slipped confining pins to curl about her slender neck and animated face. Her skin made him want to lick it to see if she tasted as creamy as her milky complexion hinted she would. Her eyes blazed with far too much confidence. The woman didn't know she was a vase—a priceless, Song dynasty one. Some lord with gentle manners and a soft touch needed to wed her—or purchase her, as it went in the upper classes. That lord needed to keep her on a high shelf in his study under lock and key where she wouldn't be at risk of being shattered by the harsh world in which she so obviously thought she could handily survive.

"What are they doing there?" Gabe asked. As the woman's lower lip began to tremble, fear unfurled in his chest. He'd been his sister's protector since he was old enough to remember. She was the only person he allowed soft feelings for because he'd been too young when they'd started to stop them, to know better. "Why are you here?"

"To...to fetch you. The men Brooke set to guard me dragged us all back in and locked us in a room, they said, for Brooke to deal with, b-but then one of the guards, Marco, came alone to the room and said, he...he wanted to see what a real lady was l-l-like under all her silk and f-finery. Your s-sister and Lady F-Frederica charged him, but he knocked Blythe out and dr-dragged Lady Frederica out of the room kicking and screaming. He forgot to lock the door again behind him, and when I couldn't wake Blythe, I climbed out the window in the study on the first floor 'cause I couldn't get out the front door. The other guard was standing in front of it, and I had to be quiet as a mouse so he didn't take note of me and stop me."

Gabe had known rage before. His temples had pounded with it on many occasions when his sister had been threatened, or he had, or someone he considered under his protection had. The rage of being treated lesser than simply because he'd been born a bastard had made his heart hammer in his chest until it had ached. The rage of being so poor there was no food to eat had seared his veins and clawed its way up his throat, leaving it raw and aching. But now all the different variations of the same emotion combined to sweep through him like a violent storm.

His gaze locked with Bear's. "Keep her here. Keep her safe. I'll be back soon to help her and deal with Brooke."

Bear arched his brows. "You goin' alone?"

"You said two men?" Gabe directed the question at Belle.

"Yes," she said, wringing her hands. "They're Brooke's personal guards."

"Not a problem," Gabe said, already heading out the door into the cold, dark night with his mind on what he was going to do when he arrived at the townhome and what he'd do to the man if he'd violated Lady Frederica. He'd kill him. That's what he'd do. Those actions made the man a pig, and pigs went to the slaughter.

Chapter Three

Of all the ways to receive her first kiss, being forced into enduring a man's unwanted attentions so she could secure his weapon and protect herself from him had never occurred to Freddy. As the man Marco's mouth smothered hers in a revolting kiss, her stomach roiled and threatened to do much more than that, but Freddy swallowed back her disgust. She almost had a grip on the dagger she'd seen at the man's hip when he'd dragged her into the bedchamber and then chased her round and round the bed.

Her fingertips brushed the hilt, but then he gripped her hair and yanked her head back, taking the dagger out of her reach. The jackanapes! If he would just release her head, she could wind her hands around his waist, then slide them to his hips, secure the dagger, and maybe she'd plunge it into his black heart. She wasn't sure if she could do it, but the desire to do so scalded her throat and made her pulse beat frantically.

The sting caused by her hair being tugged tight by the stocky man's beefy fingers relented at the same time the villain pulled his wet mouth off hers. He grinned, displaying perfect teeth, except for a single space in the front where one was missing. "How'd you like that, Mayfair?"

She'd realized right away from his scornful tone that this man's pride undoubtedly had been wounded by a proper lady in the past. It didn't matter that she wasn't the one who'd inflicted the injury. He wanted her to pay the price. "I suppose it wasn't as terrible as I thought it would be," she said. She was having a hard time feigning enthusiasm, even though doing so might be the thing to save her innocence. She'd never been any good at hiding how she really felt.

He scowled at her. "I guess I'll just have to do it again. This time open your mouth so I can slide my tongue in there."

She'd rather cut out her eyes with Papa's dull letter opener, but she managed to keep that statement to herself. Instead, she gave a nod, and then said, "Maybe if you slid your arms around me instead of pulling my head so tightly it hurts." The suggestion made her shudder inwardly, but she was able to control her disgust enough that he didn't appear to notice. Of course, that could have been because he was staring at her chest, where he'd managed to rip open her gown. Goose bumps covered the tops of her breasts, and she could feel each and every one of them.

His answer was to jerk her to him so that she let out an *oof*. But before his sloppy mouth settled over hers again, she slipped her arms around his waist, despite the fact that it made her skin crawl. Having his hands anywhere else on her would be far worse. When he tensed, she forced herself to make a sound of pleasure, which if he had any sense, he'd realize was an act. Lucky for her, the man proved what she'd long suspected: women were of far superior intelligence to men or, at the very least, they all seemed to be rendered idiots when confronted with a pair of breasts.

She moved her hands toward the dagger, wrapped her fingers around the leathered hilt, then slipped it out as she held her breath in fear of discovery. Her heart pounded a painful rhythm in her ears, and she began to shake, but she turned her head sideways, breaking contact with his mouth, and brought the point of the dagger to his side.

"I'll shove it all the way in if you do not release me right now." Her voice trembled just as much as her body did.

His surprised gaze met hers. "Well, well," he said, his sickly sweet breath washing over her face. "Aren't you surprising?"

"Yes, it's a fault I'm told," she managed through clenched teeth. "Now back up." When he didn't move, she pushed the tip of the dagger into his side a bit harder, which made her feel queasy but produced the reaction she'd hoped it would.

He scuttled backward, palms up and facing her. "There now, Mayfair. Let's not make this rough."

Her spine curled at his meaning. "Move back more," she said, shaking so hard now that the knife in her grip visibly quivered. The man's eyes went to the dagger, then back to her.

"You've never held a knife," he said, smirking.

She hadn't, blast her mother, father, and brother. They'd all acted as if she'd mortally sinned when she'd suggested she wished to learn how to defend herself. "I'll manage," she replied, taking a step toward the open bedchamber door, toward escape. When he advanced instead of staying where she'd told him to, her stomach hollowed, then vines of pricking terror spread like a weed from her stomach through her veins to her limbs. She wasn't sure she could move, but she had to.

"Come any closer to me, and I *will* stab you." She took another four steps toward the door.

It was one or perhaps two steps to the hall, then what? Even if she managed to flee the bedchamber, she had to escape the house, and there was another man here somewhere, or at least she assumed he was still here. She hadn't seen anyone since Marco had dragged her to this room. And what of Blythe and Belle? Freddy's thoughts tripped over themselves.

Think, Freddy, think.

Her only hope was to stab him or hit him with something. She cast her gaze sideways toward the bird statue on the table near the door. It looked heavy and—

"I wager I can reach you before you ever reach that statue," Marco taunted.

Freddy didn't think; she lunged. Marco slammed into her just as her fingers grasped the statue. They both flew to the right of the door, landing hard upon the floor. Before she knew what was happening, he was straddling her, his heavy weight crushing her stomach and hips as his thighs locked her in place. He twisted her hand clutching the dagger so that he came away holding it.

Damn, damn, damn. She swung the statue at his face, but he knocked it out of her hands. It smacked against the ground, several pieces splintering off, one of which caught Freddy on the cheek, slicing her skin in a stinging slash.

"I don't like women who lie," Marco said, bringing the dagger to just under Freddy's chin.

Her heart sounded like clopping boots in her ears, so much so that she almost believed someone was coming for her. She looked toward the open door, but no one was there. She frowned at the loudness of the thumping that was making her imagine things.

"You're too pretty to cut." Marco grasped her chin and forced her face toward his as the clopping continued. "I guess I'll just have to show you what happens to Mayfair snobs who visit Covent Garden."

The clopping suddenly stopped, and just as Freddy cut

her eyes to the door, a deep, dark voice filled with the promise of violence spoke. "Get off her now, and I'll let you live." A pair of shiny black Hessians appeared in her line of vision, and her heart leaped.

Marco tensed on top of her. "Beckford. I—"

"There's another man in the house!" Freddy called out, wanting to warn Mr. Beckford.

"Already dealt with," Blythe's brother said, without looking at her. His gaze bore steady into Marco. "I'll give you to the count of two," Mr. Beckford said as Freddy really took in his appearance. In the shimmering light of the bedchamber, his features appeared harsh. His square jawline was shadowed by stubble, and his full lips formed a challenging smirk. His blue eyes held a lethal glare, and the slash of a brow was raised almost in the hint of a taunt. "One. Two."

Had she blinked she would have missed the astonishing speed with which Mr. Beckford moved. He hovered over her and Marco in one motion, and in the other, he yanked the man up and off her as if he were lifting a pesky bug off the ground.

Blythe's brother moved with predatory grace and flung Marco against the wall. The thud of Marco's head resounded in the room for a moment, and the man looked dazed as he brought his head to a stop, but as soon as he did, Mr. Beckford delivered a blow straight to the man's nose that cracked bone and brought a stream of blood gushing forth. Before Marco had recovered from that, Mr. Beckford said, "Why don't you show me what it is you intended to do to the lady?"

The way he put the question made Freddy's breath catch deep in her lungs. She'd never seen a man so enraged on her behalf. It didn't frighten her, not one bit. It thrilled her. She swept her gaze over his solid form that looked as if it could not possibly be stopped by any human force. He was controlled power, and when he wanted to, he could destroy with hardly much effort.

"She's a snooty—"

Mr. Beckford's fist blurred through the air—once, twice, three times. Each hit gave a resounding smack. Marco's lip split. The skin of his cheekbone, too. "She's a what?" Beckford paused, circling his prey without ever moving from where he now held the man against the door.

"She...she..." Marco tried, his voice nasally as blood flowed from his nose. "She's a lady to be treated with respect."

"Aye," Mr. Beckford said, that slight Scottish burr she had recalled from the night she'd met him coming out. A flutter went through her as she scrambled to her feet, and he frowned fiercely.

"Belle is a lady, too," she snapped at Marco, "and you turned a blind eye when Brooke hit her."

"Brooke is my employer!" the man cried out.

"That's no excuse," Mr. Beckford said, his English once again perfect as was the delivery of another blow. This one was to the gut, and Marco doubled over. Freddy came to stand by Mr. Beckford, the power of the man giving her a new set of chills that tightened her belly. The intensity of his gaze landing on her made her mouth slip open. Before she could even shut it, he'd turned his attention back to Marco.

Freddy followed his lead and stared at the back of Marco's head, as the man was still doubled over, hands on his thighs, and blood splattering the ground and his boots.

"If you ever set foot in Covent Garden again, what I've done to you now will seem like mercy." Mr. Beckford's statement would have frozen the Thames with the chill of its delivery. "Now get out and collect your friend. He's at the bottom of the stairs."

As Marco straightened and his gaze fell on Freddy, a burning anger consumed her. It wasn't until her hand connected with Marco's cheek, sending a sting across her flesh that she even realized she'd slapped him, but once she got over the momentary shock of what she'd done, she did it once more. "In case you were wondering," she said, chest heaving, "you made my skin crawl."

Freddy tensed when Marco opened his mouth as if to speak, but Mr. Beckford said, "If you want to keep your life, you will shut your mouth and depart directly."

The man's beady eyes widened, and he turned to the door without hesitation and strode out of the room.

Freddy inhaled a long breath, and then once she could see Marco no more, she let it out in a shudder, her legs suddenly buckling. Mr. Beckford caught her, slipping one arm against her back and the other under her legs. He silently swooped her off her feet and held her to his chest. It was like being pressed against a wall, a warm one that had a heart hammering in it. She looked up at him to thank him and found his attention focused on where Marco had departed. She frowned, seeing no one there, but then the distinct tap of someone walking came to her. She tensed, but the hand curled under her legs gave her a gentle squeeze. "It's just Blythe. I heard her banging on the bedchamber down the hall on my way to find you, and unlocked the door, but told her to stay put until she was certain it was safe."

"You took your time finishing him," Blythe's voice suddenly filled the room as she appeared in the doorway. "What's this? Is she injured?"

"Are either of you?" Mr. Beckford asked, sweeping his

gaze over his sister and then turning the full intensity of his stare upon Freddy. Every time he looked at her that way her heart did the strangest flip in response.

Was she hurt? No, she wasn't hurt. Irate to have a kiss forced upon her from such a loathsome creature, furious that she had not been able to properly defend herself, but not hurt.

"No," she finally said.

Blythe's brows dipped together. "If she's not hurt, why are you carrying her?" The question was directed at Mr. Beckford.

"Her legs gave out. I imagine," he said, staring at her, "that you were frightened."

She didn't want to be frightened. In fact, she refused to be. She shoved the feelings down. "No, I'm more furious that I didn't know how to defend myself than anything."

"Well you ought to be frightened." Irritation laced his words. "You ought to be more than frightened," he continued. "If you had any sense and knew what was good for you, you would be a quivering mess. If I'd not come in when I did, that man would of—Well, he would have—"

"I know," she interrupted, knowing precisely what he was having trouble getting out. "Which is why I need to learn to properly defend myself."

"Defend yourself?" He gave her an incredulous look. "What the devil are you even doing here?" He growled the question more than asked it.

"There's no need to be rude," Freddy snapped.

"Rude?" He growled at her again.

"Yes, rude. Put me down." Her newfound irritation with him pushed away any fear that had lingered.

He did as she asked at once, then glared down at her. "Didn't I tell you not to return after last time you got yourself into trouble here?"

She set her hands on her hips and met his glare with one of her own. "You did. But lucky for me, I'm not obligated to listen to you. Your sister and I are helping women, and we have a deal."

A groan came from Blythe, and it occurred to Freddy that she'd just revealed what they were doing. But he'd riled up her temper! She gave Blythe an apologetic look, to which Blythe simply shook her head.

"You," Mr. Beckford said, pointing at Blythe, "have a great deal of explaining to do, and you will do it when I return. For now, I want you to go back to the club and see to Belle's needs."

"Do you always order people about like this?" Freddy demanded, incensed that he was bossing Blythe around.

"Yes, yes, he does," Blythe responded, looking at her brother. "Where are you going while you send me back to the club?"

"I'll be taking this one home," he said, not even bothering to look at Freddy. He simply hitched his thumb back toward her.

"My *name* is Freddy." She glared at his shoulder and tried not to snip, though she did feel rather like he needed a good bite in the arse. "In case you've forgotten."

He swung around to face her so quickly she gasped. He didn't say a word for a moment, but he didn't need to. His anger heated the space between them. She might as well have been standing outside with her face turned up to the bright sun. His gaze practically burned her, and it took a great force of will not to look away.

"I know your name, Lady Frederica Darlington," he said, his words rough. His voice had dropped low and seemed to rumble from somewhere deep in his very broad chest. "And I know where you live in Mayfair."

Her eyes widened at that pronouncement, and then her mind, fueled by her lusty imagination, imagined him imagining her, until she recalled that she'd given his coachman her address the night she'd been accosted. Mr. Beckford must have overheard it. Drat, she was the biggest of fools.

"And I know," he continued, leaning his body toward hers, consuming every last speck of space between them so that they were almost—yes, by God—almost close enough to brush noses, "you don't belong here."

That hurt more than she would ever let this arrogant man see. "I most certainly do!" she protested, and that incredulous look he'd given her moments before reappeared.

"You do not," he said, each word clipped. "You belong in Mayfair in your redbrick townhome with its twenty-six windows facing the nice, clean, safe, peaceful street and its high brick wall to keep out the likes of me."

"How do you know how many windows my parents' townhome has?" she asked, feeling rather breathless.

"I make it my business to know such things, Lady Frederica." He drew out her name so that it sounded as if he were chiding her. "That is why I belong here, and you don't. Now come along." He grasped her arm and tried to pull her toward the door, but she dug in her heels.

He could have easily moved her had he wished. She knew that from seeing the power he had unleashed on Marco without seeming to expend much energy in the doing. But he faced her once more, a strained look upon his handsome face. "Either you can accompany me out of this townhome willingly or I'll carry you over my shoulder. The choice is yours."

"I'll leave because I have to return home, *not* because you are ordering me to do so. I will be back to Covent Garden," she said. "I intend to live here."

"You wouldn't survive the night." He turned on his heel and stormed out the door.

Freddy stood there a moment, staring at his broad back and watching his long, sturdy legs carry him away. Beside her, Blythe said, "We better follow. Gabe's hot under the cravat."

"He wasn't wearing a cravat," Freddy murmured. She blinked, surprised to realize she'd noticed such a thing about him and surprised by what else she could recall about Mr. Beckford. He had, in fact, been in his dress shirt, which was loose at his neck to show a patch of tanned skin. The shirt had been partially tucked, as if he'd thrown it on in a hurry.

Blythe clicked her tongue and hooked her arm through Freddy's. "It's an expression."

Freddy could feel Blythe staring at her, so she turned to look at her and found Blythe's gaze full of surprising concern. "Are you all right?" It was almost a whispered question, as if Blythe feared the answer.

"I'm fine. Why do you ask?"

Blythe's gaze wandered downward so Freddy glanced down, remembering then that her dress had been rent open at the bodice and the tops of her breasts, scandalously near the edge of her underclothing, were exposed. She tugged the material together as her face heated yet again.

"I shouldn't have agreed to this bargain," Blythe said with a shake of her head. "Gabe's right. You don't belong here."

Freddy swallowed the large lump that suddenly formed in her throat. If she didn't belong here, and she didn't belong in Mayfair, where did she belong? Nowhere? She refused that idea.

"I do belong here," she protested. "Maybe not perfectly yet, but I'm learning. Please," she said, when she saw the wary look on Blythe's face. "Don't abandon our agreement."

"Gabe will never give you my job as bookkeeper." Blythe sounded sorrowful and as if she'd already made up her mind to relent to her brother's demands. "I'm sorry, Freddy. I don't know why he's reacted the way he has to you being here. I suppose it's because he's protective of women in general, and maybe he senses a vulnerability in you."

"Your brother cannot stop me from coming to Covent Garden," Freddy said, and when Blythe looked at her as if she'd said the most foolish thing in the world, Freddy had to clench her teeth to keep from screaming. When she got herself under control, she said, "It's not as if he owns Covent Garden."

Blythe arched her eyebrows. "What he says goes here. And that's a good thing, Freddy. The people here respect him, and they count on him. He deals with men like Marco when they threaten women, and he provides a lot of jobs."

"That may be, but he does *not* own this place. If I want to come here and live here, I will."

"You can try," Blythe said, "but I doubt you'll get very far."

"He cannot be everywhere at once. Why, he didn't even know I had been here before!"

"True enough," Blythe said, "but now that he knows you've been here, putting yourself at risk, he'll have people watching out for you. And I promise you that if you set foot in Covent Garden, someone will send you right back to Mayfair."

"What of our deal? What of your wish to become a lady?"

Blythe cocked her head. "Are you telling me that you'll not help me if I cannot help you?"

Drat. No, she wouldn't tell Blythe that. She wasn't so selfish. "No, no, of course not. But I'm going to prove to you I can get past your brother and make a life for myself here."

Blythe snorted.

"In the meantime," Freddy continued, ignoring Blythe's doubtful look, "if I don't appear at the appointed time tomorrow at the theatre where we were to meet, come to my home at Mayfair. We'll just have to continue our lessons there if it comes to that."

"Blythe!"

The booming voice of Mr. Beckford made Freddy jump.

Blythe rolled her eyes but tugged Freddy toward the door. "Come on." They started down the hall together, but at the top of the stairs, when Mr. Beckford came into view, already standing at the foot of the stairs, Blythe added, "It may hit you later what's happened tonight. If it does, have a nip of whisky. It helps to calm the nerves."

Freddy didn't think she could manage that without her father knowing, so rather than admitting that defeat, she said, "I want to learn to defend myself. Maybe your brother will teach me that if he's so concerned about the safety of women."

Blythe was still laughing when she left Freddy standing by Mr. Beckford, and the woman departed for the club as she'd been commanded.

Chapter Four

He didn't like sitting so close to her in the carriage. It stirred the desire he'd tried so hard to subdue. Lady Frederica was not the sort of woman one could bed and then bid farewell. She was a proper lady, whether she wanted to act like one or not. He had no room in his life for proper ladies and the entanglements that came with them, and he never would.

He tried to turn his mind to the club, but that made him think directly about Belle and Brooke, which circled him smack around to the enticing lady sitting across from him. He didn't steal a look at her, though he wanted to in a bad way. The image of her creamy skin, the top little peaks of her chest exposed by that bastard Marco, was now seared in Gabe's brain. Likely forever. Damn it.

The lust he was trying to ignore was screaming at him. It didn't help that every time he took a breath, he got a lungful of her spicy scent. He would not think on it. He opened the carriage window, wishing he'd sat with his coachman instead of in here, but she'd practically been ravished not long ago, and though she acted fine, had said she was, he knew well enough from Georgette and Blythe that women often said they were fine even when they weren't.

Still, the decision to sit in this small space with her hadn't been a wise one. He shifted his position, keeping his gaze on the passing streets, but it didn't matter that he wasn't looking at her. He could feel her stare from the seat across from him, and even with the window open, he still smelled her. And damn it, she smelled good—some sort of mixture of cinnamon and clove, cedarwood and musk. It made him curious if she smelled like that everywhere, and he had no business being curious if this lady, an innocent, who had traipsed around Covent Garden in the middle of the night wearing a silk gown, smelled of cinnamon under her unmentionables.

He couldn't believe she'd called herself Freddy. She was not a Freddy. A Freddy would be streetwise and dressed in breeches as Blythe had been. A Freddy would have damn well known not to—What the hell had they been doing anyway? She'd said she and Blythe were helping women. What women? Cyprians? Had to be.

Don't look at her. Don't ask her. Get your answers from Blythe.

His head turned toward Lady Frederica by some force beyond his control. She arched her eyebrows challengingly, as if she were tough, yet he noted she had her arms wrapped around her midriff as if she were holding herself together. Her loveliness struck him just as it had the night he'd met her and made him feel as if something was wrong with his chest. "Are you cold?" He wasn't sure she'd admit it even if she was.

But she nodded. "Yes."

"Shall I shut the window?"

She shook her head. "I need the fresh air," she said, but her shaking voice contradicted her words. Yet, maybe she was feeling ill now from her experience with Marco.

He frowned. "I don't have my coat or I'd offer it to you."

She gave a strained smile. "That's quite all right." Her voice trembled even more now. "I don't know what's wrong with me. I'm suddenly freezing."

"Let me close the window," he said again.

"No." The word was sharp. "I need the fresh air. I think—" She paused and glanced down at her chest, and he watched as she tried to tug the gaping material of her gown together. "I think it's my gown being torn." Her voice was low and sounded—Ah God, it sounded like she was on the verge of tears.

In one fluid movement, he shifted from his seat into the one she occupied.

"What are you doing?" Her eyes widened as he slipped his arm over her shoulder to draw her to his side and to his heat.

Excellent question. Why the hell had he moved over here? Honor. Honor and possibly a bit of that desire he needed to kill for her. "Warming you." He clutched her close so that the top of her silky head came just under his chin.

Good God, but her hair smelled better than hair had the right to smell. Like sunshine and grass. Fresh. Pure.

"This is really quite improper," she said, but she didn't make a move to extract herself from his embrace, and she was still trembling.

"I won't tell if you won't," he said, striving for lightness, but inside him, the rage at Marco had awoken once more. He'd let the man go far too easily.

She shivered even harder. "I don't know what's wrong with me."

Of course, she didn't. She came from a protected existence and had danced in light of danger. "You've had a shock, and your body is trying to adjust."

She nodded. "I felt fine before. It's just when we got in the carriage, and it was quiet for a moment, images started coming to me of...of...*him*."

Her body tensed under his arm, and his anger roiled through him like a flame.

"I never imagined," she said, her voice near a whisper, "my first kiss would be like that."

"Did you imagine your first kiss a great deal?"

Why the devil had he asked that?

She tilted her head up and to the left, her long, dark lashes fanning her cheeks. A dimple showed with her half-embarrassed smile. "Perhaps once or twice. My friend Lilias, the Duchess of Greybourne—"

"I know Greybourne and his duchess," he interrupted, disliking how much he liked her voice. It flowed like honey, sweet and warm, and it made his mouth water just listening to her speak.

"Yes, of course." She gave a throaty chuckle, nothing like the titters of most women of the *ton*. He liked it. He liked it too damned much. "She had a penchant for Gothic romances," Lady Frederica continued, "and she gave them to me when she was finished with them. And well, you see... I—That is, what I'm trying to say is—"

"The romances made you dream of kissing," he supplied, wanting to end her obvious embarrassment.

"Yes," she said, and then, "I cannot believe I told you that."

He couldn't, either, and now he had a vision of kissing that small expanse of enticing flesh that had been revealed by her torn gown. It was reprehensible, given what she'd been through, and yet, it was there because she was so damned appealing and honest. "Sometimes it's easier to tell a stranger a secret."

"Have you found that personally?" she asked.

"Me? No. I tell no one my secrets. But people often seem to tell me theirs."

"Oh." Her brow dipped in disappointment. "So, mine is one of many secrets you've heard."

"One of many, but one I'll likely not forget."

"I'm glad my secret's so memorable," she said with a self-deprecating laugh.

If she only knew how memorable he found her, she'd be shocked. Even now, his desire was presenting a problem. In fact, the sooner he moved out of her proximity, the better. "Are you warmer now?" he asked.

"Oh yes, thank you. Oddly, the only thing still cold is my mouth." A bemused expression came to her face as she tentatively licked her plump lips.

Good God, the woman may be an innocent, but she was a siren, if ever one existed. His blood moved through his veins in a hot, rushing wave. He envisioned himself hooking a finger under her chin, turning her face fully to his, tilting it up, and claiming her mouth to wipe away the rancid memory of her first kiss. He located the control he'd used to survive on the streets, and he gripped it in his mental fists.

"I hope I don't recall that kiss tonight," she said, suddenly angling toward him so that their faces were only a fraction apart. She pressed her fingers to her lips as a severe frown marred her pretty features. "Do you think I will?" She shivered then and rubbed at her arms, then darted a look at him. "I'm sorry." She gave her head a little shake as she moved her fingertips from her lips to her temples. "I'm uncertain why I'm talking of this now. I had thought I put it behind me. I had thought to take you to task for your highhandedness with me in Covent Garden."

"Had you?" He was now the bemused one. And when was the last time a woman had made him feel bemused? Never, that was when.

She nodded. "You can't keep me from going there."

"I can." It wasn't a boast; it was just a fact.

She frowned at him, even as she shivered again. He took her hands in his, brought them to his mouth, and blew on them.

"Oh. That feels lovely," she said, "but you ought not do that."

"You are undoubtedly correct. Shall I stop?"

Just as a small smile tugged at her lips, she sucked them inward as if attempting not to show her mirth. She partially succeeded, except that those dimples appeared in her cheeks. He'd not known dimples could be erotic, but hers kindled his lust to a full flame.

"Not just yet," she replied, her eyes meeting his, and the look there...

Well, that look of desire being awakened was more than a man could withstand.

"I can ensure Marco's kiss is not the one you'll remember tonight." His senses had taken full leave of his head, but he'd find them again when the carriage stopped. This was for her.

This is noble.

That was likely stretching it, but he was in no mood to analyze his intentions.

"And how can you ensure that?" she asked.

By God, if a woman could purr, Lady Frederica just had. His mouth curved into a teasing smirk. "By kissing you, of course. Are you certain you're an innocent?" She flirted like an experienced Cyprian.

She arched her brows. "Are you certain you're skilled

enough to make me forget that man's kiss?"

"I'll let you be the judge of that," he replied, sliding his hands into the heavy, silken hair that tumbled around her shoulders.

As his fingers delved through her tresses to cradle her head, she let out a little sigh of pleasure that made him hard for her. He was no green boy, but his body was responding as if he were. Her eyelashes fluttered downward to veil her eyes just as he ever so gently brushed his lips over hers. She tensed, as he'd expected having just been through what she had, so he pulled back a fraction. "If you want me to stop—"

"No." The huskiness of her voice reaffirmed the claim. "Do go on." The words were followed by her small hands coming to rest on his thighs. It was nothing, and it was everything. It drove a hunger for her straight through him.

That wasn't the plan. The plan was one kiss. One slow, thoughtful kiss to help her forget, and then he would forget her. He traced his tongue over the soft crease of her mouth, and when she relaxed fully against him, he nudged her lips open with his tongue.

Fire and honey met him, and that hunger she'd inspired deepened so that when she tentatively touched her tongue to his, then released a little mewling sound of pleasure, he forgot himself completely. He covered her mouth with his, wanting to devour her softness and to take her taste inside him. Her hands moved upward and inward along his thighs, and his body hardened further in response to her touch.

He brought his own hands from her head to her shoulders, the need to have her closer eating at him. As he tugged her near, she slid her hands to his waist to pull him toward her, as well. Her soft chest crushed against him, and the carnal need to possess her was unleashed. He broke the kiss to plant more of them on the long, slender column of her neck. She threw her head back for him, moaning, and her sound of pleasure made it hard for him to remember what it was he'd intended. All he could think was how he wanted to slip his tongue into the rip of her gown and lick her skin. He bent his head to do just that when the carriage came to a halt and reality came crashing down around him.

He set her up in the seat, shocked to realize he'd leaned her back during the kiss. He drank in her eyes, heavy lidded with desire, and the pink flush of her cheeks, the redness of her lips, and her disheveled gown.

Good lord! He yanked it as far closed as it would go as the coachman knocked on the door. "We've arrived, and the house is dark," Mr. Hanover said.

A relieved look skittered across Lady Frederica's face.

"Excellent," Gabe replied, trying and failing to quit staring at her as his mind struggled to absorb the effect she'd had on him. He had nearly lost control with her. Never, never once had he done such a thing with a woman.

"We'll be just a moment," he managed, his mind reeling. How the devil had he gone from being intent on merely seeing her safely home to kissing her senseless? He scrubbed a hand over his face, feeling her watching him.

"Yes, sir," Mr. Hanover replied. The coachman's boots tapped against the road, and then quiet fell.

Gabe cleared his throat, trying to think where the hell to begin. Best to start with the most important thing, and it wasn't the bloody kiss. The kiss was regrettable, though it had been the best damn kiss of his life. That was actually regrettable, as well. "Listen, Fre—Lady Frederica," he corrected.

"Freddy." She gave him a pointed look.

"You are not a Freddy. You are a gentle-bred lady, not a woman born to the streets. That's a Freddy. *You* are a

Frederica."

"I'm a Freddy, no matter where I was born. Just ask anyone who knows me. You are not the first person to wish me otherwise." She shrugged, but it seemed forced to him, as if it hid a world of hurt. "God simply made me different, and you'll have to take it up with Him if you have a problem with that."

He shoved a hand through his hair. She was going to be difficult. And incorrigible, and it ought not to make him want to grin, but damned if it did, so he scowled as hard as he could. "Lady Fr—"

"I must insist you call me Freddy."

"No." If he relented to seeing her as she wanted to be seen, she'd be in the bloody rookery every night, risking herself each time she came.

"You just kissed me senseless, but you won't call me Freddy?"

She had a right to sound exasperated. The kiss was tragic in that he'd initiated it, and his gut told him it was going to be damned hard to forget it. What had he been thinking? Oh, wait, he hadn't.

"The kiss was to help you forget," he said. "Nothing more."

"It certainly felt like more when your tongue traced my—"

"Enough." Good Christ, the woman didn't know the tether of control to which he was clinging. What he wanted—what he *really* wanted—was to lay her back, toss up her skirts, and introduce her to real passion. That would not, could not, happen. "Listen, Lady Frederica, there can be no more trips for you to Covent Garden. You don't belong there." He hated the hurt look that crossed her face, and he hated that his words had caused it, but they needed to be said. She needed to understand for her own safety and for him to stay as he was—detached.

Her brows dipped together in obvious consternation. "You don't know me or where I belong."

"I know Covent Garden, and it's dangerous."

"Maybe I want to live a risky life."

"Then you're a fool. Be glad for the pampered life you were born into, and stay out of Covent Garden. No more SLAR missions."

Her eyes widened at that.

"Oh yes," he said, feeling smug, "I know the abbreviation for the little society you're in. No more nighttime jaunts into my territory for SLAR, nor do I want you meeting my sister to aid women there. If those women need help, I'll aid them."

"You cannot be everywhere at once, Mr. Beckford."

"Call me Gabe." They had kissed each other senseless, after all.

"Oh, I think not." She glared at him. "Gabe doesn't fit you in my opinion."

"Are you trying to be difficult?"

"Not at all." She crossed her arms over her chest. "Gabe is short for Gabriel, yes?"

"Yes." Hearing his given name on her lips made him feel a twinge of unexpected longing. No one had called him Gabriel since his mother had died.

"Well, Mr. Beckford, Gabriel is the name of an archangel, and I think you and I both know you're no angel."

"That's true, but you're being snippy because I refused to call you Freddy."

"Perhaps, but I won't call you Gabe *or* Gabriel if you won't call me Freddy."

"Then call me Beckford."

"Then you will at least call me Frederica and drop the 'lady.' I hardly fit that mold."

He didn't like that she sounded like someone had made her feel bad about that, but he clenched his teeth on commenting. It was not his concern. Instead, he gave a nod of agreement, to which she smiled, and that smile warmed a spot in his chest that he'd forgotten existed. He frowned.

"When shall I call you Beckford?" she asked in an overly sweet voice. "When I see you in Covent Garden?"

The little minx. She was batting her eyelashes at him.

"No. You won't be seeing me there. So when we pass on the street, I suppose, if it ever occurs. Or perhaps I'll see you at the home of your sister or the Duke and Duchess of Greybourne." They were friends, after all.

"I intend to live in Covent Garden," she said, "so you will see me there."

"Was this your harebrained idea or my sister's?"

"Mine," she said. "And it is not harebrained."

"Exactly how do you plan to support yourself? I presume your parents are unaware of the future you're plotting for yourself."

"My parents are no concern of yours, and as a matter of fact, I was hoping you'd give me a position as a bookkeeper."

"A bookkeeper?" He couldn't have heard her correctly.

"Yes, your sister taught me, and she says I'm quite a natural."

He was going to wring Blythe's neck. How this woman had talked Blythe into doing such a thing, he didn't know, but he intended to find out from his sister. Too much conversation with Frederica was not a good idea. Something that felt suspiciously like admiration had lodged in his chest since the start of this exchange, and he didn't want to feel that or anything else for her. "There's no way I'll give you a position as bookkeeper or anything else." She opened her mouth, and he could see the protest balanced on her lovely lips. "No means no, Frederica. I'm not a man to change my mind. Ever."

"*Ever* is a very long time."

She hitched one perfect eyebrow. Quite a feat that was. He refused to be bemused by how lovely she looked with her eyebrow raised. Instead he said, "I'm steadfast in my decisions, if nothing else."

"Well—" she unfolded her arms and stared at him "—I don't imagine you are the only potential employer in Covent Garden."

"You'll not find employment so don't come down there. Now out you go. I don't want to see you again."

That was a bloody lie.

"You don't own Covent Garden." Her voice rose to a very unladylike bellow, which he found amusing, but he kept his face perfectly neutral. The woman had a temper. He wished he could say he didn't like that, but he did. And he would ignore that he did.

"No," he said with a calm that was not natural in her presence, "I don't own it. But you won't get anywhere there without my permission, and you won't be getting that." And since it was past time to send her on her way, he turned, opened the door, exited the carriage, and then offered his hand to help her down.

She smacked his hand away and shoved past him. "I don't require your aid, nor will I ever be in need of it again."

"I certainly hope not," he replied to her back as she walked away from him and toward her house.

He lingered there. He told himself it was simply to ensure she made it unscathed into her home, but his gut knew the lie his head tried not to acknowledge. He never allowed himself to think what his life might have been. That was a waste of his time. His parents had both died. He and Blythe had become orphans. Hawk had betrayed all of them. Georgette and the babe had died. Loss had defined his life. Even if he wanted to let someone close besides Blythe, really close, he couldn't. Hell, he wouldn't even know how anymore anyway.

Frederica had stirred his lust, nothing more, and there were ways to slake one's lust without courting problems. Yet, as he settled once more in his carriage, questions about her disturbed his peace. For instance, why exactly did she want to leave the only world she'd ever known for his? And why was it that a woman as stunning and unique as she was had not yet been kissed?

Chapter Five

Gabe returned to the club, listening as Brooke threatened to destroy him, Blythe, and Frederica for interfering with the man's private affairs, and then Gabe calmly made his own threats to the man. He was glad Belle had decided to disappear and start a new life. He'd happily given her the means to do so. Brooke seemed to be the sort of man whose pride was greater than his intelligence, which meant he'd likely try to make good on his threats. And that meant Gabe needed to warn not only Frederica but Carrington, as well. His friend and partner was the best person to watch after his impetuous sister-in-law, and luckily, the ball the Carringtons were hosting the following evening would be the perfect time to do so. He'd already been planning to attend, as Carrington was supposed to be giving him a list of candidates for Blythe to wed.

Yet, as Gabe shut the door that led from the club to the cellar and proceeded down the stairs to confront Blythe, anticipation at the thought of seeing Frederica again stirred in his chest. It wasn't a welcome feeling, but damn it all, he couldn't seem to kill it. That feeling was why he was grateful for how public the next night's ball would be. There would be no opportunity for him to forget himself and kiss her again.

Decision made, Gabe proceeded down to the cellar and found Blythe sitting on the edge of the ring with a drink in hand and an empty glass and a full bottle of whisky beside her. She flicked her gaze toward him, then scooped up the bottle with her free hand, poured him a measure, and carried the drink to him. She knew him well. He always drank a finger of whisky before bed. He took the glass from her and tilted it up, letting the whisky slide a fiery trail down his throat to spread through his chest. Maybe it would unravel the knots that Frederica's kiss had put there.

"Are you worried about Brooke?" Blythe asked, tilting her own glass back and knocking down the remainder of her drink before she swiped the back of her hand across her face.

"Yes." But he wasn't worried in regard to himself. "I'm worried about you."

"Me?" She frowned. "Why?"

"Because you take too many chances with your well-being."

"You're one to talk. You pummeled and humiliated a lord who then departed with a threat to destroy you."

"Your statement," Gabe said, "is exactly why I'm worried. Brooke threatened to destroy you too, and you don't seem to even care."

"I care about my safety," she said, patting him on the chest before padding over to the ring once more, sitting down, and stretching her legs out in front of her. "But," she continued as her gaze met his, "I have you to worry about me and watch over me, and I know you'll protect me. What worries me, *Gabe*, is that you don't seem to care about *your* safety, and you're constantly refusing to let me watch over you."

Of course he wasn't going to let her risk herself for him. Gabe rubbed a hand over the back of the knotted muscles in his neck, then joined his sister at the ring. He sat and stretched his legs out to match her position. "You seem to be confused about who is supposed to watch over whom. I'm the man; you're the woman. I'm your elder brother. Those things make me your protector."

She wiggled her finger at him. "Mama always said we protected each other."

Gabe clenched his teeth. Their mother had also told him with her dying breath, *Protect your sister as no one ever protected me.* He shoved his hand through his hair at the wave of guilt that always came with the memory of those words, words he'd never share with Blythe. She didn't need to feel the remorse he did. That thought of his mother and guilt brought Georgette to mind which led directly to Hawk. Normally, he could block out thoughts of Hawk, but tonight they pushed through his invisible wall. He'd not seen the man since the day he'd come to the club after Georgette's death, but once a year, on the anniversary of that terrible night, he got a one-sentence letter from Hawk: *Met anyone yet?*

"You're thinking about Hawk."

Blythe's matter-of-fact statement jerked Gabe's attention back to her. He opened his mouth to deny it, but she shook her head at him. "Don't bother trying to lie about it. You get a very distinct look when you think about him. I don't think he's ever coming back, Gabe. It's been four years since he disappeared."

"Oh, he will. You know he will."

"The letter."

Gabe nodded. It was a small sliver of the story that was Gabe and Hawk's tale that Blythe actually knew the truth of.

Blythe sighed. "If you met someone," she said, her words soft, as if she were walking on eggs and needed to be careful not to break them. "A lady to fill the hole in your heart that losing Georgette caused. You think he'd come back then."

Gabe had long ago ceased contemplating telling his sister the truth, not that he'd ever seriously considered it anyway. There was no point. "I know he would."

"Gabe, you can't actually intend to live alone forever. To never allow anyone in."

"I can," he said, and because he could see his sister winding up to lecture him, he added, "But what I am really thinking on now is how best to ensure your safety."

"Hawk would never hurt me if he ever came back to Covent Garden."

"I agree. It's me he hates. But I'm not speaking of Hawk. There are plenty of other dangers lurking in Covent Garden, which is why I want you to wed a lord and get the hell out of here."

He braced himself to argue with her, but she said, "I agree," surprising him. As she poured more whisky into his glass, he waited for her to continue. "Which is why *I* made the bargain with Freddy."

"Frederica," he said absently. She was a lady. She was fragile, as Georgette had been fragile. The difference was that Georgette had known it and was timid, while Frederica didn't seem to understand how easily she could die. "You agree?" he asked, knowing she'd said she did, but after all the arguing they had done on this exact point, he was finding it hard to believe.

She stared at him with wide, not-so-innocent eyes. "Didn't I just say I did?"

"You did, but I feel I must've damaged my hearing in the ring tonight."

She smirked. "Shall I recant?"

"Good God, no. I do believe this is the first time we have ever come to such easy agreement. You did say you agree that you should wed a lord, yes?"

Blythe nodded. For a woman who stated often and loudly that she never wished to wed, Gabe was certain he was missing some important fact. "Have you met someone?"

"No."

"But you now wish to wed, and a lord to boot?"

"Yes, and yes." Impatience underlay her tone. "Can we get back to Freddy?"

"Frederica," he corrected again. "Were we ever on her?" Damn, but an image of him atop Frederica popped into his thick skull.

"Gabe."

Gabe smiled. Blythe always had possessed a unique ability to say his name as a warning rather than a word simply used to address him.

"Blythe," he returned, knowing good and well he possessed the same ability. And before his sister could continue this game, he said, "Quit calling her Freddy. She's Frederica."

"Hmm..." Blythe replied, studying him. "Not Lady Frederica?"

It had been a mistake to drop the formality regarding Frederica in front of his sister. Blythe knew him too well and was too insightful and meddlesome.

"Did something happen between you and Freddy on the carriage ride home, on which you strangely insisted you accompany her?"

His body hardened with the memory of what had happened. "No. Now let's return to you and your impending betrothal."

"To return to me, we must revisit Freddy." Blythe served him a needling smile. "I would have thought you would be interested in the bargain I made with her."

He was interested—too much so, in fact—which was why he was trying not to think upon it. But it was useless. Blythe was correct. He needed particulars so that when he spoke with Frederica the following night at the ball, he could ensure she understood whatever had been agreed upon was no longer. "How is it you became so chummy with Frederica without my knowing it?"

"Well, you're very busy, aren't you? She came back to Covent Garden even after you told her not to, so somebody had to make sure the nob didn't get herself killed."

"That was very generous of you," he said, smirking. Blythe had a good heart, but he also knew his sister was cunning. One did not survive the streets of Covent Garden without knowing when to seize unexpected opportunities.

Blythe smiled. "Well, she was trying to do good for the Cyprians, and you know I have a special place in my heart for their plight."

He nodded. "As do I. Go on."

"I had been contemplating for quite some time how I could help make your life safer, and it occurred to me, after spending time with Freddy and listening to her talk about the business dealings of her father, your partner Carrington, and the many other lords she knows like your partner who make aboveboard investments in businesses in Covent Garden, it occurred to me that you needed more proper investors and less unsavory sorts so that you have the courts looking out for you."

"I look out for myself, Blythe, but I agree that it would be preferable to buy out any investors from my clubs who have ties to unlawful activities, and I've been working toward that, which was why I initially brought on Carring-ton."

"It's taking too long," Blythe said with a fierce frown. "The best way to speed it up is for me to wed a lord. That way, you will be proper by association with me."

He didn't think it would work exactly that way, but he also didn't want to tell Blythe that and have her change her mind about wanting to wed a lord. It perfectly suited the plan he'd already put into motion to find her a titled man of means who was above reproach. "How did you think Frederica would fit into this plan?"

"I need to have someone who is already entrenched in the good graces of the *ton* to introduce me into the circles. I also need some polishing."

"Just a bit," he agreed, to which Blythe glared at him.

"Freddy thinks it was her idea, but really, it was mine."

He frowned. "I'm afraid I still don't know what idea you're referring to."

"Oh!" Blythe chuckled. "Freddy's been teaching me to be a lady, and I'm teaching her how to survive in Covent Garden."

"Has she given you many lessons?" He was thinking of how Blythe had wiped her mouth with her hand earlier. He would have thought Frederica would have told her not to do such a thing. He had to admit, the idea of Blythe receiving etiquette lessons was brilliant, and it had not even occurred to him.

"Well, we've focused mostly on her so far, but she has been nagging me about my language. We were supposed to work more on my lessons this week, but now you've forbidden her coming to Covent Garden..." Blythe gave him a hopeful stare.

"No," he said. "What have you taught her?"

"Bookkeeping. She wants to live on her own here, and she wanted a way to earn a living. She's really quite good with numbers, Gabe."

"She cannot live in Covent Garden."

"Whyever not? You could hire her as your bookkeeper. You will need one, after all," she said. "I'll be far too busy being a lady."

"She wouldn't survive here, Blythe, and you know it." Never mind the fact that the woman stirred something carnal in him.

"I *don't* know it. Perhaps she would, perhaps she wouldn't. But either way, why should we force her to live in a world she detests? If we do that, then we're acting no better than all the people that tried to force us to live as poor beggars simply because we started that way."

Blythe's words hit a nerve, but he couldn't relent. "I'll find you another tutor," he said. "I'm sure Carrington's wife would be more than willing."

Blythe stood, upturning the glass she had set by her leg, which Gabe lunged for and caught before it hit the floor and shattered. As he set it down on the ring ledge, Blythe said, "I don't understand you, Gabe. You act as if you're afraid of Freddy!"

Maybe he was. He'd never before reacted to a woman the way he had to Frederica. He couldn't act on his desire, and he wasn't entirely sure the control he'd always been able to count on in all situations would hold when confronted with the temptation she presented.

Chapter Six

"*D*o your parents know you're traipsing about this ball in a gown that screams, 'Seduce me'?"

Freddy whirled toward the deep, dangerous voice that sent a tingle down her spine. Her gaze collided with Beckford's appreciative one, and her dreams of last night, which she'd awoken with full recollections of this morning, set a heated blush to her cheeks.

"This old thing? I just threw it on tonight because it's my favorite color," she said, lifting one side of the peacock-blue skirt of her gown and refusing to be appalled at herself for her obvious flirtation. When she had awoken this morning with dreams of Beckford kissing her in places on her body that had never seen the sun, she had two revelations. One, with a single kiss, Beckford had made her wanton, and two, it did not bother her a bit. Why should it? She had no interest in love. She only wanted to live a life in which she felt she belonged. Besides, from what she could tell, women of Covent Garden were not slaves of conventionality. Why couldn't she take a lover just as unattached men did?

His face was suddenly a hairsbreadth from hers. "Have you heard a word I've said?"

No. No, she hadn't.

"I'm sorry. I—" What could she say? She certainly didn't want to admit she'd been pondering what it would be like for him to toss up her skirts and kiss her under her necessities. That ache he'd first caused started anew. "I thought the next dance was starting." That was dreadfully uninspired, but it would have to do.

"Are you partnered for the next dance?"

How did he do that? Speak in a tone that slid over her skin like silk?

She cleared her throat. "No." And then the music did start, and before she realized what he intended, he had spun her about rather efficiently so that she was facing the glittering, glowing, majestic ballroom. His hand came to her back, and like a match to wood, she went up in flames. Heat danced along her spine where his palm rested, and each of his fingers singed through her silk gown and imprinted themselves on her skin and soul.

Heavens. So this was what it felt like to be in the arms of a man who did not look as if you frightened him and who did not bore you. This was what that thrill her friends and Guinevere had spoken of, the one that caused a surge of pulsing tension between her thighs.

She nearly tripped over her own feet at her wicked thoughts. Beckford's strong hands came to her waist to steady her, and then he said, "I've got you. Don't worry."

His warm breath fanned her neck from behind, and his hard body brushed her back, causing her to arch with a piercing longing as he wove her through the crowd toward the dance floor. She almost stumbled again when they passed Vivian, who was dancing with Lord Asterly and who looked radiantly happy—until her gaze landed on Frederica. Vivian's eyes widened and her face went pale, and then she looked truly as if she wished to throttle Freddy.

Freddy glared her sister into turning her attention from her, and she got a brief moment of satisfaction out of that.

Vivian had no right to be so snobby. There was nothing improper about Freddy dancing with Beckford. Vivian just didn't like it because Beckford was not part of the elite *ton*. It burned Freddy up that Vivian now cared about such superficial things. Before she'd met Lord Asterly, her sister would have scoffed at such condescending behavior.

Once they reached the middle of the dance floor, Beckford twirled her around to face him. She found herself extremely conscious of his virile appeal and the way he looked in full evening dress—like the Devil come to court her. He may have been wearing a proper gentleman's clothing—perfectly tied neck cloth, white waistcoat, long-tailed coat of black superfine, and black satin knee-breeches—but the way he wore it, all filled out across his broad chest, thick arms, and muscular legs, left no room to mistake him for a gentleman of leisure.

He'd been cut and shaped from the streets, and it was clear he was dangerous from his sharp, assessing eyes to his jaw honed like a knife blade to the way his mouth held a daring smirk. He thrilled her, and she wanted nothing more in this moment than to feel his lips on hers once more, but that would never happen. He had told her he'd throw her out of Covent Garden if she returned, so while he might desire her, he clearly had no plans to act on that desire again.

He drew her toward him, one arm encircling her back, his other hand catching hers. Rough fingers folded securely over the back of her hand, and his head tilted down as his gaze bore into hers. Being touched by him felt like standing in the middle of a storm—powerful, chaotic, perilous, exhilarating.

"I've come here tonight to warn you," he said, moving her along in the steps of the dance as if she were light as a feather. She felt rather like a feather, floating and waiting to be captured in the palm of his hand.

"Warn me?" she managed as they turned.

"Brooke threatened to destroy you and my sister for meddling with Belle."

She frowned. "How ever could Brooke destroy me?" As the question left her mouth, she blanched with realization. Did Brooke mean he was going to destroy her reputation somehow? That would ruin Vivian's chances at a love match.

"I don't know," Beckford replied, his fingers gripping her hand tighter. "And because I don't know, I see no choice but to tell Carrington so he can watch out for you."

"What?" Alarm rang through her. "If you tell Carrington, he'll surely tell my sister, and that could mean all sorts of trouble for me. You have to let me handle this. Guinevere is so unpredictable these days now that she's a mother. Why, she might tell *our* mother, and then it will be impossible for me to slip away to—" She stopped just short of telling him how she was supposed to help his sister.

That smirk on his face grew wider. "My sister won't be needing your services any longer."

"She told you of our bargain?" Freddy asked, surprised and dismayed by the finality of his statement. All her carefully laid plans to live in Covent Garden seemed to be unraveling at an alarming rate.

"She did," he said, twirling Freddy once, twice, and then bringing them back into the slower steps. "The bargain is off. I've secured another lady to help make her a... Well, a lady."

"You know what she wishes?"

He nodded. "She told me, and I can see by your face you're surprised, but it just so happens what she wants suits what I want for her."

"Which is?"

"For her to get far away from the harsh life of Covent Garden and wed to a man who will provide her a nice, safe, quiet life."

"That sounds dreadfully boring," Freddy muttered. She couldn't believe it had taken only a single night to lose her ally in Blythe.

Beckford gave her an uneasy look, almost as if something she'd said worried him. "She doesn't require your assistance any longer, so you have no other reason to come to Covent Garden."

"But—"

"No buts, Frederica. I told you Covent Garden is not for you. Let me reiterate that I will never hire you, nor will I allow you to be hired by anyone in my territory."

The good feelings she had toward him disappeared so fast it made her head ache. Anger replaced the desire, and her temples pounded. "Why are you doing this?" she asked in a low, hushed tone, though she really wanted to bellow at him. She had, after all, promised Vivian she'd behave until Vivian secured her match, and Freddy intended to uphold that promise.

"To ensure your safety, since you apparently have no care to do so yourself."

"It's not your job to keep me safe, Beckford. You are not my brother, father, or husband."

"Thank God for that," he returned so quickly that hurt spread through her chest and the familiar feeling of not being accepted gripped her.

She stiffened and tried to tug away from him, but he pulled her closer, almost improperly so. "I'm sorry." His eyes showed that he meant what he said, but her pride had been good and chipped.

"Whatever for?" she replied, refusing to let him see that his words had hurt her. It was ridiculous to allow herself to be injured by a man she barely knew. There were plenty of men she'd known all her life that already had that job. As her eyes fell from his to his lips, she thought for one more brief moment how she'd wanted him to kiss her again. That had been a foolish notion, at best.

"I'm sorry if what I said seemed harsh," he said.

"Which part?" She arched her eyebrows at him as they moved to the left and right, both automatically following the steps to the dance. "The part where you told me you'd never allow me to live in Covent Garden or the part where you said, 'thank God' you were not my husband, brother, or father?"

"Why Covent Garden?" he questioned instead of answering her. Normally, it would have irritated her, as she despised when people evaded questions, but the genuine interest in his voice and on his face was undeniable.

"I don't know for certain," she said, which wasn't the complete truth.

"Come now," he said, circling her to the right. "You don't seem the sort of woman who would make such a momentous decision without truly thinking it through."

"I'm not." Her lips pulled into a smirk that he'd state such a thing after suggesting she could not take care of herself well enough to survive in his territory.

He scowled. "Just because you think you've thought something through thoroughly doesn't mean you've come to the correct conclusion. You've chosen Covent Garden for a reason, and you think you could survive there, but I'm telling you that you could not. What I want to know, though, is why Covent Garden?"

"Because I do not fit here."

"And what makes you think you'd fit there?"

Could she trust him with her most private thoughts? For some reason, she felt she could. "Because being different seems to be accepted there."

"It is to an extent," he acknowledged, "but Covent Garden is still not the place for the likes of you. You should open a nice dressmaker shop in Mayfair."

"I don't want a nice dressmaker shop in Mayfair!" she said, feeling frustrated as the dance started drawing to an end. "I don't fit in here. I have tried for one and twenty years, and I have never belonged. The only time I came even close was when SLAR was more active. Now that SLAR is hardly doing any work, I have nothing to talk to the others about, not even my own sisters. They want to talk of babies, and balls, and teas, and I'd rather gouge my eyes out."

"That's a bit extreme," he said, chuckling.

"Perhaps," she relented. "But I want excitement, and I'm certain the sort of excitement I want will not be found in Mayfair, nor will it be found with a titled husband who demands I act a certain way, talk a certain way, be a certain way."

"You think a husband from Covent Garden would be so different?"

"I never said I even wanted a husband." A feeling of boldness swept through her. "Perhaps I simply want a lover."

Something flared on his face and made her body tingle. "That's not the sort of thing you should go around saying to men, Frederica."

She nearly grinned at the desire that vibrated in his tone. It was a heady feeling to know she'd caused it. "It's not the sort of thing I'd say to any man, Beckford." And then a perfect idea came to her. "It's the sort of thing I'd only say to a man I thought might fit a position I need filled."

"And what position is that?" His hungry gaze bore into her.

She had to seize this moment. She simply had to. "Reliever of innocence," she said, her tone low and her cheeks flaming, despite her resolve.

The smoldering flames in his eyes filled her with hope, but then he said, "I'm flattered, but that's not a position I could ever fill for you."

Shame burned her cheeks, but she had to know what it was about her that had made him refute her offer. "Whyever not?"

"It's very complicated," he said, releasing her as if he could not depart from her quickly enough. His hand came to her back as it had when he'd led her onto the dance floor, and before she even realized his intentions, he maneuvered her through the crowd and deposited her unceremoniously by Guinevere. Then, to Guinevere, he said, "Do not let your sister out of your sight. Your husband will explain after the ball."

And with that, he departed, leaving her burning with humiliation. Still, she was unable to rip her gaze from him as he strode gracefully away. She tracked his movement across the ballroom as long as she could, which was for a few minutes. He was taller than most of the men there, broader shouldered, and his dark wavy hair was longer than that of most other men of the *ton* and glistened under the chandeliers.

Beckford stopped at Carrington's side, said a word into the duke's ear, and then both men looked toward where

Freddy stood with Guinevere, before turning on their heels and disappearing altogether down a corridor, which Freddy happened to know led to Carrington's private study.

"Whatever was that about?" Guinevere asked from Freddy's left.

"I haven't any idea," Freddy lied, not wishing to face a lecture from Guinevere in the middle of the ball. Tomorrow would be soon enough, and Freddy had no doubt the lecture would likely come very early once Carrington told Guinevere that Freddy had been going to Covent Garden on her own for missions. And then, in all probability Vivian would join in on the lecturing once she discovered what Freddy had been up to, and then Vivian would no doubt make good on her threat to tell their parents about SLAR and Freddy's nightly jaunts, which were the only thing that had ever made her feel as if she belonged anywhere, and that would officially be over, though it had really unofficially been over for months.

She hated Beckford in that moment. She hated him for not wanting her as much as she wanted him, even as she knew reasonably that was not reason to hate him. So she tried to shove that aside and concentrate on being angry at him for ratting her out to Carrington. Yes, she knew Beckford thought he was protecting her, but it wasn't his right, especially when he couldn't even be bothered to consider being her lover.

Blast Beckford. No, not blast him, *damn* him. It felt good to think the profanity in her head. *Damn him. Damn him.*

Thanks to Beckford, she now had nowhere to go, and she was not certain what to do. She needed to think.

"Freddy, whatever is the matter?" Guinevere asked, drawing Freddy's attention back to her sister. "You're dreadfully pale, and you look as if someone you loved has just died."

Not someone, but possibly something—her chance for a life of belonging. "I'm simply not feeling well. I'm hot and did not eat before coming. I think I'll get some fresh air."

"I'll go with you and—"

"Duchess!" Lady Northingham waved her fan in the air as she made her way toward them. The gossiping matron, who'd told Freddy on more than one occasion she was a most odd girl, was the last person Freddy wanted to stand around chatting with. Though now that Guinevere was a duchess, Freddy knew Lady Northingham would not dare say such a rude thing to Freddy's face. She'd reserve it to say behind her back.

"Oh, dear," Guinevere said, looking between Freddy and Lady Northingham.

"You stay," Freddy said, patting her sister's hand. As much as she'd longed for the closeness she once felt to her sisters, which was the thing that had kept her from feeling like a total outsider amongst people who were supposed to be her set, that time was over. Guinevere had many obligations and little time.

"I'm sorry, Freddy. You understand, don't you, darling?"

"Of course," Freddy replied and forced a smile she didn't feel as she made her way through the crush of guests at her brother-in-law and sister's home.

By the time she reached the terrace, her heart was racing, and she felt as though she couldn't take a proper breath. She flung open the door, rushed into the cold, bright night, and made her way past the one couple outside and down the stairs to the garden below. As she stepped onto the pebbled path that led to the maze, tears stung her eyes, and her gown seemed to grow tighter and more confining, just as her life was.

What was she to do now? She ran past the orderly rows

of rosebushes toward the maze, her slippers crunching on gravel and her breath coming out in white rings in the frigid air. She couldn't simply give up, but she honestly didn't know how to go about starting a new life in a world where so few choices were available to women, and she was acutely aware that her time to create a new plan was short indeed. Covent Garden, Blythe, and a position as a bookkeeper had seemed too good to be true because it *had been* too good to be true.

She ran through the maze, passing another row of rose-bushes and coming too close to the bushes. A branch of thorns caught the sleeve of her gown and ripped straight through the material, cutting her arm as it did so. In her effort to unhook her sleeve, she got the edge of her skirt stuck in one of the thornbushes, as well, and inadvertently ripped her skirt in an attempt to free herself.

Finally, unhooked, she ran toward the center of the maze once more, slippers smacking the tiny stones of the path in a *pat, pat, pat* pattern, and the pins meant to keep her hair in place abandoned their duty. Locks of hair slipped their confines to dangle in front of her eyes and curl around her neck. By the time she reached the inner maze where the fountain was, she was panting, her hair was mostly down—tumbled, no doubt, in wild disarray about her shoulders—and her gown was not only ripped but dirty.

She stared down at herself in dismay for one moment, and then she threw her head back, tilted her face to the starry sky and started to laugh. This night fit who she was perfectly. The outsider. The oddity. Loud, boisterous Freddy, who had forever embarrassed her mother, father, sisters, and anyone close to her with her blunt words, loud laugh, and even louder voice. The sister who chattered constantly and forever ignored the manners she'd been taught. The sister who talked politics and principles to men who only wanted to know she could plan an appropriate dinner party.

In Covent Garden she was sure she could be as loud as she wanted and no one would care. And she could kick off her shoes. Freddy blinked, righted herself, and looked down at her slippered feet before actually kicking off her shoes. They flew into the bushes, and she laughed.

She'd gone mad! It was glorious! She wished she'd done this ages ago instead of trying to be someone she was not. She wanted to go even more mad! Why not? No one was out here.

The moonlight glinted off the fountain, and an outrageous, wonderful idea came to her. She wanted to stick her feet in that fountain. She'd wanted to do such a thing for as long as she could remember, but she had never dared. She bent over, pulled up one edge of silk and underskirts, and knotted it so that the gown was hiked to her thigh. She repeated the process on the other side, peeled off her stockings, and then she skipped over to the fountain, stepped over the edge, and stood in the shallow water.

It was so cold it stole her breath and numbed her feet almost instantly. It was the best feeling in the entire world because she'd chosen the act that had led to it. She inhaled a long, deep breath, filling her lungs to near bursting, then let it out in a slow release, watching the white stream of air that came from her lungs. She didn't want to go back in, but her absence would be noted eventually, and it was freezing out here. She turned back toward the house and stilled, gooseflesh racing across her body.

Lord Brooke stood at the fountain, arms crossed over his chest and a smirk twisting his lips. "You've made ruining you quite easy."

Chapter Seven

*I*t took all the concentration Gabe possessed to push the image of Frederica in her alluring, revealing peacock-blue gown telling him she wanted him to relieve her of her innocence out of his head. Christ, if only it would be that simple. He mentally willed himself to concentrate on the task at hand, and he managed to relay to Carrington what Frederica had been up to and the danger she might currently be in from Brooke.

Carrington shook his head as he leaned back in his desk chair. "I just said to Guinevere the other night, after having supper at her parents' home, that Freddy seemed unhappy to me. Of course, we both credited it to the normal tension Guinevere's mother creates when trying to get one of her daughters wed. We both assumed Freddy had someone she wished to court her that Lady Fairfax did not approve of."

"I think it's more than that," Gabe said, unwilling to reveal the private things he felt Frederica would not want made known, such as the fact that she wanted a lover, not a husband and that she felt she didn't belong in the *ton*. Never had he wanted to take a woman up on her offer more than he had Frederica in the moment she'd made hers, but that was as impossible as he'd said it was.

"Beckford, did ye hear me? I asked why do ye say that about Freddy?"

Gabe blinked and was surprised to find that there was a

glass of liquor in front of him and that Carrington held one in his hand. He couldn't believe he'd been so consumed by thoughts of Frederica he'd not even noted his friend stand and pour them each a drink.

"Beckford?"

Hell, he'd wished he'd not made that comment. "You should talk to her, or better yet, have her sister talk to her. It's not my place to relay what Frederica told me."

Carrington's brows dipped together. "And when would *Frederica* have told ye these private things?"

"She gave me leave to call her Frederica," Gabe said, feeling defensive. "Well, actually, she insisted I call her Freddy, but I refused." He paused and took a long swallow of the liquor, welcoming the warmth.

"Did she now?" Carrington replied. "And when did she give ye this leave?"

Gabe told Carrington about seeing her home after her encounter with Marco, but he left out the part about the kiss. When Gabe finished relaying the information, Carrington was looking at him as if he was about to launch an inquisition. Gabe stood and added, "If you have that list for me and Blythe, I'll take it and be on my way. You know I don't particularly care for balls."

"Neither does Freddy." As Carrington stood, his unwavering gaze assessed Gabe. "It seems ye two have that in common."

Rather than answer what seemed to be a loaded question, Gabe reached out and took the list that Carrington extended, unfolded it, and scanned the four names. He was surprised by only one—Huntley, Frederica's brother. "I thought Huntley was supposed to wed some time ago?"

Carrington nodded. "He was, but his betrothed died quite unexpectedly. Some sort of lung infection, I think it was. Huntley is a good sort with means to take care of yer sister and keep her safe. He's honorable, and he's proven with his willingness to wed the American that he does not require his wife be part of the *ton*. As for the other three men, they have means to keep yer sister in a good life and are not so ruled by the strictures of Society—or overbearing mothers—that they'd feel unable to consider marrying a woman who is not of the *ton*."

Gabe folded the paper and put it in his coat pocket. "Whether they could handle my sister is another matter."

Carrington laughed and came around from his desk. "True, and that is something ye'll have to deduce. If there's nothing else to discuss, I'd like to return to the ball and ensure Freddy is safe. Brooke was invited, and—"

Gabe didn't hear the rest of the sentence. He was out the door and striding down the hall by the time Carrington caught up with him. As the man fell into step beside him, Gabe said, "Why the devil didn't you tell me Brooke was here?"

"Because I wasn't overly concerned that Brooke would be so foolish to attempt something at my home."

"He's dangerous. Mark my words," Gabe said, trying and failing not to sound short. "And dangerous men are foolish men." He gained the ballroom and started scanning for Frederica or Brooke. "Do you see either of them?"

"Nay, but I see Guinevere. Come on."

Gabe followed Carrington toward Lady Guinevere, who happened to be standing in a small group with her brother and a man Gabe recognized as one of the men who'd been with Brooke in the basement of the Orcus Society last night. A sense of foreboding settled in Gabe's gut. "Who's the man with blond hair standing by your wife?"

"Lord Habbersham," Carrington said, and a tightness in his friend's tone caused Gabe to look at him. Carrington's jaw was clenched, and he had a fierce frown on his face.

"He is friends with Brooke," Gabe supplied.

"Aye," Carrington answered, his pace increasing to that of the urgency Gabe himself felt. When they reached the circle, Carrington hadn't even come to a full stop when he said, "Guin, where's Frederica?"

Lady Guinevere scowled at her husband. "Carrington, you remember Lord Habbersham."

"Aye." Carrington glared at the man. "Ye're not welcome in my home, and ye can take yer friend Brooke with ye."

"Asher!" Lady Guinevere chided, letting propriety slip by calling her husband by his first name.

"I'll explain later, Guin," Carrington supplied.

She nodded without hesitation, showing the level of trust between the two of them. It was a bond Gabe momentarily felt envious of, but he dismissed it and concentrated on Habbersham. "Where's Brooke?"

"Listen, Beckford," Habbersham said, throwing up his hands, palms facing Gabe as the man took a step backward. "I don't condone what Brooke did. I had no idea he was up to such a thing. All I know is that not long after we arrived, he gave me names of six people he wanted me to find, and he asked me to see that they go immediately to the terrace. I've done that, and—"

Gabe closed the distance the man had tried to create. "Stop talking." The force of his tone matched what he wanted to do with his fists. The man flinched. "Is Brooke on the terrace?" Gabe asked.

"I suppose. We were out there for a moment when we first got here, and he got suddenly very excited and asked

LADY FREDERICA AND THE SCOT WHO WOULD NOT

me to go find the six women I just told you of. Gossiping matrons, the lot of them."

What the hell was Brooke planning?

"Freddy is on the terrace," Lady Guinevere said, the mild concern in her voice not coming close to the panic that exploded in Gabe's chest. "What's going on?" Gabe heard Lady Guinevere ask, but the question came from behind him. He was already racing toward the terrace.

"No one will believe I willingly let you seduce me," Freddy said, her tone hushed but her fists pummeling Lord Brooke's back as he strode with her, thrown over his shoulder, toward the well-lit garden just below the terrace.

Brooke laughed. "Won't they? Your skirts are tied in knots, your hair is unbound, and you've no bloody stockings or slippers on. You don't look like you were trying to get away from me; you look as if you were willingly rolling on the grass with me."

Panic rioted within Freddy. He was right. No one would believe her. No one. And even if they did, it would hardly matter. There would be a scandal, and her sister's chance at wedding into Lord Asterly's stuffy family would be lost. Vivian would never forgive her, and who could blame her? All Freddy had been asked to do was behave properly until Vivian was wed, and she'd been unable to give her sister that small consideration.

"What do you plan to do?" She struggled against him once more, but it was useless. The man had an iron grip on her.

"Wait for it," he said, sounding very, very smug.

Up above, music and laughter washed out into the air,

breaking the silence of the garden. The terrace door had been opened. Then all at once, it seemed a cacophony erupted, as if the party had been moved onto the terrace. Freddy's world tilted once again, as it had moments before when Lord Brooke had captured her as she'd attempted to run from him, when the man finally set her down.

Dizziness washed over her as she came upright, her feet sinking into damp grass. Before she could lodge any sort of protest, Lord Brooke captured her face between his palms and slanted his mouth over hers. It was the second time she'd been kissed without her permission. Rage filled her, and just as she drew her fists back to pummel him some more, he was suddenly ripped away from her, and there stood Beckford, looking every inch the dangerous lord of London's underworld.

Fury flooded his features, and as his eyes swept over her, his ire seemed to become a living, breathing part of him. He roared and shoved Lord Brooke backward. Unfortunately, the man grabbed Beckford's coat, and they both went tumbling to the ground. But Beckford came up on top and then let his fists fly. They met their mark with fearsome accuracy. One hit. Two. Three. Four.

Shouting came from above her, and the clamoring of many people descending the stairs echoed around her. Freddy felt frozen, unable to move. She was in awe of the ferocity with which Beckford fought for her, and she was horrified that her foolishness had caused all this.

Beckford sprang to his feet, slamming one foot into Lord Brooke's chest. "Don't ever touch her again." He was no longer speaking but snarling. "Ever. She is under my protection."

The possessiveness in Beckford's tone made Freddy's knees feel weak.

"Do you hear me?" Beckford demanded. "She is mine."

"I heard you," came an older woman's voice, full of sharp scorn and mirth, from Freddy's left.

Freddy snapped out of her stupor and turned, meeting the shredding gaze of Lady Portsmith, the *ton's* biggest gossip. Lady Portsmith need not have told a single soul, though, for standing around her were five other gossips, as well as a host of other people, including Guinevere, Carrington, Vivian, Lord Asterly, and his mother.

His mother swept an impervious gaze over Freddy, shook her head, and said, "Come along, Asterly."

To his credit, Lord Asterly hesitated, but then released Vivian, whose arm he'd been holding. With a look of sorrow, he followed his mother away from the crowd and toward the stairs.

"Freddy, are you all right?" Guinevere asked, rushing toward her at the same time Lord Brooke was rising to his feet.

"Of course she's all right," he muttered, jerking on his cravat. "She implored me to meet her out here, and she kissed me, and then this man beat me. I'm the one who's been harmed. If I'd known the two of them had a relationship, I never would have agreed to meet her—the strumpet."

Freddy would have slapped him, except Beckford sent his right fist straight into the man's nose. The powerful punch sent Lord Brooke backward, down, and silent, but the damage had already been done to Freddy's reputation. And it was grave.

Chapter Eight

"This is worse than I predicted!" Freddy's mother declared, sweeping into the breakfast room two days later holding what appeared to be a gossip sheet in her hand.

Not for the first time in the last two days since the debacle at Guinevere's ball, Freddy wished the floor would open up and swallow her whole.

Her mother stalked toward the breakfast table, stopped at the chair opposite Freddy, and shook the sheet at her. "You have ruined yourself, and you have ruined your sister's chance at happiness!"

"Darling," her father started, but her mother turned her outraged look from Freddy to Papa.

"Don't *darling* me, Fairfax." Her dire tone and her use of Freddy's father's title instead of his Christian name, George—how she usually addressed him in private—indicated just how vexed her mother was. "You—" she pointed at Freddy's father "—will try to placate me, say I'm being dramatic, come to Frederica's defense, but I am not being dramatic, you cannot make me feel better, and there is no defense for how selfishly your youngest daughter has acted!"

With each word her mother spoke, her voice rose in pitch so that Freddy was certain it was high enough to cause crystal to break. It certainly made Freddy's ears hurt, and she sank lower and lower in her seat. Her mother was right, and her father's silence and thin-pressed lips were damning affirmations that he agreed. Papa usually did come to her defense, but now he just stared at her, eyes full of disappointment.

Her quick-witted mother smelled victory and seized it. She slapped the gossip sheet down on the breakfast table making the china rattle and Freddy twitch. "Do you know what Lord Asterly told your sister this morning?"

"I didn't even know Lord Asterly came to call upon Vivian." Freddy tried to sound properly chastised, because she was, truly, but her instinct told her to defend herself, despite her mind reminding her that her mother was correct—her behavior was indefensible. "Vivian is not speaking to me, remember?"

Her mother gave her a sharp-eyed look. "Don't be pert, young lady."

Freddy was quite sure Mama didn't want an actual response from her, so she simply nodded.

"Lord Asterly told Vivian his father informed him yesterday that he would cut Lord Asterly off if he wed her."

"Well," Freddy said, awash with guilt but also thinking Vivian might count herself lucky not to be wed to such a spineless man, "if he truly loved Vivian, he would wed her anyway."

Freddy's mother threw up her hands and shook them as she looked to the painted ceiling of the breakfast room. There in golds, silvers, greens, blues, grays, and streaks of yellow was a mural of angels and demons engaged in a battle for the gates of Heaven. "Do you see what I have to endure?!" She shook her hands once more.

Freddy glanced to her father, thinking and hoping they might share one of their special private looks they often exchanged during one of her mother's outbursts. The look that said, *We both know how silly this is,* but instead, she found him frowning at her. Things were horrid all around. Suddenly, her throat became tight and achy, and she had to swallow the urge to cry.

Her mother looked at her once more, and the sadness that settled on her face made Freddy's stomach ache. "Lord Asterly told your sister he *did* want to wed her, despite the fact that his father would cut him off and leave him penniless."

Freddy frowned. "Well, if he wants to wed her still, why are you acting as if all is so dire for her?"

"Frederica!" Her mother's shriek resounded around the room. "You live in a world that is not real! Your sister lives in reality with the rest of us." Freddy's entire face flamed. "Vivian knows her dowry would not be enough to sustain them, and she loves Lord Asterly so very much that she does not want to subject him to a life of poverty. He is a younger son. He has no title, no land of his own, no training of any sort, because he believed—and rightly so—that he would have funds from his family to live upon. The only thing he might possibly do is obtain a commission, and that might not be possible if he's wed to a woman whose sister is being called a light-skirt!"

"Georgette," her father said, his voice quiet but firm. "You know Frederica is not a light-skirt."

Well, this all explained why Vivian had thrown a brush at Freddy a moment ago when she had tried to enter their bedchamber to talk to her sister. Since returning from Guinevere's ball, Vivian had spoken four sentences to Freddy: *How could you? You've destroyed my life. You're no longer my sister.* And the last sentence had been, *Get out.*

Freddy had complied that first night after returning

home from the disastrous ball, thinking perhaps Vivian needed time to cry and scream alone and then would be willing to talk to Freddy, but that had not occurred. When Freddy had tried to return to their bedchamber later that night, the door had been locked and Vivian had not answered Freddy's repeated knocks, so Freddy had slept in Guinevere's old bedchamber. And now her belongings were there, too, at Vivian's demand. And Vivian had sent the man she loved, the man who had asked her to wed him, away today because she wanted him to have the best life possible.

Freddy knew her sister, and that deep understanding of who Vivian was at her core made Freddy's eyes fill with tears, despite her best efforts to keep her emotions under control. Vivian had not sent Lord Asterly away simply because they would be poor. No, her sister was too good, too kind, too wise to let money rule her decisions. Vivian had sent Lord Asterly away because she knew if he wed her without his parents' blessing, she would be the cause of a rift between the man and his family. Having family support was especially important to Vivian, who'd been very sick as a child and had to rely upon them to take care of her many times. Vivian would never allow Lord Asterly to lose that, even if it meant she lost him.

The tears Freddy had tried to hold back slipped their confinement and rolled a trail of searing shame down her face. She'd been very selfish. She could have put off her own desires until after Vivian was safely wed, but she hadn't.

To Freddy's surprise, her mother came around the table, pulled out a chair, and slipped an arm over Freddy's shoulder. "There, there. I know you didn't mean to ruin your sister's life, though I suspect you are not at all sad about destroying your own remaining meager chances of catching a husband on the marriage mart. And I know you're not a light-skirt, though it hardly matters what we know. Gossip and all."

Freddy smiled through her tears. Leave it to her mother to comfort and insult her in the same sentence.

Mama pressed Freddy's head to her shoulder as Freddy's tears came harder, and her father, clearing his throat and looking vastly uncomfortable, handed Freddy a handkerchief. "I blame myself," her mother said, running a soothing hand over Freddy's hair. "I allowed your grandmother to tell Guinevere all the stories of her own scandalous behavior as a hoyden, and I know Guinevere passed those tales on to you and Vivian. I suppose I should have seen the harm in it, but I didn't, especially after Guinevere landed her duke and Vivian seemed on the verge of catching a very respectable offer of marriage. But you—" Mama wiggled her shoulder so Freddy righted herself and looked at her mother. "You are different from your sisters. I've tried to subdue you, for your own good." Her mother wrung her hands. "But you seem incapable of changing." Freddy sank a little lower in her chair again as her mother prattled on. "You're so wild. Free. Bold. I both admire it in you and fear for you, darling, because of it. I don't know what you will do now."

"I'll make it right," Freddy vowed, swiping at her cheeks.

"I don't see how you can. No respectable man will have you now."

"No," Freddy said, laughing. "I mean, I'll somehow mend things so that Lord Asterly's parents will give their blessing for him to wed Vivian."

Her mother's brows dipped together, and she shook her head as she took Freddy's hand. "Frederica," she said in a patient voice, as if Freddy were still a child. "The only thing that could possibly make it right would be if either Lord Brooke or Mr. Beckford were to make you his wife." Her mother tapped a finger to her lip as she tilted her head, looking thoughtful. "Since Lord Brooke announced you were behaving improperly with Mr. Beckford, it would be best if it was Mr. Beckford whom you wed, especially given how he apparently defended your honor." Freddy stiffened, not liking where her mother's thoughts seemed to be going.

Mama smiled so big all of a sudden that her dimples showed, and Freddy's mind whirred with shock. Her mother never grinned like that about anything. "This just might work," she said, nodding.

"What might work?" Freddy and her father asked at once.

"Why, Freddy wedding Mr. Beckford, of course." Freddy opened her mouth to protest, but her mother gave her a look that would have scared the devil himself. With a curt nod at Freddy, her mother said to her father, "Do keep up! If he wed her, the scandal would eventually be forgotten!" She hugged Freddy to her, nearly crushing her, then she thrust her away just as suddenly. "I do believe fate is smiling upon us, Frederica."

It felt to Freddy rather like fate had just blindsided her. Her thoughts swirled in her head so that she had to squeeze her eyes shut. She didn't need love or marriage. Those things meant giving up her freedom, meant someone wanting to change her because she didn't suit them as she was. Of course, Beckford wasn't here. He was in Covent Garden. She was appalled she'd even had the thought, and she felt a tickle of hysteria rising in her. She had to breathe deeply to regain control.

When her mind had settled, she opened her eyes to find

her mother staring at her. Freddy swallowed. "I don't see how my marrying Mr. Beckford would appease Lord Asterly's snobbish parents." And she prayed her mother didn't, either, because if it was a viable solution, wasn't she obligated to pursue it, pursue him, for Vivian's sake? Especially given Vivian's current dire situation was Freddy's fault.

Her mother waved a dismissive hand. "He's practically of the *ton* now," Mama announced.

If Freddy were the swooning type, now would be the appropriate time to do so. She held her breath and prayed for a black wave to swallow her and take away the mess she'd made. But when nothing happened, she begrudgingly exhaled and asked, "Whatever do you mean, Mama?"

"Georgette, have you been using a tonic for your nerves again?" Papa demanded.

"Fairfax, really! Don't be ridiculous. It says right here—" she picked up the gossip sheet again "—that Mr. Beckford, 'who gallantly came to the rescue of the fallen lady, if one can still call her a lady—'" Her mother paused and patted Freddy's hand. "They wrote that, dear. I am not saying that of you. Of course, your father and I don't believe you are not still a lady. I raised you better than that, didn't I?"

Freddy scowled. It was vastly unfair that she had been tried and convicted in the court of public opinion as a light-skirt based on the claims of one deceitful man, and that Beckford was being called gallant, though he was thought to have been the partner in her scandalous behavior.

"Frederica!"

Her mother's wail brought Freddy's attention back to her. "Yes," Freddy said, "I'm no light-skirt." A searing memory of Beckford's lips on hers gripped her. His hands on hers. His smell on her. She'd been raised to act like a lady, but she'd most assuredly, in the eyes of the *ton*, her mother, likely everyone, acted like a light-skirt by letting Beckford kiss her in his carriage. By wanting him to do far more than that. It had not seemed wrong. It had seemed natural and, frankly, fair that she should take her pleasure where she found it, just as a man did. Men didn't require marriage or love for pleasure, so why must she? Why were men not labeled *light-pants* for such behavior, but women had to live by different, unfair, and very restrictive rules?

Her mother tapped on the gossip sheet. "It says right here, the very first paragraph of the gossip sheet where your reputation is brought into question, that the Duke of Carrington—" Mama paused and smiled fondly "—and the new Duke of Lionhurst, both publicly announced that they are in partnerships in very profitable businesses with Mr. Beckford."

Freddy was surprised by the mixed emotions that filled her. She was happy that Beckford had two such men, good, honorable, and incredibly influential in the *ton*, to back him. By their public announcements, they'd made silent declarations that no one of the *ton* dare treat him as if he were not accepted, but those public announcements, his new backing, did make her mother's idea viable. Freddy groaned. This was horrid. How had her plan to live in Covent Garden gone so wrong? Never had starting a new life there included embroiling a man in a scandal that might possibly lead to her needing to wed him.

"Frederica! For heaven's sake, after everything that has occurred, you must behave above reproach and comport yourself as a lady at all times. Ladies do not groan in public!"

Nails on a schoolroom slate. That's the feeling her mother's words caused Freddy. She arched her upper back but managed to keep any rejoinder between her clenched teeth.

"As I was saying, these public announcements make Mr. Beckford respectable and acceptable as a husband."

"Mr. Beckford was already acceptable and respectable, Mama." Or he was to her, which meant nothing for her problem if he wasn't acceptable to the *ton*. However, now he was, and somehow that solved part of her problem while creating a new one.

"I didn't make the rules, Frederica. I simply live by them, as we all must."

No, not everyone lived by those rules. The people in Covent Garden didn't. Beckford didn't live by rules that were so very restrictive on women. And yet, he had turned her offer to be her lover down. Too complicated. Was it his love for his dead wife that he was speaking of that made it too complicated? Or was it simply Freddy and that who she was didn't suit him at all, even for a tumble in the sheets?

She's mine.

The words whispered through her thoughts. He hadn't meant it. Of course, he hadn't. And she didn't care. Of course, she didn't. Hadn't she decided long ago that she neither needed nor wanted love? And he... He had simply been trying to ensure that Lord Brooke understood to leave her alone.

Except Beckford's words had made Lord Brooke's claim seem true. She hadn't even cared about that, not really, but what she could not dismiss sitting there now, thinking about his words, was that the idea of being his was... Well, heaven help her, it was appealing. A fissure of fear went through her. She didn't want to desire something or someone who might never return those feelings.

"Frederica, it's rude to ignore a question."

Freddy blinked and met her mother's gaze. "I'm sorry. What did you ask me?"

"I said, don't you think you should go change into something more appealing to meet with Mr. Beckford?"

Freddy's mouth slipped open. Surely, her mother was not truly serious. When her father started to rise, Freddy let out a relieved breath. He would not agree to such a thing. He was more reasonable than her mother. Among them, Guinevere and Carrington included, they could think of another solution that would lead Lord Asterly's father and mother to grant their blessing upon a union between their son and Vivian.

"George, where are you going?" Frederica's mother demanded.

He turned to face them, one foot out of the breakfast room. "To fetch my card and a pen. I think the note to call upon me to discuss Frederica should come from me, don't you?" He was not looking at Mama but at Freddy.

Her blood made an odd whooshing sound in her ears so that she could hardly think. "Papa, I cannot—"

"—choose your own desires over your sister again. Yes, you are correct." His tone was formidable. "I have faith," he said, his voice softening ever so slightly, "that you will not do so. But I do think you should have a say in whom I summon."

"George!" her mother protested.

But he didn't act as if he heard Freddy's mother. His gaze stayed trained on Freddy. "Whom shall I summon, Frederica? Mr. Beckford or Lord Brooke?"

"Mr. Beckford," she said, worry stabbing her heart.

Chapter Nine

Gabe's office door creaked open, and Blythe appeared in the doorway with two glasses of whisky clutched in her hands. She held out a glass to him, which he took, then clanked hers against his.

"What are we celebrating?" he asked, taking a sip of the whisky. Maybe it would help release some of the tension he'd been unable to shake since the ball. Worry for Frederica had plagued him every waking moment—and his sleeping ones, too. Damn it all to hell. Worry and fear for her were things he did not want.

"I thought we'd celebrate the announcement by Lionhurst and Carrington that you're their respectable business partner."

Gabe didn't give a damn about that, really, except it would make securing a match for Blythe that much easier. He appreciated both men's show of support, but he didn't need another's confirmation that he had worth. He'd defeated that demon long ago.

Blythe set her glass down and leaned forward in her chair. "You don't seem in a celebratory mood. It's the debacle involving Freddy, isn't it?"

They hadn't talked of Frederica yet. Blythe had tried and Gabe had glared her into silence every time, but his sister was not one to be put off for long. "Yes," he said, dragging a hand through his hair. He could not quit thinking upon what the scene at the ball meant for her, how his own part in it, the strange desire that had pushed him to announce in front of the *ton* that she was his, had undoubtedly made matters worse, and unquestionably made Brooke's claim that Frederica and Gabe had carried on a sordid affair appear true. She was not his, but when he'd seen Brooke with her, he'd felt a possessiveness and a protectiveness like nothing he'd ever experienced before.

"Let's talk about it, then," Blythe said.

Gabe slid his teeth back and forth, struggling to order his thoughts. Everything related to Frederica was disorderly. Unpredictable. Unplanned. She was like the wind. She'd whirled into his life all of a sudden, and he was having trouble getting her out. "There's nothing to talk about," Gabe finally managed.

"Oh yes, quite right." Blythe's smirk deepened. "We should definitely not talk about how you nearly beat Lord Brooke in defense of Freddy, or how you declared that she was yours." He glared at his sister, and in return, she grinned, kicked her feet up on the desk, and crossed them at the ankles. "We'll circle back to you. Let's talk about me for a moment."

"What about you?" he asked.

"I see no reason I should wed now. Carrington and Lionhurst can now openly cajole their rich nob associates to invest in your club. You'd be respectable by association, so I no longer need to wed and leave Covent Garden." She offered a smug, self-assured smile.

God save him from strong women who didn't seem to give a damn about their safety. He had let Blythe stay with him for too long, but her latest escapades were a sharp reminder that it was time he took control of his sister's safety. "You will still wed a lord and go to live in Mayfair.

That has not changed." He rose, went to the sideboard to pour another whisky, then faced his sister once more.

She arched her eyebrows at him. "I can die just as easily in Mayfair as Covent Garden, Gabe."

He stiffened and struggled not to show a reaction to her words, though it had hit dead center on his unstated fears, but his sister knew him too well. She rose and came to stand before him. Reaching around him, she grabbed the whisky decanter and poured herself a finger. She clinked her glass to his, then took a long swig.

"I'm staying," she said. "I only agreed to your hare-brained idea because it fit my purposes, but now my purposes have changed."

Hadn't he basically had the same thought? He thought quickly about how he could obtain what he desired for Blythe without his sister feeling like she'd been forced into something, which it was clear she would not go along with.

"You win," he said, and she grinned, thinking she had, which suited him perfectly. "But if I'm going to acquire men of the *ton* to invest in my clubs, they'll come to see the club. They won't just forget where we come from and where we live. It would help me greatly if you would act as a lady when my prospective business associates come around."

"Why does it matter now?" she asked, looking very suspicious. "It never mattered with Carrington or Lionhurst."

"Carrington and I were close friends before we were business associates, and Lionhurst has views on men of the *ton* being in business that are not typical for Society."

She snorted at that. "You mean they're a bunch of soft dandies who think they're too good to work or associate with anyone who does."

"For the most part," he agreed, though he intended to

find her a husband who was *not* like that. "And because of that, when these men eventually come to look at my clubs, you need to be the perfect hostess. You need to make them feel that the club is a natural extension of their privileged life, and the best way to do that is by behaving exactly as a Society lady would. I need you to do this for me, if you are staying." It was a dirty trick to use Blythe's love for him to get what he wanted, but he would do whatever was required to ensure her safety.

"Fine." She sighed. "If you need me, I'll do it, of course, but I do feel guilty."

"About what?"

"Well, I did practically promise Freddy she would get the job as bookkeeper."

"No." He couldn't have Frederica here. It would be impossible to keep his hands off her, and not keeping his hands off someone like Frederica would only lead to marriage. Not only would she be in danger from Hawk if she became Gabe's wife but she'd be in danger of being hurt by Gabe when he couldn't give her the proper affection.

Blythe blew out a hard breath, and the hair dangling in front of her face fluttered. She shoved it unceremoniously behind her ears. "I figured you'd say that. Well, if you won't let her be the bookkeeper, at least let her be the one to teach me to be a lady."

"No. Put your association with Frederica out of your mind. It's done nothing but cause her, you, and me trouble."

"You caused yourself trouble," Blythe said, eyeing him. "Just what were you doing dancing with Freddy at Carrington's ball anyway?"

His eyes widened. "Was that in the gossip sheet?"

"No. Bear told me."

"Bear? How the devil does Bear know?"

"You and Freddy are the talk of the *ton*, and the men who frequent this club are often of the *ton*." She gave him a look that said he should have known that. "Bear overheard some nobs discussing the fact that they thought Freddy must be exceptional in the bedchamber—"

"Blythe," he growled, his temper surging that men would talk about Frederica so.

His sister shrugged. "I'm just repeating what they said. They said she must be the best in the bedchamber for you to fight over her. They said that, despite the many times they'd come to the club, they'd never seen you so much as look at a woman. And you know, Gabe… They're right."

Now she was giving him a probing look. "Leave it be, Blythe," he said, enraged that Frederica's reputation was in tatters.

"Why?" Blythe pushed. "Because you like her and you don't want to because you want to mourn Georgette forever? Or is really because you won't pursue her because you're afraid she'll die? Because you're afraid Hawk will return and do something to her?"

Gabe slammed his glass on the bar. "All the above," he said, in lieu of truly answering. "Now just leave it be. All your pushing, prodding, and meddling won't change my mind. Nothing will."

"Beck," came a call from the other side of the door.

"What is it, Tom?" Gabe called back to his right-hand man.

"Missive delivered for ye," the Scot replied. "Bear gave it to me to pass to ye."

Gabe stalked to the door, took the missive, and thanked Tom. After closing the door again, Gabe opened the envelope and stared down in surprise at the note from

Frederica's father.

*You have ruined my daughter. Call upon me after the
supper hour to discuss what you are going to do about it.*

The Earl of Fairfax

"What is it?" Blythe demanded.

Gabe looked to his sister as his fingers curled around the
missive. "It's a summons from Frederica's father. He wants
me to call upon him tonight to discuss what I'm going to do
about ruining Frederica."

"Well, even I know you can't go around telling everyone a lady is yours and not expect someone to take it
seriously, Gabe. So what are you going to do?" She gave
him an expectant look, and he knew what she was thinking.

"I cannot wed her, Blythe."

His sister narrowed her eyes. "I don't see why not.
You're not wed. She's not wed. She's ruined. You caused it.
You like her. She wants to live here. And—"

"I told you why not already," he interrupted. He needed
a good fight. He was going to explode at any moment.

"Oh yes, ghost, guilt, and fear of yourself and Hawk."

"I'm not afraid of myself or Hawk. I know who I am,
and I accept it. And I know what Hawk would do if he ever
thought—Never mind. I am not afraid of Hawk, and I will
eventually find him and deal with him." He had been
searching for Hawk since he left, to no avail. The man had
gone underground, and no amount of prodding had
brought him up. Gabe would give Hawk this—the men
from Covent Garden who had worked with Hawk were still
very loyal, which made Gabe think they had not stopped
working together. No doubt doing illegal things. "Frederica
does not need to wed me."

"Yes, it's very sensible to let poor Freddy be ruined for

life, never get wed, be forced to live in poverty, possibly become a Cyprian to survive if her parents disown her because you're afraid to lose someone again and won't admit it."

"You are being dramatic," he said to his sister's back just before she disappeared out of the office without so much as a farewell. But dramatic or not, he could not get Frederica out of his mind. He had not compromised her—not really. He could not wed her, but he could not ignore the situation, either. He started to reach for a pen to answer the summons and say he'd come when there was a commotion in the hall.

When he stepped into the shadowy corridor to see what the noise was about, a man charged him and barreled into him with fists flying. By the time he'd evaded two punches, landed one of his own, and rolled onto the man to pin him down, he realized it was Frederica's brother, Huntley.

Huntley glowered up at him. "You seduced my sister!"

Gabe was about to claim his innocence, but he realized, technically, it wasn't true. He had kissed Frederica, and it had been a thorough kiss, one he had not been able to forget. And it was in the thinking of her soft lips under his that Huntley landed a solid punch to Gabe's right eye. He likely would have landed another if Blythe hadn't come from the darkness and hit the man over the head with a book.

Chapter Ten

$\mathcal{F}$reddy wasn't normally a coward, but when her father had forbidden her from joining him in his study to meet with Beckford, she'd been relieved. Yet, now that she could see Beckford in her father's study and she could see her father's face, which looked angry, she wished she had at least stayed inside the house, instead of retreating to the garden, so she could hear what was being said. In the house, she could have lingered near the door and listened. In fact, she still could.

She rose from the bench that faced her father's study, intent on going to eavesdrop, but before she could even turn toward the path that led to the door, a voice came at her back. "Are you trying to read their lips?"

Freddy whipped around to face Guinevere, whom she'd not seen since the ball. She'd half feared that Guinevere wasn't speaking to her, either. "No. It's too dark for lipreading. I was looking at their expressions. What are you doing here? I thought you were terribly vexed with me."

"I was," Guinevere said, "but then Asher told me how Lord Brooke had intended to ruin you because of your involvement in his Cyprian leaving him. I can hardly be cross with you that the man was successful in his endeavor, though if you'd told anyone in SLAR what you were doing in Covent Garden with Blythe Beckford, we would have helped."

"I tried to tell you," Freddy said. "Actually, I tried to tell you, Lilias, and Constantine, but I was met with much the same response from each of you."

"Which was?"

"Basically, not to bother you because you were too busy to even listen to what I wanted to say."

Guinevere's jaw dropped. "I never would have said that!"

Freddy frowned and patted her sister's shoulder, not wanting her to feel bad. "You did. But in your defense, every time I started to tell you about it, one of the children spit up or cried, and you eventually snapped at me that you were too busy to listen to trivial matters that did not involve you keeping a child alive."

"Oh, Freddy..." Guinevere's eyes filled with tears. "I'm the one who's sorry now."

"No." Freddy shook her head. "There's no need to be. I was hurt at first, but I realized that you were correct. Your life has changed, and SLAR cannot come first for you right now."

Guinevere grasped Freddy and pulled her into a tight hug. "Freddy, darling, you have the softest heart. Someday a man will—"

Freddy shoved out of her sister's arms. "Don't say it." She knew instinctively what Guinevere was going to say. "I've no interest in love." But the words seemed a tad harder to say than they had been before. Was it because now that she was faced with the prospect of having to wed, she would be foolish not to hope for it to eventually come to her?

Guinevere frowned. "You've said before, though, that you wished to find a man like Asher. Or possibly it was like Kilgore," her sister said, mentioning their friend Constantine's husband, who really was quite gallant. "Or mayhap it was Greybourne," Guinevere muttered, citing their friend Lilias's husband while pressing her fingertips to her temples. "Motherhood really has made me horribly forgetful."

"I only said that because it was expected," Freddy blurted, not surprised when her sister gaped at her. Freddy honestly felt like gaping herself. Had she truly only said that because it was expected? She was so confused all of a sudden, and she honestly felt like it was Beckford's fault. "Why are you here?" she asked her sister again, realizing Guinevere had not answered.

"I came out of concern for you, and because I wanted you to tell me exactly what your association is with Mr. Beckford. I don't believe for a moment that the two of you have been carrying on a secret scandalous affair, but my goodness, the way the man defended you the other night did make me wonder exactly what has occurred."

"Nothing has occurred," Freddy said, but the blasted kiss popped into her head and her voice got all wobbly because, well, that kiss had made her feel all wobbly.

"Freddy, you're lying!"

Considering that, at this very moment, her father was suggesting to Beckford that he wed her, she thought perhaps seeking some advice from her sister might be a good idea. She glanced over her shoulder, back toward the study window, and frowned. She didn't see Beckford anywhere. Had he and her father already concluded their business? It wasn't a good sign if they had. It would take more time than the small amount Beckford had been in there to speak of marriage contracts and her dowry. That could only mean that Beckford had declined to wed her. Dread dropped like a stone into the center of her chest.

Papa had promised her that if Beckford refused, then

Papa would ask the man to speak with her in the garden
before he departed. She would swallow her pride and beg
him to wed her, if need be, not that it would do any good,
but she had to try for Vivian. She'd racked her brain all day,
and her parents were correct. As loath as she was to admit
it, this was the best course to aid Vivian. And if Beckford
still declined her pleas, then that left her no choice but to
seek out Lord Brooke and see if he would wed her. Never
had she felt more like Frightful Frederica than in this
moment.

She looked toward the door to the garden, willing it to
open, but when it remained firmly shut, she rushed out an
explanation of what had occurred with Vivian and Asterly.
Freddy finished with, "So you see, I've no choice but to set
matters to rights."

"And you'll do that by marrying a stranger?" Guinevere
was giving her the oddest look, probing almost, as if she
were searching for some reaction.

Freddy frowned. "I know him well enough." When she
tried to glance back toward the gate that led from the
house, Guinevere grabbed Freddy's shoulders.

"Do you? Whatever could you possibly know about the
man?"

Now Freddy was getting irritated. Her sister was acting
as if Freddy were featherbrained and had not thought about
this at all. "He's compassionate." She told Guinevere
quickly of how Beckford had helped Belle. "He's considerate." She then told Guinevere how Beckford had ensured
his driver saw her home safely after she'd been accosted and
how he'd had her locket returned to her. "And he's clearly
protective and able to deliver on the instinct," she said, a
ripple of excitement going through her at the remembrance
of how he'd fought to defend her honor.

"Those are lovely qualities, but what if you and he wed, and there was no passion."

"Oh, there'd be passion," Freddy said, so swept away by the precise memory of how his kiss had felt like fire in her veins that that she didn't think to guard her words. "We've kissed, and though he's the only man I've ever *willingly* kissed, I cannot see how it could get better than how he made me feel."

"Freddy!" Guinevere exclaimed. "Do hush now."

But Freddy was determined to say what she wanted to for once without being hushed or told she ought not to. "Beckford lit me up like a chandelier."

Guinevere groaned, which made Freddy laugh. "The main problem I see with wedding Beckford is that obviously we don't love each other, but surely we could come to some sort of mutually beneficial arrangement."

"Such as?" came a deep voice from behind her.

Freddy froze for a second, certain she was imagining having heard Beckford, but Guinevere had a look upon her face, one Freddy had not seen in quite a while but that she remembered well from all the times she and Guinevere had conspired to get someone to do something they wished them to do. Freddy had been duped by her sister, though she wasn't sure exactly how or why.

"If you'll excuse me," Guinevere rushed out. "Asher must be wondering what's taking me so long out here." And without waiting for either Freddy or Beckford to respond, Guinevere hurried away, leaving Freddy no choice but to face Beckford and wonder just how much he'd heard.

He should have departed when his business was concluded

with Frederica's father. Gabe had known that full well. It would have been the safe thing to do, the intelligent thing to do, given how he wanted Frederica. But when her father had accused him of sealing her fate of ruination in the eyes of the *ton* and had demanded Gabe wed her, Gabe had actually considered it for a moment, had imagined her lips under his once again, her mouth parted, her head thrown back, and even how she felt in the most hidden parts of her body, but then he'd remembered Hawk's threat and how he'd failed to protect his mother and Georgette and how losing someone you cared for left an unfillable hole in your heart. One more hole was more than he cared to endure. So knowing all of that, how the devil had he ended up out here standing in front of Frederica?

He'd told her father he was leaving, even as the earl had asked him to tell Frederica of his decision himself before he departed. Gabe had followed the summoned footman out of Fairfax's study and down the corridor as shadows danced on the walls from the lights on the tables. And then they'd passed the damned window. If Gabe had never turned his head to the right to look outside, he would not have seen her. She shone like a star even in the darkness. She'd been standing with her back to him, but a light illuminated her figure and her hands. Those hands, gesturing with such emphasis as she spoke to Lady Guinevere, whose face Gabe could see. The duchess had seen him, too. He was sure of it. Yet she'd kept speaking to Frederica as if she had no awareness he was staring at them. Strange that, considering what he'd just overheard.

Good Christ, he'd wished he'd not heard them. He had lit her like a chandelier? Yes, he understood. She lit him, too. Dangerous, dazzling light. He was a moth, and she was the flame.

In the distance, the gate clanged shut behind the duchess, breaking some odd spell both he and Frederica had been under as they'd stood there silently staring at each other. He had to speak, to tell her he couldn't wed her but he would provide for her future, which is what he'd told her father.

Instead, he heard himself ask yet again, "What sort of mutually beneficial arrangement would you imagine us coming to, Frederica?" There was something wrong with his brain. Clearly, he'd taken one hit too many to the head if he could no longer enforce the will of his mind over his mouth.

"Just how much did you hear?" she asked.

Her bluntness spoke to his soul, which was part of the problem. She didn't mince words as most ladies did. There was no subterfuge or coquettishness, and he'd never been one for either of those things.

"Enough to know I light you like a chandelier." He could not remember a time bantering with a woman had made him desire her, but he was as hard as stone now.

"I'll not apologize for that truth, though I wish you'd not heard me say it."

He could understand that. It made her vulnerable to him, and he sensed in her the same dislike of being rendered vulnerable to anyone that he felt inside.

"If it makes you feel better," he said, wanting with a foolish desperation to do so, especially given what else he had to say, "you lit me, too."

"Ah, well, that does appease me a tad." Her low, throaty voice was the sort a man wanted to hear in his ear whispering the things the woman wanted the man to do to her. It was a bedchamber voice. "About my father calling you here, Beckford…"

"I can't wed you, Frederica." He wanted to get that part

over with as quickly as possible, but he'd actually flinched when he said the words, and his chest tightened at her slight stiffening. Her show of vulnerability caused a wave of regret to wash over him.

"Can we discuss this sitting down?" she asked. "I'm suddenly horribly tired."

He was, too, and he was never exhausted because he didn't have the luxury to be. "Where shall we sit?"

"Follow me." She turned, and he fell into step behind her, trying not to watch how her hips swayed provocatively as she walked and failing miserably. Never had he been so enchanted by the sway of a woman's hips in his life. Her skirts swished as she led him down a stone path, past orderly shrubs, scented flowers, thick vines, and around a corner past a fountain and out of the view of the house.

This was dangerous. For him. For her. For him keeping his hands off her. He should go back, and yet he went forward into the deepening shadows and onto a long path that was encased on both sides and overhead by an arbor covered in thick climbing vines. In the middle of the arbor was a bench, a wrought iron invitation to sin.

Chapter Eleven

" *I*s it done?"

Guinevere nearly jumped out of her slippers at her husband's deep voice coming from the shadows of the solar in her parents' home, which was bathed in moonlight. Her heart was still pounding in her gown from her deception of Beckford and her sister. She frowned at how horribly out of practice she was. Frederica had been correct. Motherhood had left little time for anything other than her children and husband. Though she would not change such things, Guinevere was glad she had been able to come here tonight. She was gladder still that Blythe Beckford had visited her that afternoon to tell her she thought her brother was falling in love with Frederica but resisting it. She was also the one who told Guinevere that Beckford had been summoned to meet with Guinevere's father. The "falling in love" part was certainly welcome news, considering the scandal Frederica and Beckford now found themselves embroiled in.

Guinevere glanced toward the window where Asher's form came into clearer view, and she smiled. "Were you watching me in the garden talking to Frederica and Beckford?"

Her husband waved her over. She went to him immediately, eager to have his strong arms around her. After he enfolded her in his embrace, he tilted his face to hers and brushed a gentle kiss on her lips. "Of course, I was. Ye know I like to keep a protective eye on ye."

"You must know I'm perfectly safe in my parents' garden with my sister and Beckford."

"I do," Asher replied, tightening his hold on her, "but I also know Beckford has a great many enemies. It's why he wanted his sister to leave Covent Garden for a life in Mayfair." He paused. "So is it as his sister suspects? And what of your sister's feelings?"

Guinevere grinned at her husband. "They most definitely desire each other, and I do truly believe he would be perfect for her. A man like Beckford will appreciate the qualities in her that other men, stuffy men, would not. And I vow Frederica has a tendre for him, though I don't think she's recognized it yet." Guinevere frowned then. "She seemed almost... Well, I cannot quite put my finger on it presently, but I will."

Asher kissed her forehead. "I've no doubt ye will ponder it until ye have figured it out."

Guinevere nibbled on her lip, thinking. Given the disaster at the ball with Frederica, Beckford, and Lord Brooke, giving Beckford and Frederica a push to come together seemed the best thing to do. If Guinevere was wrong about her belief that Frederica and Beckford would make a grand match eventually, there would be more than a short period of hell to pay for both Frederica and Beckford. There would be a lifetime of it.

Guinevere pulled out of Asher's embrace but grasped his hand, intertwining their fingers and turning to the garden window. His arms came around her once more, and she leaned back against his solid chest. "They've moved from where they can be seen."

"Yes," Asher replied, "but Beckford followed Frederica,

he did not lead her. I was watching. After you departed, they went in the direction of the veranda."

Guinevere smiled. "Yes, that's the most private place in the garden. Do you think we've done the right thing, coming here and intervening to ensure they had time alone?"

"Aye." Asher kissed her neck. "Especially since Beckford reacted exactly as his sister said he would."

"Yes." Guinevere pursed her lips for a moment, contemplating everything. "That wasn't very well done of him to refuse my father's suggestion to wed Frederica."

Asher snorted. "It wasn't well done of us to eavesdrop at the door. And your father didn't suggest, he demanded. No man likes to be told what to do, Guin."

"Yes, well, what did Beckford expect might happen if he declared in front of the *ton* that Frederica belonged to him?"

Asher chuckled. "I don't suspect he thought much past ensuring Brooke understood yer sister was under his protection. He's honorable, ye know this. Try not to worry. It will work out."

"I certainly hope so," Guinevere replied, worried still. "Apparently Vivian has turned down Lord Asterly's offer of marriage because Lord Asterly's family would cut him off if they wed."

"The plot thickens," Asher said, his mouth at her ear.

A chuckle washed his warm breath over the delicate skin of her earlobe. She shivered with desire, but then she said, "Do stop making light of things. I know Freddy. If Beckford won't offer for her, she'll do something foolish to right the mess she's made."

"Such as?"

"Such as going to see Lord Brooke and offering herself in marriage to the man."

"He'd take that offer," Asher said, disgust in his voice. "The man's in deep debt."

Guinevere moaned. "It's worse than I thought."

"What's worse than you thought?" came Guinevere's mother's voice from behind her.

Guinevere nearly jumped out of her slippers in surprise. She quickly disentangled herself from Asher's embrace and faced her mother. "The weather," Guinevere said, wincing at the lame explanation.

But her mother thankfully looked distracted and said, "Ah, I see. Where is Frederica? Did she take the news terribly that Mr. Beckford refused to wed her?"

"I left her in the garden," Guinevere replied, carefully avoiding the question about how her sister took the news, since she'd not told her as Guinevere had said she would when her mother had found her and Asher eavesdropping.

Her mother narrowed her eyes. "You are up to something, Guinevere."

"Me? No, Mama, I—"

"Why did you say that you came to the house at this hour?" her mother demanded.

"To ensure Frederica knew I'd forgiven her for causing such drama at my ball."

"Hmm." The single sound was full of disbelief. "I find it strange that you came here, after supper, to tell your sister that—and that you brought your husband with you."

"She hates to be parted from me," Asher replied. Guinevere knew he was trying to be helpful, but his jovial tone made them appear more suspicious.

"Hmm," her mother said again. "I don't believe you, Carrington. You sound entirely too cheerful for a man who was dragged away from his comfortable home to visit his in-laws."

"Mama—"

"Never mind," her mother said. "I'm going to speak with Frederica directly."

"Mama, wait." Guinevere made a grasp for her mother's arm, but her mother was surprisingly quick. She pulled her arm back and glanced between Guinevere and Asher.

"What is occurring here?" She sent a pointed look at Guinevere.

"Nothing," Guinevere said, desperate to keep her mother here so that Frederica and Beckford could have a few more minutes alone. The plan, which wasn't very elaborate at all, given the short notice, had been to come here, and if Beckford had declined his duty to wed Frederica, Asher had thought time alone might push him toward changing his mind, especially if he desired Frederica as much as Blythe seemed to think. Yes, it was improper for them to be alone, but what was propriety in the face of scandal?

"I say," Guinevere's father suddenly boomed, coming into the solar, "the footman just informed me that Mr. Beckford hasn't left yet. His carriage is apparently still here. I sent the man to the garden to tell Frederica he'd not wed her, and—"

Guinevere's mother let out a shriek. Then she gave Guinevere an accusing look and dashed out of the solar toward the garden door.

Chapter Twelve

*S*itting would be the height of idiocy, so naturally, Gabe sat and nearly laughed at himself when he did so. His leg brushed hers, and yearning swished through his veins and made his fingers curl reflexively, aching to touch her.

She turned to him, her face almost completely in shadow except for a flash of white teeth as she bit her lip. He could just see the self-conscious gesture in the filtered moonlight. "I've gone and ruined my sister's life, and I cannot allow that."

He was struck speechless that she would wed him in an effort to aid her sister. It was rare in his world to come across selfless people. "I'm afraid you'll have to elaborate. Your father merely told me I had helped to thoroughly ruin you in the eyes of the *ton*, and it didn't matter that I hadn't actually ruined you. Then he informed me I needed to wed you or live with the fact that I had left you without prospects for the rest of your life."

"And you said you'd live with it."

He hated the tentativeness he heard in her voice. He knew enough of her to know she was not a tentative woman. That he was making her feel that way pained him. "I said I'd ensure you had means for your life. I'll be settling a large fortune on you."

She slumped a little beside him, and he felt her defeat deep in his bones.

"Your money won't save my sister's dream." Her voice was barely above a whisper. "And I don't want your money." Her volume rose with conviction. "You must listen to me." And now the self-assured woman had returned. He almost smiled in relief. "I've never pleaded for anything in my life, but for my sister's happiness, I'll plead." He didn't want her to feel she had to plead for anything. He'd pleaded in his life. For food. For shelter. For work. The humiliation left a scar on your soul that never fully faded, but he couldn't give her what she wanted, so he sat in silence.

"You see, Vivian was almost always ill when we were younger, and Guinevere and I filled her with tales of romance to keep her going. We told her she must live to one day find her true love, and she did. It doesn't matter that I think he's boring and that I can't see what she sees in him. I didn't understand that until today, so I went on foolishly and recklessly doing what I wanted. But now I truly see that she loves him. She gave him up because of me. She gave up the man she loves to spare him pain caused by a mess I created. His family told him if he wed her, they would cut him off, and he told them he didn't care. Don't you see? He's honorable and brave and loves her."

He did. Frederica had a huge heart. It made his chest tighten. "Yes, I see." Her pain made his chest tighten in a way he didn't like. It felt suspiciously like caring. He barely knew her, yet it felt strangely as if there were an invisible tie suddenly binding them. No, that could not be right. It was the moonlight. This damned arbor. Her spicy-sweet scent. Her husky voice. Her bloody honor and bravery. All things that tempted him to kiss her, to touch her.

"She's the best person I know," Frederica said. "She is willing to give Lord Asterly up to ensure his family does not cast him aside, and I wasn't even willing to behave properly until she was wed. That's all she asked of me."

"She asked you to be someone you aren't, Frederica." He didn't like that she was putting all the blame on herself.

"Yes, but only for a short time. I could have done that, but I chose to be selfish."

"And now you want to sacrifice yourself to a marriage you never wanted with a man you barely know?"

She grabbed his hand. Her warm skin against his quickened his breathing, his heartbeat. He'd been careful not to touch her after the initial leg brush, and her hand on his was like a red-hot poker to the inferno of desire he had for her. "I know we'd have passion," she said, little innocent lamb that she was. Oh yes, they'd have passion. He wanted to consume her on the spot now. As she spoke, he took deep breaths. "Or at least I think we would."

Deep breathing was not helping at all. His craving for her climbed within him like flames licking and reaching for oxygen long denied. He struggled to find control, but then she placed his hand on her hammering heart. Ah damn. His mind went blank as to why he should not touch her and lust thickened the blood in his veins.

"This," she whispered, "is how you make me feel."

Each beat of her heart thumped through her silk gown, seeped into his skin, and echoed through him to the chambers of his own heart. He wanted to get lost in her. It scared him how much he wanted it. He was like a drowning man, but he was drowning in his craving for her. He struggled against it, searching for the strength to break contact, but the strength eluded him. His body became hotter, harder, his mind turning over all he wanted to do to her. He wanted to settle her over his lap, ruck up her silk skirts, and claim her. Slowly. Thoroughly.

No, no, no. He squeezed his eyes shut, his senses sizzling in his ears.

"I know you must think worlds separate us…" she said.

Yes, damn it all. That was it. That was the lifeline to reason he had needed. He was at once bloody relieved and angry that she'd said it. He didn't know where he found the will to pull his hand away from her, but he did. Her soft exhalation of disappointment filled his ears like a loud roar.

"If I were to wed you," he said, hearing how his lust strained his voice, "you'd be in danger, Frederica." It was the absolute truth, though not the whole truth of why he needed and wanted to keep a distance from her. "And even if I did wed you, Frederica, I have walls up that I cannot let down. Eventually you'd hate me. I can't allow that life for you, even if you're willing to accept it for yourself."

"You could wed me, and we could live apart. Then you wouldn't have to worry about your walls at all."

The suggestion was tempting and ridiculous.

"That wouldn't work for me, Frederica. I'm not the sort of man to part with what I've acquired."

"I see," she said, her tone wounded. "I do believe you've managed to make me doubt my desirability more than I ever did before."

Good God, her hurt struck a chord deep within him. "Frederica—"

"I shouldn't have said that. Never mind. I thank you for listening to me." She started to rise, but compelled by yet more madness that she inspired, he caught her by the wrist before she turned away.

"Why would you doubt that you're desirable?" he asked.

"Well, I have a particular knack for sending gentlemen running from me at balls. The barbed tongues of the *ton* labeled me Frightful Frederica."

He wanted to pummel every man who'd ever said that about her and push the jealous harpies into the nearest fountain. *Frightful.* He clenched his teeth, his temples beating in time with his temper. She was not frightful; she was magnificent. She was different, and that scared them. She was free, where they were constrained. Bloody asses, the lot of them. One thing he could do for her before he left was show her how desirable she was. "I cannot think a man could meet you and not want you, Frederica."

She smirked at him. "Please don't offer me platitudes on how my eyes are like a storm cloud, or my smile the sun, or my hair makes you want to unpin it."

"I wouldn't dream of it," he said, steeling himself against succumbing too far with what he was about to do. He pulled her so close that her softness crushed to his hardness, and awareness of her body ripped down the length of him. It was like plunging himself into warm water. He wanted to float there, allow her to cover him, become one with him. He brought his hands to her face—it was far too dangerous to allow his hands to rest anywhere else— and cupped her perfectly carved bones. "What I like most about you is your bluntness, your stubborn and inquisitive mind, and your fierce loyalty to your sister. Any man who has ever run from you was too weak for you, and the women are simply jealous. They wish they had the bravery to live their lives as they want to, instead of how they think they ought to."

"Are you including yourself in that bit about the men?" she asked, her warm breath fanning his face.

"I promise you, Frederica, it is not you. It's me." And before he said too much, he slanted his mouth over hers and kissed her. She was like discovering a rare, exquisite whisky of which he could only get his hands on enough to have one small sip. Every cell within him fired to life in a way he'd only experienced with her.

She'd had chocolate at some point this day, and something tart that made his tongue tingle. She was like basking in the sun and soaking up the rays. She parted her lips on a soft moan, and he plunged his tongue inside, a desperation pushing him forward. He felt the same sort of urgency in her, too. She met each stroke of his tongue with one of her own, and though he kept his hands on her face, she slid hers down his back and splayed her fingers against him, palms flattened as if in surrender.

She broke the kiss, and he thought to be glad of it because he'd been getting carried away, but then she threw her head back, inviting him to plunder her neck. He couldn't turn away. He kissed a path down her hot skin, knowing the direction was danger, but he descended lower and lower to bliss, until he stood on the precipice of sanity and sweet surrender.

One touch.

A warning slithered through his head, hissing like a snake. He slid a finger under the top edge of her bodice, past some stiff undergarment, and brushed her hardened nipple. She sucked in a sharp breath, her fingers curling hard into his shoulders. Desire vanquished all thoughts but to slide his tongue over her hardened peak. He couldn't say how it happened next, but she made the most enticing sound of pleasure from deep in her throat as he stroked his finger over her bud, and his need grew so great to taste her skin there, smell it, feel it in his mouth, that with some tugging on strings and hurriedly undoing of clasps that he found at the back of her gown, the material loosened enough that he freed her left breast.

In the dark night, it was a glimmer of creamy flesh. It was the apple in the Garden of Eden. He took her in his mouth, and he felt much like Adam must have when he bit into that apple. He didn't care in that moment how far he fell. All he wanted was to bring her pleasure and take his own. He suckled her in long pulls and nips as she tangled her hands into his hair, and she alternately tugged at his head and pressed him closer.

"What are you doing?" she panted.

Excellent question. His mind had deserted him. Before he could pull his wits together to release her and answer, she said, "I ache, Beckford. So very much."

He knew how to assuage that ache. He abandoned his ministrations to her breast to her protest. "Beckford, don't stop!"

"Shh," he assured her, his voice thick with desire as he bent to gather her skirts up. The fingers of his left hand grazed her warm, silky thigh as he did so, and with his right hand, he found her unmentionables, tugged them down her shapely legs, and rid her of them, tossing them to the side.

She gasped as his fingers delved into her silken hair between her thighs, and he located the pleasure point that would make that ache go away.

"Oh my heaven, that feels good," she said, her voice breathy, one hand clutching his back and her other hand coming to his wrist. "Beckford, we shouldn't."

"No," he managed to force out as disappointment flooded him, and he stilled. "We most definitely should not." His words came in ragged spurts around his labored breathing.

"What are you doing?" she demanded, her fingers fluttering against his hand before disappearing and joining her other hand at his back. "Why have you stopped?"

"You said we shouldn't," he replied, perspiration break-ing out on his forehead from the control it was taking not to keep going.

"I didn't say stop, though!" Her words were a rush of fury and excitement. "I said we shouldn't."

"Ah, my mistake." He grinned, his fingers touching that perfect pearl that made her quiver once more. "I forgot about the language of women."

"I will be offended later," she said on a moan. "Now I simply want to feel the pleasure."

"Do you mean the pleasure when I touch you here?" He ran the pad of his thumb over her nub ever so gently.

"Yes, yes. More."

"Like this?" he teased, stroking faster and in circles.

"Yes, yes, just like that. Beckford—"

"Gabriel," he demanded, his heart pumping blood so hard he'd probably be deaf from his desire tomorrow. "Call me Gabriel." He had gone and jumped off the edge of a cliff. He had not allowed anyone to call him Gabriel since his mother died, not even his sister. He was no angel—far from it. But he wanted to hear his name on her sweet lips.

"Gabriel." She clung to him, her thighs clenching to-gether to press against his hand. "Gabriel, don't stop. Don't you dare stop."

"Even if someone comes down the path," he said, offer-ing a provoking smile then glancing down the long, dark, pebbled passage just to be certain they were in no danger.

"Maybe then," she said on another moan, and she tensed, her fingernails digging into his shoulders for one breath, two, three, before they loosened and her entire body sagged forward. Her cheek came to his chest, and her hand settled over his heart. He tried to will the damn thing to stop hammering, but it was useless. He was wound with need and desire tighter than any coil.

"I will never forget this, Gabriel."

And before he could answer, a shout cut through the night. "Frederica!"

Reality punched him hard and fast like the fool he was. He never let desire rule him. Never. Not until her.

Frederica bounded away from him like a cat thrown in water and yanked up her gown. "It's my mother!"

What had he done? He couldn't believe it. He knew better. Frederica was an innocent, and he was so far from it he might as well be reaching to Heaven from Hell.

She fell to her knees by his feet. "My unmentionables! Where are they?"

Good God. Was this what a woman you were truly drawn to could do to you? Steal every ounce of sense you possessed? He'd touched her in a way he should never have let himself do. He'd touched her in a way that bound him to her now for life. He couldn't let anyone else touch her like that. He'd trapped them both.

Clenching his teeth, he bent and scooped up her un-mentionables from where he'd dropped them, his pulse ticking even faster. "Here." He extended the garment toward her, and just as he did so, light flooded the dark passage.

She lunged toward the garment, snatched it from his hand, and dropped it, crying out and reaching for it just as he did. Their heads nearly collided, and she tipped back-ward, but he grasped her, tugging her toward him, their chests smashing together as footsteps stopped behind him and light illuminated them, as well as her unmentionables sitting beside them.

A pregnant pause came for one breath, and Gabe drank Frederica in. She looked well sated and beautiful. It made him want to ruck up her skirts again. It was not the moment for the thought, but it was there in his head, stirring his desire once more.

"Papa," she breathed out, and the single word locked in Gabe's fate.

Behind him, a voice, deep and angry, said, "Either you will wed my daughter, or I'll meet you on the field of honor tomorrow and one of us won't live to leave that field."

"Papa!" Frederica gasped, scrambling to her feet, clutching the very material Gabe had pulled off her supple body. "Papa, no! It's not what you think."

Her father's face twisted with fury, an emotion the man had every right to feel. Frederica scuttled backward, and Gabe stepped forward, grabbed her by the waist, and pulled her behind him, shielding her.

"You do not need to protect my own daughter from me." The earl's voice vibrated with anger. "You, on the other hand, I've a mind to kill."

"Papa!" Frederica tried to come out from behind Gabe, but he stuck out his arm and blocked her, his instinct to protect her still too strong to deny.

"You've every right to be enraged with me," Gabe said. "But your daughter—"

"Is an innocent whom you have clearly compromised," the earl said, spitting each word out as Frederica's mother began to wail. "You will wed her, or we will duel. I'll accept nothing less."

⚜

"Papa!" Frederica yelped. She'd wanted to set things right for Vivian, but she certainly had not wanted to trap Gabriel into wedding her. She'd hoped he'd come to the decision of his own accord. "You cannot force the man to wed me!"

"You are certainly right, but if he doesn't, I will ruin him as you will be ruined."

"She could wed Lord Brooke," Guinevere, who had just appeared with Carrington behind her father, said in an odd, almost cheerful tone.

"Yes!" her mother agreed, her wailing pausing mercifully. "Yes, yes! If this scoundrel won't have her, I'm sure Lord Brooke will do what is right so that Vivian and Asterly can still wed."

"Indeed," Guinevere said in that same inappropriate and overly cheerful tone. "Lord Brooke is in a great deal of debt, I hear." Was it Freddy's imagination or was Guinevere spearing Gabriel with a challenging look? "I'm certain," Guinevere continued as she stared at Gabriel, her eyebrows arching, "that once he discovers Frederica's great dowry, he'll snatch her up like the prize she is."

Freddy felt her jaw slip open. What the devil was Guinevere doing? She knew that Brooke was a horrid man. Why was she suggesting Freddy wed him?

"I will kill Brooke before I let him wed your sister," Gabriel snarled.

Freddy's lips pulled into a smile, which she just managed to cover. It was horribly unfitting to smile at a time like this, but, well, Gabriel *did* sound as if he didn't want Brooke to wed her because he himself wanted to possess her. That was something. Something good, she thought. It wasn't love. Of course not. They hardly knew each other. But they wanted each other, enough that they'd been unthinking fools. Enough that he didn't want another man to have her.

Couldn't love spring from that?

She blinked in shock at the errant thought. Did she

want it to? Hadn't she decided after her disastrous entry into the marriage mart that she didn't care about love, didn't need or want it? Hadn't she lain awake in her bed after being labeled Frightful Frederica and cried hot tears, vowing she would gain her freedom from life in the *ton* and live where people would accept her as she was? Marriage had not been part of her plan, and yet, here she was. She would be the biggest fool to want a marriage of convenience with a stranger rather than a partner, indifference rather than caring, coldness rather than warmth. Could Gabriel accept her as she was? Did she care, truly?

Before she could ponder it more, her father shoved his finger so close to Gabriel's nose, he almost touched it. "Either you will wed my daughter or Lord Brooke will. You and I both know what a man deep in debt will do."

"I'll wed her," Gabriel said, and with those three words, her fate—and Gabriel's—was sealed.

Chapter Thirteen

"Frederica, stop it!" Freddy's mother grabbed Freddy's hands just as she was about to rub her sweaty palms against her silk wedding dress once more.

"I'm so nervous, though," Freddy grumbled, tugging her hands away from her mother's grip. Freddy eyed the closed door of the drawing room. Gabriel was in there with Freddy's family and his sister, waiting for Freddy to enter and wed him. Was he as nervous as she was? She didn't know because she hadn't seen him since the scene in the garden three days prior. Her father had forbidden them from doing so until the wedding, and he had positioned her brother to sleep outside her bedchamber door while her father assigned the footmen outside to guard the house at night. It was the height of humiliation, though no less than she knew she deserved.

"You've made splotches on your beautiful gown," Vivian said, leaning toward Freddy to grab at her skirts and shake them.

Freddy smacked her sister's hands away, and when Vivian gave her a hurt look, Freddy said, "I'm sorry." She wasn't vexed with Vivian. Truly. She was glad her sister was speaking to her again, and she was equally glad that Asterly had come to see Vivian that morning, after Vivian had sent word to him that Freddy was to wed Gabriel today. And Freddy was thrilled that Asterly's parents had indicated that he could offer for Vivian without fear of being cut off from them—*after* Freddy was good and wed. So it seemed the mess Freddy had created was going to be set right, after all. Freddy was thrilled, just thrilled.

Except she wasn't. She'd merely managed to trade one mess for another.

She hadn't been able to sleep or eat since Gabriel had agreed to wed her, and she did so love her meals. The realization that she'd trapped Gabriel, inadvertently or not, and that he'd despise her for it forever was making her ill.

"Just look at your hair!" her mother exclaimed. "You've done nothing with it!"

Freddy shrugged, her thoughts stuck on her and Gabriel. She was about to wed a man she barely knew anything about, except that his kisses and touches fired her blood. She was sure she could come to care for him, but it would be nice to know if he believed he could come to care for her.

As she stood there, her thoughts tumbling around her head, her mother and sister fussed over her hair, tugging, pulling, and twisting. Freddy let them, glad for the time to think, before her mother pronounced, "There! You look much better."

When her mother glanced to the parlor door, as if about to open it, Freddy's panic grew.

She had to speak to Gabriel alone. She would not back out of the wedding—she would not do that to Vivian—but she needed Gabriel to know she had not meant to trap him.

"I need to speak with Beckford," she blurted.

Her mother frowned at her. "You'll have a lifetime to speak with your husband."

"No." The word came out sharper than she'd intended. So sharp, in fact, that her mother gasped and Vivian's eyes went wide. "I need to speak with him before we are wed.

Alone."

"Your father will never allow that," her mother said, her tone now equally as sharp as Freddy's.

"Mama!" Freddy sucked in a breath for patience. "I have trapped this man into marrying me!"

"Trapped him?" her mother repeated, her tone incredulous and gaining in volume. "Trapped him? He seduced you! You are an innocent. You—"

"Mama!" Freddy bellowed. "Beckford did not seduce me! I think it highly probable that *I* seduced *him.*"

And just like that, her mother fainted.

A loud thump came from outside the parlor door, which Gabe welcomed as a nice break from Frederica and her mother yelling at each other. As Frederica's family rushed from the room, Gabe felt Blythe's stare on him. He glanced at her as the vicar pretended to busy himself with more wedding preparations, though a moment ago the man had been standing there impatiently waiting for Frederica and the others to enter.

Blythe hitched her eyebrows at Gabe and grinned. "She seduced you, eh?"

"Hardly." Gabe tugged on his cravat. He damned well hated cravats. They were confining, and he hated to be confined. Flashes of Frederica's eyes, her mouth, her lips danced before him. She had not seduced him, his little wanton fool. They'd seduced each other. He'd come to that conclusion over the past three sleepless nights as he'd come to accept that he was getting married, despite the fact that he'd planned never to do so.

Wedding was what a man had to do when he could not

keep his hands off an innocent woman, and they were caught in a moonlit garden with her unmentionables removed. The cravat seemed to grow as tight as a damned noose around his neck, choking off his air. Outside the parlor, the commotion grew louder, but he forced himself to face the truth. He had compromised Frederica. He had compromised her knowing somewhere in the back of his head what it might lead to, and he'd still taken that chance. No. No, that was not right. He'd been unable *not* to take the chance. That was different. There hadn't been a choice. His reaction to her was physical, and it controlled his mind whenever she was near.

He'd not been prepared for it, for her, because he'd not known such a reaction was possible. He'd never been drawn to a woman as he was Frederica. When she'd said she would wed Brooke, he'd known down to his marrow that he could never allow that. Brooke was a bastard, and Gabe couldn't live with himself if he let Frederica sacrifice herself to a life with a man like Brooke. Except now, she'd sacrificed herself to a man like him, one who didn't want to feel soft emotions, one who didn't even know if he could anymore. One who had an enemy who would come for her.

Good God, what had he done? To her? To himself? To both of them. He shoved his hands through his hair, reeling as he had for three days. And then he forced himself to take measured long breaths. There was no going back. Only forward.

They'd wed, and he'd install her in the house in Mayfair he'd purchased yesterday. She'd stay in this world where she would be safe, and he'd stay in his. Part of his problem was solved, which left Hawk for Gabe to deal with. He would have men watch Frederica day and night, and when

Hawk finally appeared, Gabe would make his move. He
would swoop in, snatch Hawk, and take him to the
Henderson Home for the Mentally Impaired, right here in
London. Gabe had personally funded a new ward at the
institution over the last four years, knowing the day might
come when Hawk tired of waiting for Gabe to attach
himself to a woman and simply returned to get his revenge
on Gabe. He would then need two physicians to sign their
names to papers saying Hawk was dangerous to society and
needed to be committed. Whether that was for life or not
would depend on Hawk and his willingness to face the
reality of what he'd done to Georgette, not to mention
Gabe's determination of if the man was still a threat to
Frederica.

"Gabe, shouldn't you go see what all the fuss is about?"
Blythe asked.

Before Gabe could answer, the parlor door swung open,
and Frederica strode in. "Beckford, I need to speak with you
in private."

Her appearance in a rose-and-white gown that fit her
curves to perfection, her hair swept up to reveal her kissable
neck, would have been enough to trip up his thoughts. But
it was, in fact, the way she speared him with her intense
gaze, set her hands on her hips, and gave him an expression
that dared him to deny her request that made his head spin
and admiration fill his chest. Frederica might have been
reared in the protection of Mayfair and taught to be a
proper lady, but he would wager she could hold her own
with any Covent Garden–bred woman or man any day.

She arched her eyebrows. "Beckford?"

"Yes, of course," he replied and glanced to Blythe and
the vicar. "We need a moment."

The vicar looked prepared to protest, but Gabe narrowed his eyes upon the man, who wisely followed Blythe out of the room. Once the door shut, Frederica whispered, "I didn't mean to trap you into wedding me." She glanced down at her hands instead of looking at him.

The woman before him continued to astound him. She might possibly be the finest woman he'd ever met. Here she was, about to wed a virtual stranger, and she was worried that he might think she'd tried to trap him. He moved toward her, the desire to discover all the layers that made up this woman strong within him.

He hooked a finger under her chin and raised her face until their eyes collided. The worry in the depths of hers stirred him. "You didn't trap me, Frederica. I did that myself, the minute I touched you once more. I could have possibly walked away from you before the garden, but after—"

"You feel obligated to wed me because of my father's threat?"

He shook his head. "No. I am obligated to wed you because I compromised you, and I could not stand by and watch you sacrifice yourself to a man like Brooke."

She looked stricken. Women were so bloody perplexing. "That's very noble of you," she said, sounding glum.

He frowned. "And that makes you unhappy?"

"No, of course not. I'm unhappy because we don't know each other. I was so concentrated on saving my sister's dream of wedding Asterly that I didn't truly consider that, in wedding you, I'm wedding a stranger. I never even thought to wed. I thought to move to Covent Garden and live as I pleased in a place I would finally feel accepted for who I am."

The best to thing to do in accordance with his intent to keep her at a distance would be to offer her vague reassuring words. Words that didn't draw them closer, yet he found there was no chance he could do that to her, knowing how worried she was in this moment. So instead, he tucked an errant lock of hair behind her ear, and she smiled shyly at him, making his chest tighten. "We won't remain strangers, Frederica." They could be friends, of a sort.

"Yes," she muttered, still looking worried.

"What is it?" he encouraged her.

She nibbled on her lip for a moment before answering. "What if we find we don't like each other? Marriage is for life."

"I don't think we'll have that problem," he said, and because she still looked concerned, and was once again nibbling her lip, he brushed a light kiss there, driven by the desire to set her at ease.

She exhaled slowly, and a small smile tugged at her lips. "Desiring someone is not the same as liking them," she said, her voice soft and filled with trepidation.

A knock came at the door, followed by her father demanding to know if they were ready.

By the earl's impatient tone, Gabe knew the man was not of a mind to give them much longer. Gabe took in her face, suddenly very white. He caught her fingertips in his, unsure if she was more worried that she would not like him or that he would not like her. Whichever case it was, he wanted to reassure her. He brought her fingertips up and kissed them. "We've little choice in the matter to wed at this point, do we?"

"No," she said, looking glum. "I am sorry. I would offer to back out, but I cannot. Yet, if you wish to, I will not hate you."

She was giving him a way out, but it was one he could never take. "I may have grown up on the streets, but I'm a man of honor, as I told you, and I wouldn't be if I backed out."

"Yes, yes. It's good and solidified in my mind. You will wed me because you're oh so honorable. Thank God above for us both," she said, sounding anything but thankful. Could he blame her though, given the circumstances they were in, and given that he was not offering words of any love to come. Guilt jabbed him, especially given she didn't even yet know he intended for them to live apart. "Listen, Frederica, I need to tell you—"

The parlor door banged open and Frederica's father stormed into the room. "You'll wed my daughter now, Beckford," he said. "Or we will meet for that duel."

Chapter Fourteen

" *Frederica.*"

Her name in her ear woke her with a start. Frederica jolted up, blinked the sleep from her eyes, and glanced around, unsure for a moment where she was or why her head felt as if someone had stuffed cotton in it.

Gabriel's gaze met hers through the dancing shadows of the lantern that hung from a nob to light the inside of the carriage. He looked disturbingly, wickedly handsome and withdrawn. Memories pelted her at once. Her quick wedding ceremony, the long wedding dinner where toast after toast was given to her and Gabriel's happiness. How after each toast, he seemed to draw further away from her, though he was seated right next to her. And then there was the champagne…

She'd never drunk it before, but tonight she'd had two glasses to drown her anxiety and her fear that she was now trapped in a marriage with a man who desired her but did not like her. Or possibly, hopefully, it was more apt to say he did not *want* to like her because he still loved his dead wife. While she had been quite sure for some time that she neither wanted nor needed love, she was not as certain now that she was good and wed, and she was most definitely, most absolutely certain that she, at the very least, wanted her husband to like her, accept who she was, and allow her into his world.

"Frederica."

His deep voice startled her out of her thoughts. "Yes?"

"You're at your new home." Gabriel said, rapping on the carriage door, which was immediately opened to reveal his coachman standing at the ready to help them alight from the conveyance.

Something about his words made her frown, and if her blasted thoughts were not so muddled, she would know what immediately. As it was, it took her a moment to pick the sentence apart. When she did, and she got at the heart of its meaning, her air felt suddenly cut off and she had to force a breath. Surely, he could not mean he was putting her in a home in Covent Garden other than his? She had wanted her freedom, but she'd meant freedom to be herself. Not freedom from all ties. No, no. He most definitely could not mean that.

Still, her pulse would not settle. "My new home?"

His gaze settled on her once more. If eyes could have shutters, then Gabriel's were closed. There was a protective covering that now hid his emotions. "Yes," he said, raking his hand through his hair, the only indication he was feeling anything at all. "I tried to tell you at your house, before the ceremony, so it wouldn't come as a surprise—"

"Tried to tell me what exactly?" she asked, her pulse now at a full gallop.

He glanced over his shoulder to his awaiting coachman, and she thought he might dismiss the man since he stood within hearing distance, but he didn't. Instead, Gabriel cleared his throat and faced her once more, a determined look now upon his face. "I purchased a home in Mayfair the day before yesterday."

Freddy's brows drew together. "Whatever for?" she asked like a fool, but there could be only one answer. He was never planning to let her into his world. He thought to force her to live in a world where she didn't belong. A spasmodic trembling began in her that she could not control. She could not be right. She could not be.

"For you to live here."

"Alone?" She blanched at how wounded she sounded, and she had to blink to stop the tears that suddenly wanted to come. She bit down on her lip until the sharp pain overtook the ache in her throat that was urging her tears to unleash.

"Yes, I'll live in Covent Garden."

He could have struck her, his words hurt her that much. He was rejecting her. Her nickname whispered through her head. *Frightful Frederica.* She shoved down the self-pity that tried to rise. How dare he reject her before he even truly gave her a chance!

"You said we'd not remain strangers."

A long silence stretched, and with it, her nerves, but then he finally said, "We won't. We have a lifetime to become acquainted."

Acquainted. As if they were business partners and not husband and wife. She wanted to scream and slap him. Instead, she bunched her skirts in her hands. "I gave you the opportunity to back out of this," she accused.

He had the good grace to flinch at her words. "I told you I could not do that."

"Oh yes," she said, her words as bitter on her tongue as lemons. "Your honor would not let you. But that honor does not require you to live with me."

He shifted, looking wholly uncomfortable, no doubt, with her not meekly agreeing to this preposterous arrangement, and a man in livery appeared by the coachman. She snapped her attention from him back to Gabriel. "Let's speak of this later," he said. "I've urgent business at the club."

"More urgent than this?" she asked, unable to temper her incredulity.

"Yes, Frederica. More urgent than this. I'll see you tomorrow at the latest."

"How very honorable of you!" She shoved past him to exit the carriage and nearly fell out of it in her haste. His strong arm slid around her waist in a flash, and he pulled her back into the safety of his embrace. Her body's instantaneous reaction to him irritated her to no end. She wanted to hate him, but she desired him. She did not want to care that he didn't want her around him, yet she cared so much she ached with it.

What was happening to her?

"I've got you," he whispered, his warm breath washing over her neck and ear to make heat pool low in her belly.

"Got me," she muttered, squirming out of his grip, needing time to think, to sort the confusion rioting in her head. "If this is how you will 'have me,' I think perhaps I'd rather be lost." With that, she pulled away from him and lumbered down the stairs of the carriage, taking the extended hand of the man she assumed was the footman.

Once she was on solid ground, the footman released her hand. "My lady, I'm Morgan. If you'll allow me to show you to your bedchamber, I'm sure your exhausted."

She was too furious and confused to be exhausted, so she simply nodded and followed Morgan toward the front door, not bothering to truly look at the home. She had no intention of remaining here in Mayfair.

Stationed on either side of the door were two men who stared straight ahead until she was nearly upon them. She frowned and turned to Morgan, whose understanding look said he'd anticipated her questions. "Mr. Beckford placed these men here to guard the house."

The house or her? She recalled Gabriel mentioning an enemy. She glanced over her shoulder to ask him about it and felt her mouth slip open. The carriage door had been closed and was pulling away. Well, she was certainly not going to chase after Gabriel. She had her pride, even if she did not have a husband who wanted to live with her. She sniffed at that and followed Morgan into the home, noting the grandeur without much interest. She had not picked these things and had no sentimental ties to them, nor had Gabriel chosen them because he knew her. He did not.

With every step toward her bedchamber, her despondence grew, but when the footman opened the door to her appointed chamber, she gasped. It was decorated in colors of peacock blue and gold, with an elaborate raised platform bed and miniatures from her bedchamber at her home, of her family, were sitting on the table beside her bed.

She swept her gaze over the room, but it stalled at the dressing table where her favorite hair combs and brush were arranged just so. "Did my... Did my sister Guinevere come here and do this?" she asked, befuddled.

"No, my lady." The footman grinned. "Mr. Beckford oversaw this himself. He had the room decorated yesterday. He told the decorator that peacock blue was your favorite color, and he had all the staff in a frenzy to collect your personal things after the wedding ceremony today so you would not know until you arrived here and felt at home."

A maelstrom of emotions overwhelmed her. He'd remembered her favorite color, and he wanted her to feel at home here. He *did* care. A man who didn't wouldn't remember such a thing or go to such trouble. And yet, she didn't want to live in Mayfair, and he knew that. He had done all of this, bought this home here in Mayfair, decorated it to make her feel welcome, to keep her out of Covent Garden and to ensure they had separate lives.

Her thoughts spun as she thanked the footman, closed the door behind him, and sat on the bed. She had long ago told herself that she didn't want or need love, and yet here and now, when faced with the prospect of a loveless marriage, her heart ached. Why? If she truly didn't care, then why?

She was a fool, that was why. A fool who had lied to herself.

But why?

She pondered that question until her temples pounded but could not solve the puzzle that was herself. Yet, she did know several things for certain. She was wed now, and since she was, she did not want to live separately from Gabriel, whom she desired. She still wanted to live in Covent Garden and make a life where she felt as if she belonged. And she wanted her husband to like her as she was—no, more than that. She wanted… She wanted him to possibly fall in love with her because she suspected she could quite possibly fall in love with him.

She fell backward onto the bed and blinked up at the ceiling in amazed wonder. How could she make all that happen? She suspected the first thing she needed to do was get him to lower his guards. Were they raised because he was still in love with Georgette, or were they raised because he thought Freddy didn't belong in his world, that he was somehow protecting her? Or was it both reasons? The second was by far the easiest to tackle presently. Perhaps if she could show him she *belonged* in his world, then he'd truly let her into it, and maybe, just possibly, he'd open his heart to her, to them, to possibility.

᷐᷐᷐᷐᷐

"What are you doing here?" Blythe straightened from the ledgers she'd been hunched over at Gabe's desk and scowled as he entered his office.

"This is my office and my club, last I remember." He tugged off his cravat as he shut the door and then walked to the sideboard and poured himself a drink. He needed it. He had several images lodged in his head, and he couldn't get them out. They kept revolving across his mind, one after the other, repeatedly.

Frederica appearing so worried as she spoke with him in the parlor before their wedding. Frederica looking achingly beautiful standing by him saying her vows. Frederica sitting at the supper table as they listened to each toast, her smile fading, awareness rising in her eyes as he started the necessary and surprisingly painful process of putting distance between them. Then Frederica asleep in the carriage.

That was the worst image of all. Conjuring it sent hot heat through his veins and a pulsing need to return to her this very moment and spend himself in her arms, then watch her sleep again. Her dark eyelashes fanned her cheeks when she slept, and every so often, she would scrunch her nose as if a dream bothered her.

He would stay here tonight because of how very much he had wanted to remain with her. He hated that he'd hurt her earlier, but she'd suffer more if she came to expect tender emotions and deep attachments from him. He would do his duty, but beyond that, he would not give more and form bonds that would bring pain if he were to ever lose her. He'd had enough pain for a thousand lifetimes.

He'd not been lying when he'd said he had urgent business. He did. Now that he was wed, he was sure Hawk would return. He'd already set two men to guard Frederica tonight and tomorrow, but those men would need breaks. He wanted to pick out two other men to rotate the duty to, and that was his biggest priority—her safety.

"Pour me one, too," Blythe said, bringing his attention back to his sister.

"You're supposed to be learning to be a lady. Ladies don't drink whisky. Haven't you had a lesson with Lady Guinevere yet? I arranged it."

He turned, holding a now-full glass, and stared at his sister, who had a decidedly suspicious look on her face for a breath before she wiped her expression clean. Blythe was exceptional at not showing what she was feeling. They'd both learned very early that to survive on the streets one could never show weakness or divulge what one was truly feeling.

Blythe stood, which alerted Gabe to the fact that she was wearing pantaloons, and then strode to the bar, stepped around him, poured a finger of whisky, and drank it down in one gulp. "She mentioned the lessons." Blythe set her now-empty glass down. "But I told her that since you were now wed to Freddy, she could give me the lessons. Of course—" Blythe arched her eyebrows "—that was before I knew you had purchased a home in Mayfair and settled Freddy there. How'd Freddy take that? Is that why you're here?"

Damn it. He didn't want to talk of this. The question brought Frederica's stricken face back into his mind. It had made him want to forget his plan to keep her out of his world. He couldn't relent simply because he didn't want to hurt her. That plan, two houses, two lives, would keep the walls firmly between them.

Blythe's eyes widened. "You ran from her!"

"I did not run." He swigged his own drink down, then set his glass beside Blythe's. "You can come to the Mayfair house tomorrow for lessons with Frederica."

"Gabe!" She set her hands on her hips and somehow managed to look down her nose at him, though she was a head shorter. "Don't tell me you are planning on living a separate life from her!"

"Why are you wearing pantaloons?" he asked instead of answering the question.

Blythe glared. "I had a mission for a Cyprian."

"No more missions, for God's sake! I've enough to worry about now with keeping Frederica safe!"

"Don't fuss like a mother." It was something they'd said to each other often over the years. They paused and looked at each other, knowing they both wished they had their mother with them to fuss over them. Blythe broke the silence first. "I took a guard with me."

"Who?"

"It doesn't matter."

Blythe's ambiguousness was more vague than usual. "Good God! Please don't tell me you've taken up with a rookery man. I don't want to sound like a hypocritical ass, but your innocence must remain intact if—"

"Shut your trap!" Blythe's face turned such a shade of scarlet that he was reassured her innocence was still her own. "I'm as innocent as I was yesterday."

"Does that mean—"

She slapped a hand over his mouth, glaring. "Yes."

He pried her fingers away and squeezed her hand. He had played the part of brother and parent so long it was hard to recall when he'd taken up the second role. "Who was your guard, then?"

"I'd rather not say."

"Then I'll ask around. You know I'll find out."

She gave him her cross look, the one that scared half his employees. "Huntley."

"Frederica's brother?"

"Do you know another?" She turned from him, went to the chair in front of his desk, and plopped down into it, legs sprawled like a man. Frederica had her work cut out for her, but he realized standing there, staring at his nearly mannerless sister, that he was glad it was Frederica who would be teaching Blythe to be a lady. No, Frederica did not always act precisely like a lady herself, but she behaved precisely like the sort of lady he wished Blythe to become. One with a heart, who could play the part of the lady when she deemed *she* needed to do so, not when told to do so.

"When did you and Huntley become friends?" He crossed to his desk and sat behind it, glancing down at the ledgers. He was surprised to see that the figures were completed already. It normally took Blythe two days after the close of the week to finish the tally. He wanted to ask her about them, but he wanted answers about Huntley first. "Blythe? Huntley?"

"We're not friends, per se." Her blush said otherwise. "But we became acquainted when he attacked you and I hit him over the head with the book."

"Do you mean after I left Bear to take care of him?" Gabe had needed to depart to one of his other clubs for an emergency flooding problem.

"Yes. Bear had to break up a fight here so I waited for Huntley to rouse, and when he did, he had a pounding head, which I pointed out he deserved. But I took pity on him and gave him a compress."

Gabe's jaw must have dropped open because he suddenly sucked in cold air. "You took pity on a man?"

She shrugged, but her blush deepened. "He's different from other men. I don't find him tiresome. He actually admitted he should not have attacked you, and then he explained he was just trying to protect Freddy. He got me in my soft spot." She said the last part begrudgingly.

"You've a soft spot?" This was a Blythe he had never seen. This was a vulnerable Blythe, a feminine Blythe. Thank God. He'd feared greatly she didn't exist, and that would make it damn hard to wed her to a man of the *ton*.

"You're my soft spot, you big oaf," she snapped. "And his behavior reminded me of how you always protect me." She shrugged once more. "So I decided I like him."

This wasn't a bad thing. In fact, it could be a very good thing. Huntley was from a good family. Huntley would inherit. And if Huntley had one tenth the honor that Gabe knew Frederica possessed, then Huntley would be a fine match for his sister. But he couldn't let Blythe know he thought so. The minute he did, she'd decide she didn't like Huntley.

Blythe leaned forward and set her elbows on her knees and narrowed her eyes on him with a suspicious look. "Don't you have anything to say? You always have something to say."

He had a lot to say, but nothing he could speak of now. "I still don't understand how you and your newfound *friend* ended up going on a mission together."

Blythe's blush deepened to the color of a ripe berry.

"I tried to send him back to Mayfair, but when he realized I was going to aid a Cyprian, he insisted on accompanying me. The man is rather muleheaded."

It took all Gabe's will not to laugh. Somehow Blythe had stumbled upon the perfect match for herself. "It must run in the family," he finally managed to get out while keeping his glee for his sister out of his tone.

"Speaking of his family…" Blythe probed him with her gaze. "Why did you leave your wife on your wedding night?"

Wife. The word made him still. It wasn't the first time he'd heard it. The vicar had repeated it during the ceremony, but Gabe had been expecting it. Frederica was his *wife.* He didn't like the way the word made his chest constrict.

"Gabe?"

He snapped his gaze to his sister's concerned face, uncertain when he'd looked down at his hands and away from Blythe.

"Why did you leave her alone?" she asked again. "And don't even try to tell me you don't want her."

"Ladies shouldn't talk of such things." Especially because talk of his desire for Frederica stirred it painfully. He didn't plan not to have passion between them, but he needed to approach it with control of himself.

"Good thing I'm no lady yet, then," Blythe said, eyebrow raised. "So?"

"You're a thorn in my side."

Blythe grinned. "And you're a pain in the arse. Now answer me."

Gabe sighed. "Because I was setting the precedent for how it will be. She'll live in her world, and I'll live in mine."

Blythe snorted. "Good luck with keeping her away from Covent Garden."

Yes, he knew it was going to be a challenge. Frederica was not one to be easily deterred. It was one of the things he admired most about her so far. But to Blythe, he said, "You know very well that Hawk will return now and come for her. She's safer in Mayfair. He'll look here first, and that will alert me to his return, and then I'll swoop in and snatch him."

Blythe's expression sobered, and she nodded. "So you've a plan?"

"Yes. I've been funding the Henderson Home for the Mentally Impaired since shortly after Hawk left and made his threat against me."

"So you did think you might one day meet a lady you could love!" Blythe said.

He shook his head. "No. I assumed Hawk would eventually tire of waiting and return to simply take revenge on me."

"You mean to kill you?"

"Yes. He's shown remarkable patience, but I planned on the day his patience expired."

"I'm both glad and sad at once," Blythe muttered.

"Don't fret for me, Blythe. I'm fine."

She snorted. "You're far from fine. You're a self-made emotional iceberg. But I suspect Freddy will thaw you."

"Frederica will not thaw me, Sister." She'd damn well heat him to near incineration, but that would be confined to passion in the bedchamber.

Blythe changed the subject. "Why are you funding the Henderson Home?"

"So that I'll have somewhere to put Hawk and two physicians willing to sign papers committing him without an exam or question."

"That's a good plan," Blythe said, "except the part where you wait for him to show himself or strike first."

"I'm not waiting for him to come for Frederica, Blythe. I've set dozens of men out in Covent Garden as of the day the bans were read to watch for his return. The minute I hear of it, I'll find him."

LADY FREDERICA AND THE SCOT WHO WOULD NOT   155

"Assuming you can. I think a better plan would be to use Frederica to lure him out."

"No." The word came out harsh, but the idea of putting her in danger was intolerable.

She smirked. "Ah. Seems to me you've already formed an attachment to Freddy."

"No, no, I haven't," he denied, even as his pulse spiked. "It's my protective instinct, is all. She's my wife. Protecting her is my duty."

"If you say so."

He opened his mouth to say he did say so when a knock came at his door. The door swung open, and Bear stood in the threshold.

Gabe rose. Bear never left his post at the door to the club when the club was open. "What's the matter?"

Bear strode into the room and held out a folded note to Gabe. "This was delivered for you just now. I recognized the man—Alex Peterson."

Gabe's breath caught. If Hawk's old crony in running underground card and dice games was delivering Gabe a note, there could be only one reason why. Gabe took the paper, unfolded it, and read.

> *I like your new home in Mayfair, and your new wife is pretty. Too bad she'll be gone when you return home.*
>
> *Hawk*

"Goddamn it!" Gabe roared, shoving past Bear to get out the door and to Frederica. He'd made a mistake, a terrible one. He prayed to God he wasn't too late to protect her.

Chapter Fifteen

Freddy punched the pillow for the dozenth time, tried a new position, and stared at the ceiling while reciting old etiquette lessons. When that failed to put her to sleep, she knew nothing would. Huffing, she climbed from the bed and wound her hair into a knot to fan her damp neck, but the meager swoosh of air against her heated skin was not nearly enough relief. She made her way to the window, drew back the heavy silk curtains that she'd pulled shut before getting into bed so that the sun would not wake her in the morning, and she screamed.

Staring back at her was a man with a long, crooked nose, a square chin, and hair dark enough to blend in with the night, except his pale skin showed the inky strands across his forehead. When he drew up a knife and tapped it against the window, she screamed again. She scuttled backward, tripping over the slippers she'd left in the middle of the floor and landing with an air-stealing, arse-bruising thud.

Behind her, her bedchamber door banged open, and she jerked, twisting around, not sure what she'd find, so when Gabriel appeared, she cried out her relief. Before she could even fully inhale a ragged breath to tell Gabriel of the man at her window, Gabriel was there, scooping her into his arms and encircling her body in a protective shield. His dark eyebrows slashed down over his eyes as he swept his gaze over her, then glanced around the room. "You screamed."

"There was a man at my window," she replied, curling her fingers into his solid shoulders.

He tensed and whipped his head toward the window. "Bear!" Gabriel shouted, and the man from the Orcus Society who she knew manned the door from seeing him the times Blythe had sneaked her into the club, the one Blythe said never left his post, appeared suddenly beside her, as if conjured by Gabriel speaking his name.

"Tell the guards to check outside," Gabriel ordered. "You go with them. And send Blythe up here."

"I'm already here," Blythe replied from behind Freddy.

Freddy looked over Gabriel's shoulder to see Blythe with a pistol in her hand. "What's going on?" Freddy asked, a tingling sensation sweeping over her body.

"Are you hurt?" Gabriel asked. "Can you stand?"

"No, I'm not hurt." Well, technically her bottom was throbbing, but she kept that information to herself. "I can stand. What's happening?"

Gabriel was already setting her down and pushing her toward Blythe. "Guard her."

"Gabriel!" Freddy said to his back as he strode to the window.

Blythe pressed a finger to her lips. "He'll tell you after."

After? After what? After someone tried to attack them? Was this the enemy Gabriel had spoken of?

Coldness struck Freddy at her core, and she shivered. Then she gasped and ran to the window Gabriel had opened and now was climbing through. "Gabriel!" she said, clutching at his arm. "You'll fall!"

"I've climbed a lot more dangerous things than this tree, Frederica," he said, not turning back toward her. Below, in the darkness, light suddenly bobbed, and she saw four men standing there.

"Bear," Gabriel called down.

"He got away," Bear replied, seemingly knowing who the "he" was whom Gabriel was referring to. And of course Bear knew. Everyone was privy to the information but her.

"Damn it all to hell." Gabriel turned toward her, leaning away from the tree branch he stood on and toward the window ledge. She thought to aid him, but before she could figure out how, he was inside once more, standing before her but looking out the window. "That tree," he growled, shoving his hands through his hair, then settling them on the back of his neck. "I should have realized that tree could be used to get in here."

"Gabe," Blythe said, moving past Freddy to stand behind her brother. "She's fine." She set a hand on Gabriel's shoulder. He jerked visibly at Blythe's touch and swung toward her, his gaze bouncing from his sister to Freddy to the window.

"I should have realized," he repeated, misery in his words. "I've gotten soft. Christ." He yanked his hands through his hair again and finally looked at Freddy. Her heart thumped at the worry in his eyes. "If he'd taken you—"

"He didn't," Freddy said, stepping around Blythe to stand in front of Gabriel. She set her hands on his chest, feeling his muscles twitch under her fingertips. She didn't even know who "he" was, but in this moment, it hardly mattered. "I'm fine, as Blythe said."

"Yes." His attention was beyond her now, toward the bedchamber door, and a fierce frown creased his face. "I miscalculated. Gravely." Suddenly, his eyes settled on her again, something intense in their depths. He grabbed her gently by the arm. "You'll be coming with me."

"Where are you taking me?" She had a sudden horrible

fear that he was going to try to return her to her parents. That was ridiculous, wasn't it?

"To my home," he said, tugging her toward the door. His home. Not theirs—*his*. But it was the place she wanted to be and a move in the right direction.

Still, on the threshold she dug in her heels. "Gabriel!" she gasped. "I cannot go out like this!"

He glanced over his shoulders and swept his gaze down from her face to her feet and back up. When his eyes met hers, she shivered once more, but it wasn't from the cold. It was from the hunger on his face.

⁂

The notes of a pianoforte woke Freddy. She sat up with a start and blinked into the darkness, her mind taking a moment to recall where she was—Gabriel's home in Covent Garden. No, her home now too. Pleasure rippled through her, but then she frowned, recalling he'd had his butler install her in a guest bedchamber. She'd attempted to ask him questions on the short ride here, but he'd put her off, telling her they'd talk tomorrow, and then they had entered his home, and he'd surprised her by handing her off to the butler with orders to put her in the guest bedchamber.

Gabriel intended for her to stay here temporarily, but she, however, did not. She debated for a moment whether she should remain abed, but curiosity to know if it was Gabriel playing at this late hour had her rising from the bed, pulling her wrapper over her night rail, and following the music down the hall and the winding stairs, all the while half expecting to encounter one of Gabriel's, no—*their*—servants. The music drifted from the parlor, or at least she thought she recalled that the parlor was to the right. She tiptoed through the darkness toward the room, and as she neared it, the music rose in volume and light spilled out from under the cracked door.

Freddy carefully opened the door, and her breath caught as her stomach tightened. Across the room at the pianoforte, Gabriel sat shirtless, head bent and hands flying over the keys. His absorption in the music made him oblivious to her presence. Moonlight and an orange glow from the nearby candelabra slashed across his face. His body moved fluidly in time with his playing, and every half breath, his face would appear in the light, and she found herself gazing with a slack mouth. His playing was beautiful. It would not have been something she would have expected from a man born and reared on the ugly streets of London.

She moved just inside the doorway and gently shut it. This was a side of Gabriel he never would have willingly showed her. His dark hair gleamed in the light. It was cut shorter than when she'd first met him, but she liked it. The shorter style suited his strong jaw. Even from where she stood across the room, she could see his chest and stomach muscles rippling as he moved. There was not a bit of fat on the man, and simply looking at him made heat gather in her belly and an ache pulse to life between her legs.

She wanted him, but not just for physical pleasure, and she wanted answers. To break down the barriers between them she had to be brave. Her heart fluttered wildly in her breast, making her eardrums throb with rushing blood. She took a breath and then a step. And then another. And when she was halfway across the room, he suddenly glanced up, his eyes locking on her. The music came to a halt, the silence crashing in on her, and her lungs constricted with fear that he'd send her from the room. Yet, he didn't say a word as she walked toward him. He turned around fully on the bench to face her and watched her with a hungry, guarded gaze. When she came to stand before him, the intensity in his gaze sent a shiver down her spine.

Without a word, he hooked his hands around the backs of her legs and tugged her toward him, sliding his palms up her legs to settle on her bottom. His heat seeped through the thin material of her wrapper and night rail. Her insides vibrated as he tugged her still closer until he grasped one of the ties of her wrapper with his teeth, and with a tug, loosened the wrapper. She bit her lip, her pulse skittering, when he bent his head and did the same to the other tie, causing her wrapper to fall open.

His strong hands circled from her bottom across her hips, settling there as his eyes drank her in, making her feel beautiful in a way she'd never felt.

"I meant to wait before touching you again," he said, his voice husky.

She frowned. "Why?"

"It doesn't matter. Not now." His gaze raked over her, making her toes curl. "I can't wait. Not with you here before me. You rob me of control."

He didn't sound as if he liked that one bit, but he was proceeding forward, so she bit back any comment as he slid his hands up across her stomach and between her breasts, his arms stretching, muscles straining against his skin, before he cupped her breasts. At the same time, he stood to tower over her. "Are you afraid?"

"I want very much what's to come," she said, sensing he was speaking of them joining.

A hint of a smile pulled at his lips. "My bold lass," he said, the burr that so rarely was heard coming out.

He lifted her, setting her on the top of the pianoforte, her feet on the keyboard. Lyrical notes punctured the silence, even as he opened her legs and rucked up her gown. The air around her became electrified, the desire between them crackling like lightning. Her breathing grew shallow and fast.

"You're so damned beautiful." He skimmed the tender inner flesh of her thighs with his fingers and made her insides turn to liquid. "I want you so very much." His hand hovered at the juncture of her thighs, as if he'd not delve there, into her silken curls where her hidden spot lay, without her permission. She appreciated the gesture on a deep level. He was giving her power in a world where women had precious little.

She wanted his touch, just as much as she sensed he wanted to give it, but she also wanted to know one thing. "Why did you leave me in the bedchamber alone on our wedding night?" Never mind that he'd left her alone *twice* on their wedding night. It was a triviality.

His gaze suddenly dropped, but he said, "To give you time to calm from your fright."

She brought her hands to his shoulders, allowing her fingers to curl there over the taut muscle and solid bone. "Do you know what I think?" she asked as her pulse drummed hard.

Slowly, his gaze came to her. "What?"

The word was heavy, reluctant, but she didn't let it stop her. She couldn't. "I think you were the one who needed time to recover."

His gaze flicked wider by the barest of slivers, but it was all she needed to know she'd struck on a truth.

"It's my job to protect you, Frederica, and I almost failed."

She wouldn't push him, not now. This destroying of barriers was a delicate process. "Well, I'm here, unharmed. You didn't fail. So show me, if you dare, what happens next between us." She had never said such a bold thing in her life. The thrill of it left her breathless, and the smile he gave her made her dizzy.

"Wee, wicked lass," he growled, drawing off her unmentionables in an astonishingly adept manner. Cool air hit her below as he pulled her to the edge of the piano top, so that she was almost hanging off. He shoved the bench out of his way, then gently parted her at her center and lowered his head toward her most private area.

The action rendered her speechless and rushed adrenaline through her, and when his fingers spread her and his hot breath wafted over her core, she clutched him. "Do you mean to—"

"I do indeed mean to..." He offered a salacious smile as his fingers touched her bud, firing off a million sensations within her. Her bottom clenched and a moan escaped her. "I assume that's you giving me permission to proceed?" he teased.

She barely got a nod out, as she forced herself to loosen her clenched thighs on either side of his upper torso. Before she could even fully relax, his tongue traced up her sensitive flesh, branding her and making her whimper at how wonderful it felt. Gabriel, the intelligent man, took her whimpering for what it was in the moment—full submission.

He stroked his tongue up her center slowly and repeatedly until her throat ached to scream her satisfaction, and then he circled the pearl, making the need and knots build and tighten with each slide of his tongue against her flesh. Blood rushed in her ears, heat swept through her body, and her pulse increased at a pace that left her panting. She lifted her hips to meet him more fully, to force his mouth harder upon her, to get that completion that he'd given her before.

A great wave built slow and delicious, and then crashed upon her. Yet, even in the chaos, she knew it would not be enough. "Gabriel, please, I want you to make me yours."

The dark look of primal triumph he gave her as he tugged her away from the keyboard to the other edge and slid her toward him made her quiver. "Look at me," he commanded, and she did, locking gazes with him. "It will just be one moment of pain, and if you want me to stop—"

"I won't. I'm ready."

He captured her mouth with his hot one, slanting a ravenous kiss over her lips and plunging his tongue inside her while he lifted her toward him and plunged himself inside her. She gasped and stilled, digging her nails into him. She'd known. Of course she had. She'd made it a point not to be naive. Even as the thoughts flitted through her head, her body started to relax, to stretch, to accept him and conform around him.

"Frederica?" he said, the restrain in his voice obvious.

"I'm fine."

He pulled back to look at her. "Just fine?" He raised his eyebrows.

"More than fine," she whispered, leaning forward to kiss his chest and his neck. A low growl emanated from him as if she'd pushed him toward some edge with her ministrations, and when he gripped her legs harder and slid slowly inside her from his base to his tip, she realized she'd pushed him toward losing that grip on himself he always held so tight. It was exhilarating, and becoming more so the faster he moved, the more pleasure it built within her.

Even as he moved within her, he brought his teeth to

her night rail, tugged the material down over one shoulder to bare her breast, and took her nipple in his mouth to suckle. It was too much perfect torture. Her body arched like the string of a bow about to be shot, and she could not stop her scream of pleasure as waves of heat flooded over her. As her muscles clenched repeatedly around him, his own movements grew faster and faster, until he too tensed and growled and seemed to bury himself impossibly deep within her. And then hot liquid filled her. She sagged against him with a laugh, and he surprised her by lifting her, her gown falling from where it had been pushed up to her hips, and he slipped an arm under her legs while tugging her gown back down to cover her.

His eyes held hers for a moment. "You're beautiful, and I don't mean simply your outer appearance, though you're right damned lovely. You've an inner light."

She frowned. "You sound unhappy about it."

He opened his mouth as if he was going to respond, but then he shut it, and instead of speaking, he carried her across the room and managed to open the parlor door.

"Where are you taking me?" She looked around warily for servants, but the halls were dark and quiet.

When she glanced to him once more, she found him studying her, a guarded but soft look in his eyes. "To your bedchamber."

Hers, not *theirs*. A little knot of sadness hardened in her throat.

Gabriel frowned. "You needn't worry about the servants seeing us."

Frankly, she wasn't. She ought to be if she were the right sort of proper lady, the sort her mother had tried to raise her to be, the sort that all women of the *ton* were. Even Guinevere, for all her adventures, would be scandalized if the servants witnessed Carrington carrying her through the house. Freddy suspected she'd be slightly embarrassed but mostly annoyed. That was the problem. She was the problem. The way her mind worked never would have allowed her to be a proper *ton* lady, but a Covent Garden lady she was sure she could master as long as Gabriel didn't try to stop her, which was almost certain he would.

She wouldn't say any of that. Not yet. Instead, she made light and teased, "Did you threaten them not to come out of their rooms?"

He laughed, seeming to readily accept that she had been concerned about the servants. And why wouldn't he readily accept that? He didn't know her, and she barely knew him. But she was determined to rectify that.

"No, but that's a sound idea." He flashed a grin then sobered. "Even if they came out, my carrying you through this house won't scandalize them as it would the Mayfair servants you're used to," he said as he took to the stairs.

"Gabriel, now that I'm here in Covent Garden, I want to stay."

He hesitated just outside her bedchamber door. "This is temporary."

Her chest tightened with his words. As he opened the door, proceeded inside, and moved to the bed, where he gently set her down, she asked, "So you plan for us to live separately forever, once you've dealt with your enemy? Assuming that's what tonight was about, given I have no notion."

"I think it's best."

The man wouldn't know what was best for her, or even them, if it slapped him in the face. She refrained from arguing that point just yet. Instead she said, "So was your plan when you decided to wed me to keep me at arm's length from you? To never give us the chance to be close?"

The startled look he gave her made her heart feel very likely that if someone blew on her heart, it would shatter. "I see," she said and then to her horror, her throat constricted and began to burn, and before she could stop the instinctual reaction to cry, her vision went blurry. She turned her face down quickly, but above her, Gabriel inhaled sharply, and then the bed squeaked as he sat down beside her. His hand came to rest by her thigh, but he didn't reach out to touch her. Still, his heat enveloped her and sparked a longing, a need to feel understood and wanted, that she had tried to bury. She'd almost been successful until he'd kissed her in the carriage—quite possibly before that, though. Perhaps the lies she'd told herself had started to unravel the very night she'd met him and he'd intrigued her.

"I'm sorry," he said, and she knew he was. Remorse underlay his tone, but his remorse would not change the wall he wanted to keep erected between them. She could try to tear down some of it, though ultimately, he'd have to rip down the rest. She wanted that truly, and just how much took her breath. She didn't just want a life in Covent Garden. She wanted a life in Covent Garden with him by her side. But was she competing for him with his dead wife or was she competing with fears he had of getting close to someone again? She wasn't sure one was any less problematic than the other, though the first one, his dead wife, made Freddy shamefully jealous.

"How long will I be staying here in Covent Garden?" She needed to know how long she had to change his mind and get him to relent to letting her live here.

"Until I've captured my enemy."

"The man at my window tonight."

Gabriel nodded.

"Tell me of him. Who was he?"

The relief that swept his face would have been comical, except she suspected that he was so relieved because she'd not pursued the line of conversation about how their marriage was to be. She bit her lip on the sharp ache in her chest.

"His name is Phillip Hawkins. He grew up in the orphanage and on the streets with Blythe and me. We were once the best of friends—Hawk, Blythe, myself, and my first wife."

"Georgette," she said, the name of the woman Gabriel had been wed to before her coming easily to mind. The woman he'd loved. The one who had died four years ago.

Gabriel frowned. "How did you know—"

"Blythe told me," Freddy interrupted, not particularly wanting to linger too long on the topic.

He eyed her with suspicion. "What exactly did Blythe tell you?"

"Just that you'd been wed before and that she died," Freddy lied, not wanting to say aloud that Blythe had told her how much he'd loved Georgette, nor did she want to give him a reason to confront Blythe and possibly cause his sister not to share anything else with Freddy. She needed an ally, and Blythe was definitely her best option.

He scrubbed a hand across his face. "We watched out for each other, the four of us. Kept each other alive. Comforted each other. And then things became complicated."

"How?"

His lips thinned. "I wed Georgette, and Hawk didn't like it. He fancied himself in love with her."

"Did you know that he loved her?"

His brows drew downward in a frown, and his gaze went unfocused, as if lost in the past. "I didn't betray him, Frederica."

She wanted to ask more about it, but his shuttered look told her he'd not welcome the questions, and she didn't want to push too much. "But he thought you did?" she supplied, thinking it appropriately neutral.

"He convinced himself I did," Gabriel said, his tone bitter. "It's easier to blame someone when things don't work out the way you want than to look at yourself and accept what you've done."

"What did he do?" she asked, unable to stop the question before it slipped out.

His mouth went tight and grim. "It doesn't matter now. The past is the past."

But it did matter to her that he would not share it, confide in her, but she pressed her lips together on saying so.

"What matters," Gabriel continued, "is that Hawk tried to kill me one night by blowing up my warehouse."

It was said so casually that she realized it wasn't shocking to him. What sort of hardening of himself had he had to do to survive and thrive? No wonder he didn't want to let her in, and yet, he had let Georgette close. Was it because she was from the same place Gabriel was? Would it be easier for him to let Freddy close if she could show him she could survive here, as he had, that she truly belonged here, as he did?

Freddy swallowed. "And what happened when he blew up your warehouse?"

Pain twisted his features. "Georgette was the one to open the door that triggered the explosion. She was supposed to be home in bed, but she'd come out late at night to the warehouse because—" He halted his explanation suddenly and shoved his hands through his hair. A long pause followed, and he finally said, "Because she'd asked me to do something, and I hadn't yet, and she was fretting about it."

He blamed himself for her death. She didn't need to hear him say it. It was painted in the lines of his drawn mouth. It was apparent with the flare of his nostrils, his rigid posture, his darting gaze. She ached for him, but she didn't offer comfort because he wouldn't welcome it. Instead, she sat, clutching at her night rail, and prayed he would continue.

"The explosion didn't kill her instantly, but soon after." His eyes had taken on a glassy look, and he was staring down at his hands. "I held her as she was dying."

Freddy's insides twisted.

"She made me promise not to kill him." His skin bunched around his eyes as if he could see her. "Even in death, even after all he'd done, Georgette was the best person I'd ever known. She was pure and kind, and she needed me to protect her, and I failed." He finally looked up, his gaze spearing her. "I won't fail to protect you, Frederica. I didn't want a wife."

She blanched at his truthful statement and the ensuing regret that flittered across his face, and tears suddenly filled her eyes. He grabbed her hands, just as she was thinking of getting up and asking him to leave. It all seemed too impossible in this moment.

He squeezed her hands. "I didn't want another wife for many reasons, but I also couldn't keep my hands off you, so now here we are."

She grimaced. "Yes, here we are."

"Hawk disappeared the day after Georgette died or I would have dealt with him before. I've tried to find him for four years, but he kept eluding me. He's been waiting, you see."

She frowned. "For what?"

Gabe's gaze locked with hers. "For you."

Chapter Sixteen

" For me?"

Gabe hadn't meant to say it like that. Hell, he hadn't even meant to be this truthful, but he was still reeling from earlier, and Frederica did things to his brain that made it malfunction whenever she was near. He needed to concentrate, to focus.

"Yes," he finally said. "He's been hiding in the shadows, waiting to seek the revenge he thinks I deserve."

She frowned. "Which is what?"

"To take away the woman he thinks I love, just as he thinks I took Georgette from him."

"Simply get word to him that we wed out of necessity," she said, her voice suddenly tight.

They had. It was the truth, and yet, when he'd gotten that note and read Hawk's words, Gabe's heart had stopped and it hadn't beaten properly again until he'd seen Frederica was safe and touched her himself. He didn't like his reaction. He didn't like it one bit. It had been too strong for a woman he barely knew, had only just wed, and had no intention of getting close to. And yet, none of that changed what his reaction had been. He clenched his jaw, unsure how to proceed now that he'd brought her here.

He'd had to, he reminded himself. The house in Mayfair wasn't safe like his home here was. It had been yet another foolish decision in the long list of reckless ones he'd made where Frederica was concerned. He'd spent four years ensuring his home in Covent Garden was as impenetrable as possible, and he should have accepted that she needed to be here until Hawk was captured. But only until then.

Gabe would not allow himself to get used to her being there. He would not allow himself to come to want her presence in his home, but he didn't want to hurt her, either. What a damned tightrope. How the hell was he to walk it without falling off? She was his wife. He desired her.

No, hell, he craved her as if she were an addiction. Maybe that was the answer. Little doses of her every day would make him want her less. Maybe coming together in the bed would eventually temper his lust. It had to.

"He wouldn't believe that," Gabe said, finally answering her.

"Then we lure him out."

He didn't like the word *we* she'd just used. "You'll stay out of it, Frederica."

"I'll not! He's after *me*. He wants *me*. It makes the most sense to use me to lure him out."

Cold fingers curled around his heart and squeezed at the thought of her putting herself at risk. "You will stay out of it, or I will send you under guard so far away from here not even a map could lead you back."

Her jaw went slack at that. Good, she understood. She didn't like it, given her sudden pressed lips, narrowed eyes, and flared nostrils, but she understood. Now, whether she would comply or not was another matter.

"I'm going to have my men here watching you at all times," he said. Flames sparked and danced in her beautiful eyes. "To keep you safe from Hawk and yourself."

"How very considerate of you," she replied, her tone as sharp as a well-honed blade.

"I do try," he teased, hoping to lighten the mood, but she was having none of it.

She pursed her lips and cocked her head. "What is your plan, then, if you don't like mine?"

"My plan is to hunt him down. I'm going to enlist everyone who owes me a favor to aid me. I will get him. Don't fret."

"I'm not fretting," she replied, sounding too damned calm for his liking.

He didn't want her to worry, but damn it... "You should be fretting!"

"You're very contrary, Gabriel," she replied, a smile tugging at her lips, which had the unwanted effect of making him want to kiss her. He'd never been a contrary man. Ever. Not until her. "What will you do with him after you find him? You aren't planning to kill him, are you?"

He shook his head. "I vowed to Georgette that I'd not kill him." Though, if Hawk was about to kill Frederica, Gabriel would break that vow to save her. But he was going to do everything in his power to avoid it.

"Oh, I see." She sucked in her lower lip. "I understand." There was an odd note in her voice he couldn't place, but before he could decide whether to ask about it or not, she said, "That's good. But what will you do with him?"

"Put him in the Henderson Home for the Mentally Impaired. I've funded the place for years to ensure that I would have somewhere to lock Hawk up in the eventuality that he returned to seek his revenge. He hasn't lived in reality in a long time."

She nodded. "It sounds like a good plan, except for the part where you do not let me aid you. It would be so much faster if—"

"No. I mean it, Frederica. I was not making an idle

threat earlier. I will send you away. Do you understand?"

She scowled. "I'm not a numbskull."

"And you will comply with what I've asked of you?"

"Do I have a choice?"

"No."

"Then I suppose I will do what I must."

He didn't think she was going to give more of an agreement than that, so he nodded and started to rise to go to his own bedchamber. She grasped his hand, and her skin upon his made his damned blood heat. He looked down at her as she turned her face up to him, exposing the long, delicate column of her neck. Her pulse ticked in the blue vein just visible beneath her porcelain skin. He could have lost her tonight. The reality had him sitting back down beside her.

That was a mistake. Her thigh pressed against his, and her shoulder grazed his arm. Her sweet, spicy scent filled the air, his nostrils, his head. He wanted to strip her night rail from her and—He squeezed his eyes shut on the thoughts and breathed deeply to gain control of his body and his mind. "I'm exhausted, Frederica," he said. "What is it you wanted?"

"I want you to teach me to defend myself."

He opened his eyes slowly and turned to her. The set of her jaw told him she was prepared to argue. His initial reaction was to tell her no, but that was foolish. If Hawk or any of his men did ever manage to get near her, it would behoove her to know how to defend herself. "Tomorrow morning," he said.

"Thank you!" she burst out and took him by surprise when she wrapped him in a hug.

Heat from their bodies radiated in his chest and his desire for her reawakened, but he tamped it down. He had to exercise restraint when it came to her or he'd find himself soon out of control. He reached behind his back and gently took her wrist, unlatching her arms from around him. The sense of loss made him grit his teeth, and the hurt look that flashed in her eyes, the one she tried to hide by glancing down at her lap, made him want to explain, to offer comfort, but no explanation he could give would comfort her.

He rose, and when she finally looked up, her expression was blank. He didn't know what was worse, the fact that he knew he'd injured her feelings or that she felt she had to hide her injured feelings from him. He was an arse, and this, this moment, was exactly why he'd never even considered wedding again. It hadn't been simply about Hawk; it had been about him, too.

"Good night, Frederica," he said, forcing himself to turn from her and walk out the door, leaving her staring after him. By the time he got to his own bedchamber to undress and climb into bed, his mood was sour. He stared up at his ceiling, recalling the way she smelled, the way she looked when in the throes of passion, her bravery in facing him.

"Damnation!" he cursed, flipping onto his side and trying to force his mind to focus on tomorrow and the meeting at the club he'd asked a few people to attend— people he thought might be able to aid him in finding Hawk in London. But his thoughts kept returning to Frederica. That wasn't how it was supposed to be. It was only supposed to be desire, but already it wasn't. There was concern—too damned much—and admiration that seemed to be growing by leaps and bounds, not to mention a genuine liking that made him want to be around her far more than was wise.

How the hell was he supposed to keep a wall between

them when everything about her chipped away at it?

"Again," Gabriel said, his tone just as no-nonsense as it had been since he'd started training Freddy several hours ago. She wiped the sweat from her brow and tried to ignore the sting of hurt. What had she expected? That in one morning together Gabriel might lower the guard he'd erected between them just a bit?

Yes, that was exactly what she'd hoped, but clearly, it was going to take a great deal more than one lesson. Gabriel had his plan, and she had hers. She would show him she belonged here. He had told her not to involve herself in locating his enemy, but she was the very best person to do so since the man was after her. And once she captured Hawk for Gabriel, there would be no way her husband could send her away because he didn't think her capable of surviving in Covent Garden. If he sent her away then, it would be because he simply didn't want to get close to her, but after the passion they'd shared the night before, she had hopes that he did. At the moment, it might be mostly about desire for him, but given the thoughtful gestures he'd made so far, she was sure there was more to it.

"Frederica!"

She blinked and gawked at him. "Sorry. I'm ready."

He was before her in a flash, and his hands came around her neck, squeezing and cutting off her air. For a breath, she panicked as she'd done every time, despite the fact that he'd told her exactly what to do.

"Frederica, think. Push the fear away. You want to survive. You need to survive. You have to survive. Picture who you have to survive for."

She closed her eyes, heart thumping in her ears, and Gabriel's face danced before her lids, making her belly flutter. She stepped back as she dipped her body forward, toward Gabriel, and then she turned, stepping out of his grasp.

"You did it!" Gabriel boomed, sweeping her into his arms and off her feet, and twirling her around.

She laughed as he set her down and stared at her. "Well?" he asked, hitching his brows.

She laughed. "It was just as you said!"

He nodded. "My hands may be around your neck, but the strength in my thumbs, or any man's, is not a match for the strength of your body."

"Teach me more maneuvers, Gabriel!"

He laughed now. A rich, deep laugh that warmed her chest. "Tomorrow morning. I promise. I've got to go to the club now."

She bit her lip on protesting. Instead, she asked, "Will you be home late?"

He opened his mouth to respond, frowned, and closed it, looking as if he were contemplating what to say. "Yes. Don't wait up for me. And Frederica, just in case you are planning anything you ought not be, let me remind you, I have guards at the front door, and they aren't stationed there to watch the house."

"I've not forgotten," she said.

With a nod, he departed the garden. She watched him go, considering her mood. She wasn't angry at him, which surprised her. He effectively was taking away some of her freedom, which was one of the very reasons she had thought she didn't need marriage or love. But he was doing it to protect her, which was an act of caring, whether he admitted it or not, and she found she liked that very much.

She certainly had no intention of becoming a wife that had to bow to the orders of her husband. Never that—gawds!

But she didn't think Gabriel would ever expect that, given how he'd relented rather easily to showing her how to defend herself, which was something her brother, father, almost no man in the *ton* would have ever done. But Gabriel was not of the *ton*. He was logical, whereas logic seemed to escape most men of the *ton*, the only exceptions being her brother-in-law; her friend Constantine's husband, Lord Kilgore; and her friend Lilias's husband, Lord Greybourne.

Gabriel also had been patient with her this morning during their lessons, but he had not treated her as if she were breakable. He'd put real force into the moves he'd used. That told her he saw her, who she really was, and it didn't scare him.

She hoped he would come to lower his guard soon because she was most definitely falling for her husband.

⚜

The second Blythe entered Freddy's new home that afternoon, Freddy sprang on her. The footman hadn't even closed the door behind Blythe before Freddy was taking her sister-in-law by the hand and pulling her to the parlor so that they could speak in private.

"What's so urgent, Freddy?" Blythe growled and tugged her hand out of Freddy's hold.

"I need to show Gabriel that I can survive in your world before he sends me back to Mayfair, and the best way I know to do that is to catch Hawk, and to do that, I need your assistance."

"And why should I help you do that?" Blythe asked,

sitting down on the settee, kicking her legs out in front of her, and folding her hands across her stomach.

Freddy took it as a very good sign that Blythe had not immediately denied Freddy's request. "You know as well as I do that the best way to catch Hawk is to use me as bait, which your brother has refused to do."

"What did Gabe tell you exactly?" Blythe asked, leaning forward and setting her elbows on her knees.

Freddy took the seat opposite Blythe and quickly re-capped what Gabriel had told her. When she was done, Blythe said, "Is that all?"

Freddy frowned. "Is there more?"

Blythe nodded. "Georgette was with child when Hawk killed her."

The news rendered Freddy speechless.

"She had gone to the warehouse that night because Gabe was supposed to have retrieved the cradle, and he hadn't done it yet, and she couldn't sleep because of it. The cradle was being stored at the warehouse."

"Good God," Freddy whispered. "No wonder Gabriel blames himself."

"Yes," Blythe agreed, "though it's not his fault." She paused. "I actually suggested to Gabe that he use you as bait…"

Freddy arched her brows as she stared at Blythe. "I don't know whether I should be offended or compliment-ed."

Blythe chuckled. "Complimented, Freddy. I'd have never suggested he use you if I didn't think you possessed the necessary mettle for such a thing, but he refused the suggestion flatly. He cares for you, you know."

A jolt went through Freddy's body at hearing Blythe voice what Freddy had only hoped. Blythe smiled. "I see you aren't certain, but that the thought pleases you, and *that* pleases me. I want to see Gabe happy again, and I think you can make him happy. But what do you want? If it's still just to live in Covent Garden and have your freedom, well, that's not enough of a reason for me to risk my brother's rage, which will be great when he discovers I've helped you catch Hawk."

"I'm pleased to hear you think we can catch Hawk," Freddy said, her thoughts whirring in her head at Blythe's question. What did she want, truly? It was time to solidly answer that for herself.

"Of course we can, now that he's resurfaced. We're smart, resourceful women, and he'll underestimate us as most men do. But you didn't answer my question, Freddy. What do you want?"

Freddy swallowed. "I want Gabriel to lower his guard."

"Seems a wise thing to want since you're married to him. But why? Why do you want him to lower his guard?"

"I think," Freddy said, her pulse seeming to tick up. "I think I might have gone and developed a slight affection for your brother."

Blythe snorted. "I think it's more than a slight affection, Freddy. I think you love him."

Freddy opened her mouth to deny it, to say that she hardly knew him and that it would take time to fall in love with her husband. But a feeling so intense swept through her that she promptly shut her mouth and simply sat gaping at Blythe.

Blythe rose, came around the table, and sat by Freddy, taking her hand and patting it. "Poor Freddy. You love him, and you just realized it."

Did she? Her thoughts spun. Her heart squeezed. Perspiration gathered at her neck, her breasts, her forehead.

She couldn't properly breathe. She felt her entire future happiness depended on convincing Gabriel that he could let her into his life, let down his guard, and together they could build the life she'd been imagining in Covent Garden. The one where she was accepted for who she was and loved for it. The one where she had freedom, but that freedom now included a husband by her side who did not expect her to be a proper lady of the *ton*. How had she fallen in love with him when she hardly knew him? When had she? It hardly even mattered. It didn't change the fact that she was in love with him. She alternately wanted to cry and laugh at once. She never imagined she'd find love. Not truly, and she hadn't found love. It had found her.

"I love him," Freddy whispered as she stared at Blythe. "I love him, and he loves a ghost." She bit down hard on her lip.

Blythe sighed and patted Freddy's hand. "I think he just needs a little push to return to the world of the living. And from what I've seen of his reaction to you, you're the perfect person to do it."

Freddy laughed and swiped at the tears suddenly rolling down her cheeks. "I hope so. We are wed, after all."

"So shall we get to planning? I can tell you Gabe is already doing so. He was having a meeting at the club with Carrington, Kilgore, and Greybourne when I left. I think he must be procuring their aid."

"But you don't think they will help him, do you?"

"Maybe eventually," Blythe answered. "But I know we can do it quicker, and the quicker, the better. Hawk swore to take you from Gabe, but the longer he's denied his revenge, the more reckless he'll become. I worry that he or one of his cronies will try to kill Gabe."

"Yes, I'm very worried for Gabriel, too," Freddy said.

Blythe grinned. "I know you are. You're so worried that you'd risk yourself for my brother, which is how I knew you loved him."

Freddy frowned. "Then why'd you ask me?"

"Because you needed to realize it, silly. Now, not that I don't trust in our abilities, but I think we'll need someone else to aid us. Muscle, if you will, and I took the liberty of cajoling Huntley into aiding us."

"What? I hadn't realized you really knew my brother, and I just told you my plan!"

Blythe smirked. "I told you I thought of it first, remember? I proposed using you to Gabe. Did you think I'd simply forget my brilliant plan just because he told me to?"

"Well, no, but—"

"Exactly," Blythe interrupted. "I felt almost positive once I spoke to you about it that you would answer as I wanted you to, so I simply got things moving in the right direction."

"And how do you know Huntley?"

"He came to the club to defend your honor after the incident at the ball. I hit him over the head with a book, and the rest, well—" Blythe shrugged. "We've become friends."

"Friends?" She scrutinized Blythe, who was the color of a berry now.

"Well, he did ask to court me."

"Court you?" Freddy gaped.

Blythe scowled. "Don't sound so surprised."

"I'm surprised that he is willing to court at all. He was to be wed before, you see, and—"

"He told me."

"He told you?"

"Yes. We've had many long talks over the last week. He insisted upon accompanying me on missions to protect me."

"And you agreed to that?" Freddy couldn't seem to quit gawking at Blythe.

"Your brother has a way of making me want things I never thought I would."

Freddy knew a thing or two about that. "So did you agree to his request?"

"I told him I'd think about it." Blythe bit her lip. "What if I fail at being a proper lady? What if I hate it? What if Huntley regrets asking to court me?"

Freddy ticked a finger up. "You can learn the rules of etiquette easily." She raised another finger. "You may hate it. I can't say you won't, but you won't know unless you try it."

"As you tried my world?"

Freddy nodded. "Yes. I knew immediately I felt at home there."

"What of your parents, though?" Blythe asked, her tone worried.

Freddy gave a dismissive wave. "You've a fat dowry. Papa won't refuse that for Huntley, though he has no need of it, and Mama would part Heaven itself to see Huntley wed. Now, I'm not suggesting at all that you need to change who you are, but if you want me to teach you what the *ton* suggests makes a lady, then I can."

"Teach me. It will be the perfect cover in helping to keep what we're really doing from Gabe."

Both women looked at each other and dissolved into laughter. When they were silent once more, Freddy asked, "How should we go about luring Hawk to us?"

"I think the best way is to propose a meeting with him. We don't want to wait around for him to try to take you," Blythe said. "I can send a message through some underground connections, old business partners of his, to let him know that you and I want to meet with him. I'll word the message so that he thinks we're worried for Gabe's safety—"

"Which we are," Freddy said, to which Blythe nodded.

"And that we want to meet with Hawk to try to persuade him to forget his revenge. I do believe Hawk will think Gabe never told either of us that Hawk is after you and not Gabe, so Hawk will come to meet with us simply to take you."

Freddy nibbled on her lip. "He wouldn't try to hurt you, would he? I don't want to endanger you."

Blythe shook her head, a sad look settling on her face. "Not only did I once save Hawk's life so he owes me a life debt, but I mothered him. So no, I know Hawk would never hurt me. He never blamed me for Georgette and Gabe being together. In fact—" Blythe scrunched up her nose "—he only ever blamed Gabe. It always seemed odd to me that he didn't hold anger toward Georgette for not loving him but Gabe."

"That is odd," Freddy agreed, but she didn't think they'd ever know why the man had reacted the way he had. "Where should we meet with him?"

Blythe drummed her fingers on the table for a moment. "Somewhere close to the Orcus Society so that once we've captured him, I can race over to the club and let Gabe know. But it can't be the club. Hawk would never go there unaccompanied. And we'll have to make it clear in the note that we'll only meet him alone. Now, the other great problem I see is getting you past the guards that Gabe has set here to watch you, but there's a window in the cellar that you can climb out of, and Huntley and I can provide the distraction you'll need when the time comes. We can stage a row and then simply leave as if we are both storming away."

"That's brilliant, Blythe!"

Blythe grinned. "I thought so, too."

"Where will we tell Hawk to meet us, then?"

Blythe quirked her mouth back and forth and then said, "The orphanage we all once lived in. It's abandoned now, but I know the place as well as my own face. We can hide and watch for him coming, and if he's not alone, we can flee."

"Don't you think he'd do the same?" Freddy asked.

"No." Blythe shook her head. "Hawk has long thought himself invincible, which is why I think he may come alone, but if not, as I said, we'll flee."

In the meantime, Freddy would try to show Gabriel in small ways how she could fit into this world, and maybe then he'd open up to the possibility that he could love again. "Blythe, could you bring the books later today? I'd like to show Gabriel that I can do them."

"I brought them."

"What sort of things do you think would make Gabriel see I could survive in his world? That I belong here?"

"Well, you could swear a lot." Blythe grinned. "And wear some pantaloons. And learn to gamble. Oh, and swig Gabe's whisky! The women of my world aren't afraid to use their charms, either. When he returns tonight, you might consider seducing him, if you're not too timid." She snickered.

Freddy knew just what to do to seduce Gabriel, thanks to her sister and friends in SLAR. She'd go see Madame Toussant today and procure a special night rail made just to tempt a man, and she'd have whisky on hand for both of them. And how hard could it be to learn some bawdy language before tonight? She already knew words such as *damnation* and *hellfire.*

"I need some direction," she blurted.

Blythe's eyes went wide. "I hope you don't mean on seducing Gabriel."

"No!" Freddy's face heated. "I need you to teach me some bawdy words."

She gave Freddy an approving look. "I can teach you gobs of bawdy words, but a word of warning about the whisky..." Blythe eyed her. "You've never really imbibed, have you?"

"No. Ladies aren't supposed to. I've had a sip here and there, and I did have champagne after my wedding."

"Those few times won't make your body used to it. Have no more than *two* fingerfuls. I can have three and just feel the effects so you should keep it to two. Oh, and don't talk of the heart and emotions or expect Gabe to act like a dandy. People in Covent Garden don't talk of soft things. Come to think of it, I don't think I ever once heard Gabe or Georgette speak of their love for each other or even tell the other any words of love. In fact, Georgette was rather reserved with her emotions. The best advice I can give you is to make Gabe think you only want him for bedroom pleasure, and then, once his guard is down, you can win his heart."

Chapter Seventeen

$\mathcal{G}$abe glanced around the table at the men he'd asked to aid him. He counted each of them as a friend, but none of them had he ever let too close. Carrington was closer than any, but there was still a barrier there. And yet, they'd come and stayed all day and late into the night, working together to concoct a plan to find Hawk.

As the men rose to leave, and return to their homes and wives, the tight band that had been squeezing Gabe's chest since Hawk had shown up at the Mayfair home loosened a bit. He would find Hawk with help from the men gathered here—Carrington, Kilgore, and Greybourne—as well as Gabe's men from Covent Garden, whom he'd already set to the task of scouring the streets and keeping their ears open for word of Hawk. Carrington had connections at Scotland Yard with a man whose job it was to seize petty criminals in the rookeries, and he would check in with the man for any information he might discover.

Kilgore knew the leaders of one of the biggest under-ground crime rings, as well. He didn't explain how and Gabe had not asked. What Kilgore had done was offered to ask the man if he'd heard whispers of Hawk returning to Covent Garden, and if he had, where he might be staying or if he could get his comings and goings. And as for Grey-bourne, he was well acquainted with a physician who happened to specialize in serving unsavory sorts in St. Giles rookery, which was where Hawk had last lived, before he'd disappeared. Greybourne would check with the physician for any news and report back to Gabe.

Gabe felt good about the plan. What he didn't feel good about was how eager he was to return home to Frederica or how much he'd thought about their time together this morning. He'd enjoyed it too damn much for a man who was supposed to be keeping his wife from getting too close to him. She seemed to be slipping under his skin, despite his efforts, so as everyone rose to leave and filed out of the room, he kept his seat behind his desk.

Carrington was the last out of Gabe's office, but the man paused at the door, turning back toward Gabe. "It won't work, ye know."

Gabe frowned. "What won't work?"

"Trying to keep yer life separate from Freddy's."

Gabe gritted his teeth. "It will work because that's how I want it."

Carrington arched his eyebrows. "Is it? I think not. Ye've been making choices to tangle yer life with Freddy's since the night ye met her."

"Like hell I have."

Carrington smirked. "Ye had yer coachman take her locket to her."

"How the devil do you know about that?"

"Yer sister told my wife, who then told me."

He was going to give Blythe a verbal lashing when he saw her.

"Ye also took her home yerself the night Brooke's man attacked her. And I'd wager my fortune that it wasn't an innocent carriage ride."

Gabe yanked off his cravat and glared at Carrington, whose smirk grew in response.

"Ye came to warn her at the ball when ye could have just told me, and that ye felt compelled to ensure her safety at all was verra telling."

Damn it. Carrington was correct.

"Then ye declared to the *ton* that she was under yer protection. And then ye had yer little garden incident. And then ye wed her. And then—"

"Enough," Gabe said, going to the sideboard and pouring himself a finger of whisky, which he threw back in one gulp.

He met Carrington's eyes. "Ye already care for her."

"Of course, I care for her," Gabe said, his blood roaring in his ears. "She's my wife. It's my duty to see to her protection and needs."

"I wonder how long ye'll lie to yerself."

Gabe slammed his whisky glass onto the sideboard. "And I wonder how bloody long you'll stand here annoying me. Don't you want to rush home to your wife?"

That damned smirk of Carrington's got even bigger. "Don't ye want to rush home to yers?"

Good God, he did, and just how much made his heart stutter. He needed to find Hawk quickly so he could get Frederica out of his house. His efforts to keep her at a distance were made a thousand times harder with her so near.

Gabe entered the house late that night, expecting and hoping to find it in silence. What he found was a very loud rendition of a bawdy poem set to tune by his wife. It was undeniably Frederica singing at the top of her lungs from somewhere abovestairs, likely her bedchamber, and she was slurring the words of "The Plenipotentiary." She sounded rather foxed. He didn't know how a woman raised as Frederica had been would know the words of a bawdy poem.

He eyed his footman, who blanched and scuffled back a few steps, and then Gabe glared at the two guards, who both held their ground with him but tensed. "Where the devil has my wife been today?"

"Only to the seamstress," the footman responded. "And straight home from there."

"And who's been to call on her?" he asked.

"Just your sister," the other guard answered. "She came and went and came again."

What the hell had Blythe done?

Gabe gave a quick nod, then headed for the stairs, stopping midway up in shocked amazement at the words Frederica was singing and just how ridiculously horrible a singer she was and how her merry singing in his home made him smile and put an undeniable warmth in his chest. *Damnation.*

> "When to England he came, with his prick in a flame,
> He shewed it his Hostess on landing,
> Who spread its renown thro' all parts of the town,
> As a pintle past all understanding.
> So much there was said of its snout and its head,
> That they called it the great Janissary:
> Not a lady could sleep till she got a sly peep
> At the great Plenipotentiary."

When Frederica started the same verses all over again, Gabe shook off his stupor and took the stairs two at time, following the sound of her voice straight to her closed bedchamber door. He swung open the door and came to a halt, jaw sliding open once more and his own prick hardening at the sight of his wife in the sheerest creation he'd ever seen. It displayed her body in all its superb glory. Her head was thrown back, her eyes closed, dark hair cascading in waves down her back to touch the top of her perfectly rounded bottom, and her bare arms were slung wide as she spun around. One hand made small circles in the air, and in the other she clutched a snifter of dark amber liquid, which was sloshing over the edges as she spun.

She circled once more, head still back, eyes still closed, and stopped so that she was fully facing him. Her hard nipples showed through the sheer white material of her night rail, as well as the outline of her lush breasts and full hips. His mouth went dry with desire. He hadn't wanted a wife, but now he had one, and the need to possess her strummed through him. Every moment in her presence was putting cracks in his wall.

He gritted his teeth. "Frederica."

She jerked her head upright and snapped her eyes open.

Damnation, but her eyes were lovely. Like silver fire across a twilight sky. They warmed him through and not with simple lust. It was a wanting. A dangerous one. Just as he hardened his resolve, she grinned and melted his determination.

"Gabriel!" She dashed toward him and essentially tripped into his arms. He caught her, acutely aware how touching her, embracing her, made not only his groin ache but his damned chest constrict.

"What are you doing?" He plucked the snifter out of her hand just as she brought it to her lips to take, he presumed, another drink. Instead, he swigged it back in one gulp, surprise registering that it was whisky. "Why the devil are you drinking whisky?"

"Because," she said, nuzzling his neck.

His first reaction was to let her, but his short history with her had taught him it was unwise to allow his instincts to rule him where Frederica was concerned. He needed to take a breath and temper how hot she made his blood run. Except her lips on his bloody neck felt better than anything he could recall ever feeling. It took him until her lips had made a trail down one side of his neck and up the other before he could force himself to pull back and get the answers he needed.

"Frederica." He grasped her shoulders and held her far enough away that her lips could not tempt him. He couldn't damned well think straight with her mouth on him. Actually, if he was honest with himself, she'd been wreaking havoc on his ability to concentrate all day. "Why are you imbibing in whisky?"

She gave him a lopsided grin that made him want to laugh. "Well, I was only supposed to have two fingerfuls." She held up two fingers between them and stared at them as she fluttered them. He tried not to laugh, but he couldn't help himself. She was so deep in her cups. Her brows dipped together in a frown, and she poked him in the chest. "You're not supposed to laugh at me," she muttered. "You're supposed to want me madly in this night rail."

"I think," he said, his hands sliding down to her waist with a will of their own, "that we've already established that I want you madly. You don't need to don a night rail such as this to make me burn for you." She could be wearing a potato sack, and he'd suddenly want to live on a diet of potatoes only. When she frowned, he added, "However, I do like you in it very, very much."

"I'm glad." She grinned again. "But I froze my arse off

waiting for you in it, which is why I had the third finger of whisky. The first one warmed me so much, I thought three might chase the cold away for good."

He frowned at her use of the word *arse*. Not that he had innocent ears, nor did he really give a damn if she cursed like a sailor or not—it just sounded wrong coming from her for some reason. "But why did you have the first fingerful?" he asked, rubbing her back purely to ensure she was warm. Not at all because it felt so bloody good to touch her.

She tilted her head, looking as if she were having trouble remembering why she drank the whisky to begin with, and then she said, "Oh yes. Because of you, you cocksure jackanapes. I found myself nervous about seducing you, which was quite surprising, and I decided whisky might be just the thing to settle me and is one of the ways to show you I belong here."

"Was the whisky Blythe's idea?" She nodded, and then hiccupped. Bloody Blythe. He was going to stuff a rag in her mouth. "And the cursing?" Freddy nodded again. "And did Blythe teach you some bawdy words?" Another nod and a sway. "Cocksure jackanapes?" He hiked his eyebrows at her.

"Did I use the words incorrectly? I've loads more where those came from if I did." She hiccupped again and leaned into him, pressing her cheek to his chest, and that small gesture of trust made more than his chest constrict. His entire body hardened.

"You jumbled it just a bit." He told himself not to stroke her gently, lovingly, but his hand smoothed over the delicate curve of her head anyway. "I assume Blythe taught them to you today?"

"Yes," she murmured, her voice heavy as if sleep were near.

"All to show me you belong here because you don't

want to live in Mayfair?"

"I do belong here." Her weight settled further against him. He tightened his arms, prepared to keep her upright and then pick her up. She was a slip of a woman who was not used to imbibing. "But it's not just that I don't want to live in Mayfair." She raised her head, swaying as she did, and set her hand upon his heart. She tapped her fingers against his chest and settled her hand over his heart as a sad look settled on her face. "To my consternation, I've discovered I want this beating organ to beat for me," she murmured, "but I don't truly know how to get it to do that."

A flush of adrenaline shot through him. She wanted his heart. Good God. A longing pierced him, making him stiffen. Suddenly, she slumped against him, and her body became instantly loose and heavy. He reacted immediately, glad to think of her immediate needs and not how she made him feel. He scooped her off her feet and into the safety of his arms. Her head lolled backward, revealing her long, slender neck and her pale skin. He could just see her veins hiding underneath her skin. The pulse there beat strongly, but he knew how fragile life was. And she wanted his heart. She wanted him to let her in and accept all the pain that could come with that if he were to ever lose her.

He shook from the thoughts as he took her to the bed, laid her down, and stared at her, his own heart thudding in his chest while he warred with himself as to whether to stay with her or go to his own bedchamber. But when she shivered and moaned, there was no choice in his mind. He kicked off his shoes and settled behind her, pulling her into his arms. She wiggled, pushing her soft bottom into his groin, and then she let out what sounded like a contented sigh.

An unexpected smile tugged his lips, and he surprised himself by pressing a gentle kiss to her bare shoulder while slipping his arms around her midriff. A strange sensation filled his chest, as he lay listening to her deep breaths, inhaling her scent—a mix of flowers and vanilla and oak from the whisky.

She wanted into his world, and he was denying her. And she wanted *him*. She had turned herself inside out tonight in an effort to get those things. It killed him to see her hurting. He had made a grave error in not considering how his actions might hurt her and what effect that might have on him. He was supposed to be protecting her, but he was a danger to her himself. Not a physical one, but that made it no less powerful. Could he allow her in? Could he accept the risk that would bring?

Chapter Eighteen

*T*he question plagued Gabe throughout the week. He strove to avoid Frederica during the day by leaving the house before she woke and tending to business at the club until evening. At night, he took to the streets with the men he'd tasked with keeping an ear open for news of Hawk, and when those efforts proved fruitless, he accompanied first Kilgore, then Carrington, then Greybourne to talk to their contacts. But there was no word of Hawk—not even a sighting. Ice set in Gabe's veins, and it kept him up at night when he finally dragged himself home, exhausted.

After a week of little to no sleep, Gabe made a critical error: he failed to wake up before Frederica.

Opening his eyes to bright sunlight in his bedchamber, he frowned and blinked. Why was the sun out? He hadn't seen daylight in the morning in seven days. He sat up, stretched, then looked around the room and froze. Across from his bed, in the chair by the window, with sunlight filtering in on her shining hair, sat his wife.

Frederica smirked at him and stood. His half-asleep body roused in an instant, going hard all over. "Where did you get those breeches?" he asked, unable to tear his gaze away from how the material molded her luscious hips. Each step she took beckoned him to strip those breeches off and bury himself in her, as he'd longed to do all week. Avoiding her had been torture for his body, as well as his mind.

She didn't speak as she moved toward him, but when she was standing right beside him, she bent down, scooped up the breeches he'd tiredly discarded by his bed the night before, and dropped them on his chest. "Blythe loaned them to me. You promised to teach me to defend myself, and yet, I have only had one lesson. Hawk could have tried to get at me again, and I would be defenseless. Unless he tried to choke me face-to-face, that is, so I could use the one move you taught me." She plunked her hands on her hips. "Don't you care that I'm vulnerable?"

"Of course I care," he replied, finding it hard to concentrate with her so near. His unquenched desire for her was threatening to drown him.

"Then you will not mind making time for me this morning to teach me more maneuvers."

Good God. He couldn't be around her this morning— touching her, smelling her. There'd be no way to resist his need for her, and he did not yet have an answer to the question of if he could accept the risks that would come if he let her further into his life. "I can't this morning, I—"

"You," she said, her eyes narrowing and her perfectly kissable lips turning down into a frown, "are not a man of your word."

Bloody hell. She had him. And she knew it. "Fine," he said, to which she grinned, swooped forward, and kissed him. He'd have stopped her if there'd been time, but once her lips were on his, the tether he had on his self-control snapped.

He didn't know if she had parted her mouth or if he had demanded entry, but suddenly, their tongues were swirling and he was drinking in her taste. Damn it, if Frederica didn't taste like temptation incarnate. How the hell was he supposed to resist that? The one thing he'd known from the night he'd met her was that he wanted her, and that bloody wanting had only grown stronger with every moment in her presence.

He thought to gently push her back and tell her he'd meet her in the garden to practice, but when she made a desperate sound in her throat as his mouth slanted hungrily over hers, any thought of resisting her disappeared. Her hands came to his shoulders, and she dug her nails into his flesh, tugging him closer.

He didn't just deepen the kiss in response. That would have been too sane. Instead, he encircled her waist and broke the kiss long enough to haul her onto the bed. He settled her over his thighs, and the material of her breeches that covered her entry met his hardness, sending a primal need to possess her spiraling through him.

She wore a white men's shirt open at the collar. "This shirt is bloody brilliant," he growled as he kissed a path down her neck and tugged the collar open and over one breast, which he found shockingly bare. A pink nipple and her creamy flesh greeted his eyes. "You meant to seduce me," he said, his gaze capturing hers.

Fine lines crinkled around her eyes as she smiled. "Yes, well, I… Are you vexed?"

"I want you too damned much to be vexed, Frederica," he said right before he took her rosy nipple in his mouth and suckled. Her moan was the sweetest sound he'd ever heard in his life. He sucked and nipped and swirled his tongue around her bud as she squirmed and grasped him with her hands, pulling him closer.

His lust battered him, demanding he unleash it, but he strained against himself, trying to go slower, not to scare her or be too rough. But when she suddenly pulled away, rolled off him, and yanked her trousers off to reveal her complete nakedness, the beast within him fiercely took over. He yanked back his coverlet and enjoyed the widening of her eyes and her gasp.

"Do you always sleep without anything on?" she asked.

"I do," he said, rolling off the bed and coming to stand in front of her. Her breasts brushed against his chest, and he tried to hold on to the small amount of control he had left. "Freddy."

Her lips parted and then formed a beautiful smile. Christ. Where had that slip come from?

He cleared his throat. "Frederica, my control is hanging by a thread. The things I want to do to you..." He wanted to rut like a street-born beast. No pretty manners required. No lineage. Just two people desperate for each other. But he didn't want to scare her. For all her talk of living in Covent Garden, she was still Mayfair born and bred.

"I want you to take me," she said, her throaty voice making his cock twitch. "Take me without fear. Without control. I'll meet your need."

She didn't know what she was saying, but he was too far gone to fight his need for her. "You might be offended by what I want to do. You might be—"

"No." She pressed her lips to his, and he tasted just how much she wanted him when she slipped her tongue inside his mouth. She pulled back and raked her nails down his chest, making him groan. "I won't be offended or scared. Take me." A wicked grin twisted her lips. "But you must call me Freddy as you do it."

She drove a devil's bargain, but in that moment, he would have sold his soul to have her. "You've got yourself a bargain, Freddy," he said, setting his hands on her shoulders and turning her gently toward the bed so that her back and her perfect, plump arse were facing him. "Put your hands on the bed and lean over."

"Lean over?"

"Yes, *Freddy*," he said, but it came out like a growl. "This won't be polite, but I can promise you, it will be pleasurable."

She set her hands on the bed and leaned forward, and all he could do was stare openmouthed for a moment. "Freddy," he said, splaying his palms over either side of her low back and allowing his fingers to curl around her hips. Gooseflesh rose on her skin, and her back arched ever so slightly.

"Mm-hmm," she said, turning to look over her shoulder at him. Her eyes danced with mischief, and a rosy flush touched her cheeks.

"Christ, Freddy, you are the damned prettiest lass I've ever met. And the boldest. By God, you are."

"That's the nicest thing you've ever said to me," she replied.

Was it? He had a burning need to rectify that. He'd been so busy avoiding her this week, but in this moment, he wanted to ensure she understood how wonderful she was. He leaned down and slid his hands up, up, up her back, savoring her silky skin under his fingertips. He didn't stop his pleasurable glide until his hands rested on her heavy breasts. He cupped them and started to gently stoke her flame by circling her nipples with his fingers so that her need would match his when he took her.

"Good God, that feels good," she moaned, pressing her breasts harder against his hands.

He followed the clues she was giving him, continuing to lavish attention on her breasts with gentle circles and tiny pinches, and as he did so, he kissed his way up her spine. His chest seemed to expand with each kiss he gave her.

He used his left knee to nudge her legs farther apart, and then he reluctantly released her left breast to guide his cock to her entrance. Heat met the tip. "You have to be the best thing I've ever felt," he said, sliding his now-free hand around her hip and through her soft hair to find the spot he knew would make her more than ready. She gasped as his fingers parted flesh and settled on her pleasure point, and then he began to stroke her. Each moan from her brought his own lust closer to the edge. "You're so wet and ready, Freddy," he said, his voice now ragged from trying to hold back from taking her.

"I am ready," she panted. "Take me, Gabriel."

"Not yet," he replied. "Soon." He wanted to bring her almost to completion before he did. He delved a finger inside her, nearly crying out as her quivering flesh tightened around him.

"Gabriel Beckford," she growled, "if you don't enter me right now, I will never allow you to do this to me again."

He chuckled at that, withdrew his finger, and pressed his mouth close to her ear, even as his gripped her hips and slid slowly in her. "Liar," he whispered as unspeakable pleasure washed over him, consumed him, and stole all his thoughts except one: she was his.

With that in his head, he slid in and out of her, the friction and her tightness making all his muscles coil and demand to be released. She pushed her bottom back toward him, and he could see her hands gripping the coverlet. When she threw back her head and screamed and her body clenched around his cock, he found his release in an explosion that threatened to bring him down upon her and drive them both flat against the mattress. He smacked his palm against the bed as he filled her with his seed, and never, never had he felt closer to another person in his life.

It stole his ability to breathe and then left him trembling.

It took him a moment to gain control, but when he had, he withdrew from her, and she turned to face him. "Do you know what I'd like to do now?" she asked, smiling shyly at him.

"What?" he asked, fighting the way that simple look from her made his heart squeeze. But it was useless in this moment.

"I'd like to lie in bed and while away the remains of the morning with you."

He should say no, yet he found himself motioning to the bed, and when her eyes lit up, he could not make himself regret or question it. Together, they climbed into bed, and he stretched out his arm to allow her to lay her head on his chest. As she settled against him, slinging her leg over his, placing her hand on his heart, his throat constricted and his breath became trapped in his lungs. It could be like this with her every day if he let it. Unless, that was, he lost her.

He gritted his teeth, unwilling to ponder the question he still had no answer for. He wanted simply to enjoy this one moment. She was like the sun warming him when she was near. She was so achingly lovely. He trailed his gaze down her back, recalling his hands on her smooth skin, and then his gaze wandered over her rounded hip and her calf. She had the most alluring calves he'd ever seen. In fact, she was the most beguiling woman he'd ever met. She was a free spirit in a world where conformity was prized.

"Are you staring at me?" she asked, turning her face up to his.

"Mm-hmm," he answered, reaching over and tucking a lock of her hair behind her ear.

Her eyes shimmered like the color of a dove's wings.

"The hue of your eyes reminds me of the doves that I could see out of the one window of the room Blythe and I lived in with our mother."

A sad look settled on her face. "How did she die?"

"From poverty." He didn't intend on expanding. Hell, he'd not intended to say as much as he had, but Freddy's eyes shone with such sympathy that he said, "We were poor, and I couldn't earn enough money to keep us warm and fed." He didn't know why he'd told her that. He'd never spoken of it to anyone other than Blythe. "I watched her waste away in front of me. I sent Blythe out every day to sell flowers so that she wouldn't have to watch her die."

"Oh, Gabriel." She touched his cheek before simply laying her head back on his chest. "You've been protecting people all your life, haven't you?"

"I've tried." He didn't say more. To say that he'd failed would invite more conversation, more revelations, and he'd already said more than he'd intended. And yet, a lightness touched him now.

They lay in silence for a long time, and Freddy traced her fingers back and forth over his chest as heaviness creeped into his limbs and his eyes closed.

"Gabriel?"

He struggled to make himself open his eyes, but when he looked to her, she was staring up at him with a hopeful look. "I'd like to start every morning like this, doing what we did earlier, exactly as we did it."

She wanted him to say she could stay, but if he said that, he'd be lost to how she made him feel. There was no way he could keep her out if she was here every day. He wasn't even sure he was keeping her out now. His heart took on a different cadence when she was near, but he couldn't say the words she wanted to hear. Not yet.

Instead, he reached over and stroked a hand down her cheek. "You were right, and I was wrong."

Her brows dipped in confusion. "About what?"

"You're most definitely a Freddy."

For Freddy, the next month went by in a blur of secret meetings with Blythe and Huntley where they relentlessly went over every detail of what could go wrong if and when Hawk agreed to meet her. She also had daily lessons from Gabriel before he'd leave for the club each morning and stay there all day. Freddy didn't love that, but at least he was returning home at night before she fell asleep.

She also didn't love that he had still given no indication that he wanted her to remain in Covent Garden after Hawk was found, but she tried to take comfort in the fact that he now called her Freddy. It implied a monumental shift and showed that he thought her at least a tad capable of being a part of his world, and she reminded herself of the worry he had to be feeling with Hawk still out there.

Blythe had assured Freddy that she'd gotten word to the most appropriate of Hawk's old acquaintances, but they had not heard from the man yet. Freddy knew from Blythe that Gabriel had not had any luck securing information about Hawk's whereabouts yet, either.

Gabriel also still slept in his own bedchamber and had not invited her to join him. She didn't want to push him to do so. She wanted him to do it of his own accord. She wanted him to want her there with him, as she wanted to be there, and at night, when alone in the dark, she couldn't help but fret over what might happen to her heart if he didn't ever want more.

With each day that passed, each time they joined their bodies, each self-defense lesson he gave her, her heart expanded more and more, making room for him. She was perilously close to being one of those hopelessly in love heroines she'd read about in those Gothic romances Lilias had given her.

Perhaps that knowledge was what drove her to storm out of the house on that particular afternoon carrying the ledger for the Orcus Society, the figures which she had done in Blythe's stead. Freddy didn't want to be the only one in her marriage hopelessly close to being foolishly in love. She had to do more to make Gabriel understand that she truly belonged in Covent Garden with him, that he could let his guard down so that they could fall ridiculously in love together.

She was surprised to learn that Gabriel had directed the guards not to let her leave the house, but she was pleased to realize they were afraid to physically restrain her. So when she refused their command to stay put, they could do no more than follow her as she marched the short walk from the house to the Orcus Society. She was feeling rather proud and brave until the moment Bear showed her into Gabriel's office and his lips parted in surprise.

His brow furrowed, and a dark, dangerous look settled on his face. "Is the house burning down?" he asked.

The calm in his voice did not match the burgeoning fury on his face and made her want to turn and leave, but she stiffened her posture and stood her ground. "No. And before you say more or proceed to shout at the guards, they told me of your new orders." She clutched the ledger she wanted to show him tight to her chest. "Am I to be a prisoner in our home now?" She purposely used the word *our*. She wanted him to get used to it, but the wariness that flashed across his face dismayed her.

"You are a *guest* in my home until I have captured Hawk."

She wasn't the crying sort, but there was only so much a person could take. Tears filled her eyes, and despite her effort to blink them away, they mutinously spilled over and rolled down her cheeks.

Damnation. He hated himself in this moment. He was a bloody bastard.

Freddy turned and mumbled an excuse that she was suddenly struck by a megrim and would return to the house. Gabe rose and headed toward her, and just as she reached his office door and gripped the handle, he captured her by the shoulders. She stiffened under his fingers, which gutted him, and the fact that it gutted him worried him. The struggle not to open up to her increased tenfold every day, and he had woken that morning wanting only to spend himself in her and then spend hours in bed talking to her. The realization had left him cold, so he'd vowed to keep his distance. But faced with the pain he was causing her now, distance was impossible.

He pressed a kiss to the back of her head, inhaling her sweet-and-spicy scent as he did so. "I'm sorry, Freddy. I'm in a foul mood."

That much was true. Despite his relentless efforts over the last month, he'd been unable to locate Hawk. There had been sightings of him, however, in Covent Garden over the last week, which had led Gabe to decide Freddy had to remain at home unless he was personally accompanying her. If he could find Hawk and put him safely away, maybe then he could decide if he could truly let Freddy into his world and his heart.

"It's fine," she said, but her injured tone told him she was lying.

He turned her to him, determined to smooth things between them as best he could, given the circumstances. "What do you have there?" he asked, his attention catching on the book she was clutching to her chest.

She bit her lip but extended the book to him. "It's your ledger."

He frowned. "How did you get—Blythe?" he guessed.

Freddy nodded, shifting from foot to foot. "I wanted you to see... I'm very good with numbers, and I thought perhaps if you saw... Well, I thought perhaps, it might show you that..."

He opened the book and stared down at the neat rows of numbers. It took him a few moments to go over her calculations, but they seemed to match the ones he'd done himself.

Good God. He shoved a hand through his hair. She thought her capability at doing the books might make him reconsider allowing her to stay in Covent Garden. He didn't want to hurt her more, but he couldn't let her think something like this would change things. "It's not about how capable you are, Freddy," he said, looking up and wincing at how her shoulders dropped. He wanted to quit speaking, but he had to make her understand. "Over these last couple of weeks, I've seen how capable you are of surviving here. You're very capable. But then so was Georgette."

He didn't know what had made him say that. Why was he offering her another glimpse into what was truly holding him back? He'd told her of his failure to protect his mother, and now he'd practically told her how his failure to protect Georgette haunted him.

She flinched as if he'd hit her, and his own shoulders dropped under the weight of his self-loathing. Then she poked him in the chest. "You! You and your damned heart that you bloody well refuse to open can, can…go to the devil, and…and you can sod off, you arse!"

She turned and strode out, and he stood there for a moment stilled by her rage and her very creative use of foul words.

His damned heart that he refused to open? She knew. Of course, she did. His Freddy was the most intelligent woman he'd ever met.

His Freddy.

The words resounded in his head, battering his mind and demanding acceptance.

"Boss!" came a call toward the office door. "Do you want us to follow your wife?"

Good God! Gabe raced from the room, nearly colliding with the men he'd set to guard Freddy. He shoved them both out of the way, and as he did, he said, "Bloody idiots! Follow her everywhere at all times!"

He bounded down the passage, and as he rounded the corner, he could just see Bear sitting alone at his spot by the door. Gabe's heart pounded as he yelled, "Did Freddy leave?"

"Just," Bear called. "She said she told you she was going home."

That clever little minx. She was a Covent Garden lady if ever there was one. But that didn't make him feel a bit better knowing Hawk was out there, waiting for his chance to snatch her.

He ran past Bear and threw open the door, turning

toward his house, and then he bellowed in rage. There in the middle of the street was Freddy wrestling with a man by a stopped curricle. As Gabe hurdled toward them, she ducked as Gabe had shown her and twisted her body out of the man's hold. But then she turned to run, giving the man her back and leaving herself open.

"Freddy, no!" Gabe roared, his voice sounding inhuman to his own ears.

But it was too late. The man knocked her over the head with a pistol, and she fell to the ground, her head hitting so hard that it bounced back up. Gabe's vision went momentarily red, and he sprinted toward them as the man dragged Freddy onto the seat of the curricle and then sat himself and took up the reins. The conveyance started to move just as Gabe reached it.

Gabe didn't hesitate. He grabbed on to the back, being dragged for one moment, before he managed to find a foothold and pull himself onto the single seat, reserved normally for the servant, at the back. Freddy's assailant turned back to look at Gabe just as Gabe jumped over the seat onto the man. Gabe reared back his fist and he let loose a punch so hard it sent the man flying off the seat and onto the ground. Gabe jerked the carriage to halt, gave a glance over his shoulder to find Bear towering over the man. "Take him to the club and keep him there," Gabe ordered Bear, and then Gabe turned back to Freddy, who was slumped in the seat with her eyes still closed. He gathered her into his arms as images of his mother still and white on her cot and then Georgette bloodied on the street flashed through his mind. He shoved the images down, but they left him shaking as he lifted her and started to the house, his chest seeming to constrict more with every step.

As his boots clopped against the ground, a certainty

filled him. Freddy was not only in his head, but she was in his heart. It had never been his choice whether to let her in or not. She'd stormed her way in. And it scared the hell out of him because the thought of ever losing her was a reality he knew he could not survive.

Chapter Nineteen

"You're certain?" Freddy asked the doctor who'd been called in to examine her at Gabriel's insistence, though she'd woken up from being knocked out soon after Gabriel had brought her home.

The doctor smiled at her and nodded.

She'd assured Gabriel she felt fine except for a pounding headache, but he had refused to listen to reason. He had, in fact, been acting particularly tense since they'd arrived back home. He'd also refused to leave the bedchamber until the doctor had insisted. She was glad of that now. Her hand fluttered to her belly. *A babe.*

Her breath caught in her throat. "But that's impossible." It was a stupid thing to say. Of course it was possible. It was just that she'd not once considered what would happen if she were to get with child. She'd been so focused on creating a place for herself in Gabriel's world and getting him to open his heart to her, she'd not given a single thought to what all their lusty joining might result in, nor had she spared a moment's worry for her missed flux.

She settled her other hand on her belly, too, and bit her lip. How did she feel about this? Frightened. Most definitely. And the thing that most scared her was that Gabriel might never be willing to give her his heart and put himself at risk for loss again. Or… She bit her lip as hope rose. Perhaps this child would be the hope he needed, the thing to make him love her as she loved him.

"Do you want me to send your husband in?" the doctor asked, interrupting her thoughts.

Freddy nodded, and he inclined his head, turned, and quit her bedchamber. Before she could think any more on the news of the babe to come, the door opened with a swish, and Gabriel filled the doorway, his jaw set and shoulders stiff. He strode to the bedside and swept his gaze over her, but not, she noted, touching her. A sliver of apprehension swept through her.

"Dr. Hughes says you are fine, but you look pale." He shifted restlessly from foot to foot.

Just blurting the news might be the best way to tell him, she reasoned, given how cagey he already appeared. "I'm fine, and so is the babe."

His face drained of color, and his gaze flew to her stomach. "Did you say *babe?*"

Her lips pulled in a tentative smile and that little bubble of hope within her expanded. "Yes." When Gabriel looked up, her stomach clenched tight at the agony in his eyes.

"I can't." He shook his head and backed up several steps.

She frowned. "What do you mean, *you can't?* There's no choice, really." But there *was* a choice. He could lead a separate life from her *and* the babe. She knew plenty of husbands of the *ton* who carried on as if they had no wife or child, but she'd not considered that possibility until this second.

"Damn it, Freddy." Gabriel shoved his hand through his hair. "Letting you in was already too much risk. But a babe too?"

Her breath stalled at his words, and she tracked him as he began to pace in front of her bed.

"But you pushed and pushed every step of the way. I told you not to come back to Covent Garden after that first night we met, but you came anyway. I told you that you didn't belong, but did you listen?" His voice was rising with each word.

"No," she said, her voice quiet, "I did not listen."

"Precisely!" He squeezed his eyes shut for a moment and pressed his knuckles into his forehead as if trying to contain something in his mind. What? His anger at her? His fear to love again? Or his sadness that she was not Georgette? Freddy wanted to rave at him, but she *had* pushed him. He was correct.

"You came and got yourself in trouble, and what was I to do?" he went on.

She watched him continue to pace the room, not sure if he really wanted her to answer.

"I had to save you, that's what." He stopped mid-stride and glared at her before continuing again. "I had to save you. And then you went and sat close in my carriage—"

"I think *you* sat next to *me*," she inserted, but he was wearing a path on the floor as he muttered to himself and didn't seem to even hear her.

"And you smelled so bloody nice. And then you shivered." He paused again and narrowed his eyes at her as if shivering were the worst sort of offense. "And then you told me how that kiss from that sod was your first kiss." He swung toward her and pointed an accusing finger. "You damn well knew I could never let that stand."

"I damn well did not!" she said, scowling, but he was still pacing, muttering, and jerking his hand through his hair. At this rate, he'd go bald if he kept it up.

He stopped once more, but this time he was facing the door, and she had a sudden worry that he'd simply walk out of her life, and she'd never see him again. "You and those little sounds you make at the back of your throat."

Her brows dipped together. She hadn't realized she made sounds at the back of her throat.

"You've the spirit of a siren. You seduced me. Put a spell on me."

Had she? She at once liked that he thought she could, but he slung it at her like an accusation.

"The way you kissed me," Gabe said. "Well, no man could damned well resist that. And now we come to the bloody ball."

She bit her lip. He was going through their history in a rapid, alarming fashion.

"I came to warn you, and what did I get for my troubles?"

"No one asked you to warn me," she snapped. "I did not ask you to come to my rescue! You came of your own will."

He swung toward her, gripping the edge of the bed, his nostrils flaring, his jaw tense. "Of course I would rescue you. Was I to let you be ravaged? If you'd only listened in the first place, our lives would have never intersected again."

Ice infused her veins at his words and spread like vines of despair through her stomach.

"If only I'd not touched you, had kept my bloody hands off you and left your unmentionables in place. My honor has been my downfall. First with Georgette and then with you. But you...you are nothing like Georgette."

He couldn't have said anything more hurtful to her. "Get out!" she yelled. He stood there, staring at her, eyebrows dipped as if confused about why she was suddenly so angry. Frightful Frederica had a husband who was afraid to love her. Or maybe he simply did not want to. It was all too much. This moment of her heart shredding was why she had never, ever wanted to be in love.

Shaking, she reached over to her nightstand, picked up the brush from the table, and threw it at him. "Get out!" she screeched, not caring how she must sound to the household staff. "Get out. Get out. And don't come back! I don't need or want you in my world!"

He opened and closed his mouth several times, filling her with hope that he might apologize, might say he actually did love her, had not meant what he'd said—even saying he had not meant it like it had sounded would have sufficed—but he didn't do any of that. He clamped his jaw shut, turned, and left.

With a pounding heart, she scrambled out of the bed and rushed to her bedchamber door, pressing her ear to the wood and listening as his boots thudded down the stairs. When she knew he'd reached the bottom, she opened her door and raced to the top of the stairs just in time to see him leaving through the front door without a backward glance. Then, and only then, did she allow her tears to fall. She sank down at the top of the stairs and cried until she fell asleep.

Chapter Twenty

"*B*ear tells me ye spent the last night two nights at the club," came Carrington's voice from the doorway of Gabe's office.

Gabe looked up from the day's ledgers he'd read a dozen times, but still could not damn well tell what they said. Staying away from Freddy had not been easy, but he had stayed away because the need to be with her was an all-consuming, gnawing ache. He loved her. The moment he'd seen her fall in the street he'd known it. It had been a dagger straight into his heart. And now she was with child. How could he bear it if he lost either of them? He didn't know that he could, but he also knew he could not imagine his life without her in it every damn day.

"Do ye plan to spend tonight here, as well?"

Gabe frowned and looked to the window, his lips parting at the hues of blue and purple in the sky indicating it was dusk. *Plan?* He only had one plan and that was to find Hawk, and it was bloody well not going as he'd hoped.

"I spent the first night here attempting to get information from the man who tried to snatch Freddy."

"And did ye?"

"Yes," Gabe said, then frowned. "And the information I got was that the man was just a lackey who has no idea where Hawk is. Hawk paid him to watch this street and snatch Freddy if he should see her, then take her to the old orphanage where we used to live. There, he was to light five candles in the window, which would serve as a signal to Hawk to come for her. I did all of that last night and nothing. Hawk didn't come."

"Undoubtedly, the man's heard about yer stopping the carriage and saving Freddy," Carrington replied. "So he knew it was a trap."

Gabe scrubbed a hand over his face. "Yes, undoubtedly."

Carrington entered the room and sat opposite Gabe. "I've seen a great deal of yer sister the last two days. Did ye know Huntley is courting her?"

Gabe nodded. "She mentioned it. I'm pleased." He studied Carrington. "You came all the way here to see if I knew that?"

"I'm here because my wife informed me that I'm to be an uncle, and I was surprised I'd not heard the news directly from ye." Gabe flinched at the spasm of happiness that cramped his chest just thinking of his unborn child. "I was even more surprised to discover that Freddy has agreed to her mother's suggestion that she should spend her months awaiting the child at their country home," Carrington added.

Gabe jerked his gaze back to Carrington from the window where he'd diverted his attention. "What?"

Carrington nodded, studying him as sweat broke out on Gabe's neck. Freddy couldn't leave him. He knew he'd said all the wrong things, but he needed her here. That was the damned problem. He had not wanted to need her, and now he did, and it scared him just how much.

"Beckford, I've never offered ye advice, but ye gave me some once with my wife, which helped me, so I'm going to return the favor."

"Do I have a choice?"

"Nay," Carrington said with a chuckle. "I've known ye for a long time, and the one thing I've always known is that ye harbor enormous guilt for things ye could not control. Neither yer mother's death nor Georgette's was yer fault." Gabe opened his mouth to protest, but Carrington held up his hand. "Hear me out."

Gabe nodded.

"Ye distanced yerself from everyone after Georgette died, except yer sister, and I suspect ye would have distanced yerself from her if she'd allowed it, but she wouldn't. And then along came Freddy."

Gabe couldn't stop the smile that came to him just thinking about her. "She forced her way into my life."

"That's our Freddy." Carrington nodded. "Listen, Beckford, ye don't have to feel guilty because ye've come to care for Frederica. I think Georgette would want that. I—"

"That's not it," Gabe said, deciding to finally break his promise to Georgette to never tell why they had truly wed. He quickly told Carrington the tale. "It's not guilt. It's... Well—" Devil take it. He could not speak of how he was feeling to his friend, but Carrington gave him a knowing look.

"If it's loss that ye fear, ye'll lose her certainly if ye refuse to let her close. She'll still be yer wife legally, but there are technical marriages and then there are real ones. Trust me. I've had both, and ye don't want the first one."

Gabe thought about everything he'd said to her, how he'd reacted to the news of the babe. It had struck an even greater fear in him that he would fail them both, be unable to protect them from the dangers of the world, and when she'd ordered him to leave, he'd taken the opportunity like a coward. He was afraid of himself, of what she made him feel. But sitting here now, thinking on her, thinking on the babe, he knew without a doubt that he'd rather have this fear than a life without her and his child.

He'd feel better if he found Hawk, but Hawk was not the only danger in the world. He'd used Hawk as an excuse to hide from more pain, but in doing so, he had robbed himself of living. He wanted to live fully with Freddy. "I need to go talk to her."

"Aye, ye do, but she was at my house when I came here so ye don't need to rush. But when ye do talk to her, ye might want to explain how ye came to marry Georgette. Freddy seems to think that one of the reasons ye are keeping yer distance from her is that ye are in love with a ghost."

He frowned. "Where'd she get that idea?"

Carrington laughed. "From ye, ye thick skull! And yer sister apparently, who agreed with her that ye must still be in love with Georgette."

"I'm going to need a fingerful of whisky before I face my wife and grovel."

"Smart man," Carrington said. "Pour me one, as well, and I'll tell ye what I've learned about the art of groveling to one's wife."

"Guinevere!" Freddy said in surprise as the footman announced her sister, whose house she had only left a short time ago. But a lot had happened since departing Guinevere's. Blythe had arrived and Huntley had arrived and told her Hawk had contacted Blythe and would meet Blythe and Freddy at the orphanage tonight. Freddy glanced at the dark, sensible gown she'd donned for the mission to capture

Hawk, and then she glanced over at Huntley and Blythe, who were both aiding her, standing at the sideboard. They looked frozen in surprise at Guinevere's appearance. Freddy willed them not to do something foolish that would reveal what they were about to do. She was positive Guinevere would race to her husband and tell him, and then he'd tell Gabriel, and Gabriel would stop her. He may not want to love her or want her in his life, but he thought it his duty to protect her.

"What are you doing here?" Freddy asked her sister, giving the footman a nod that he could go. As he departed, Guinevere entered the room, eyeing Freddy, Huntley, and Blythe with narrowed eyes.

"I didn't feel like our talk at my house was finished." Guinevere came to stand in front of Freddy but cast her gaze to Blythe and Huntley. "Huntley," Guinevere said, amusement in her voice, "I never would have believed you would be involved in whatever shenanigans Blythe and Freddy have plotted."

He opened his mouth, looking as if he were about to protest, but Guinevere held up her hand with a chuckle. "Don't bother denying it. I'll not ask what the three of you are about because I know I won't get a truthful answer, but I'll remind you two," Guinevere said, sounding stern, "and you," she added, looking at Freddy, "that Freddy is with child and needs to act accordingly."

Freddy scowled at her sister, even as her hand fluttered protectively to her belly. "That is at the forefront of my mind, I assure you, but being enceinte does not render me an invalid."

"Quite right, Freddy. Doing it your way as usual, I see, but I'm glad of it. That's what makes you, you. And you are special."

Freddy frowned. "What's this about?"

Instead of answering her, Guinevere turned to Blythe and Huntley, who still stood at the sideboard. "Might I have a moment alone with Freddy?"

Blythe and Huntley nodded and departed hurriedly. When the door closed, Guinevere said, "My, how love has changed Huntley. He's actually become aware of others' wants besides his own."

"Yes," Freddy agreed, pleased. She loved her brother, always had, but he had been rather self-absorbed and self-indulgent before he'd met Blythe. Before, he had not wanted to be bothered with Freddy, Guinevere, or Vivian, other than to chide them, which he'd done to Freddy, in particular, a great deal, telling her repeatedly that she was embarrassing not only herself but him when she behaved, well, like herself.

"However, I am not here about Huntley. I'm here about you. I had hoped marriage to someone like Beckford, who I felt certain could appreciate a woman with your gusty nature and even complement it, would help you accept yourself, but our talk earlier at my house made me sure it hasn't."

Freddy frowned. "I beg your pardon?"

Guinevere sighed. "Frederica, I'm going to be blunt. There is nothing wrong with you."

"I never said there was!"

"No," Guinevere agreed, "you didn't, but in the past month, sitting in the quiet nursery and rocking the children to sleep by myself, I have come to see that we—Viv, Huntley, Mama, Papa, myself, even our friends—might have made you feel that way through the years. I always thought you so sure of yourself, truth be told, too sure. But talking to you at the house a bit ago, when you told me that you were fleeing to the country rather than staying to make a life for yourself somewhere you love, I realized that you are not sure of yourself at all."

Freddy's mouth slipped open and her mind turned over her sister's words.

Guinevere squeezed Freddy's shoulder. "What do you remember most about childhood?"

"Oh, that's easy," Freddy said, "the words *do stop* linked with my name."

Guinevere bit her lip. "Yes, that's what I recalled, as well. How often we would all say, 'Freddy, do sit still.' 'Freddy, do stop chattering.' 'Freddy, do stop humming.' 'Freddy, do stop running.' 'Freddy, do be quiet'—especially when Vivian was ill."

Freddy's stomach tightened. "Yes," she said, her voice quiet, and a flush heating her as she recalled when Vivian was at her most ill, and her family at their most cross, the scoldings became more severe and frequent. That was when she started to feel like there was something wrong with her, that she did not truly belong in her family, and then later, when she made her debut, that she did not belong in the *ton*.

Tears filled Guinevere's eyes. "I'm sorry, Freddy. You were different from the rest of us—more boisterous, exuberant, talkative, more of *everything*, especially full of life—and I think, for my part, I was a tad jealous. I know Viv was, as well, being ill and unable to be so lively, and I think Mama and Papa simply didn't know how to contain you, so we all had a hand in making you feel there was something wrong with you."

Freddy inhaled a sharp breath. She had felt that way, as if she were odd and out of place, and she had hated thinking she might never feel like she belonged. So she had made it about Mayfair and eventually set her sights on living in Covent Garden. Her pulse skittered. No place or person could ever make her feel like she belonged. Only she could do that by accepting herself and loving herself, even if Gabriel never did.

"I don't want you to go to the country to await your child or to live there permanently, as you suggested earlier. You'd be miserable there."

"Yes, I would." Freddy sniffed and wiped at her cheeks, which suddenly had warm tears rolling down them. "I never expected to fall in love," she whispered to her sister.

"Whyever not?" Guinevere asked.

"Because," Freddy said, admitting something out loud she had only just truly understood, "I couldn't see how someone would ever possibly love me, so I convinced myself I wasn't interested in love, only in living somewhere I was accepted and felt I belonged. And then along came Gabriel, and I fell in love with him."

Guinevere hugged Freddy. "You're more than worthy of love."

Freddy rested against her sister's comfortable shoulder for a moment. "If only Gabriel would see that he can love again."

"Well, he won't be made to see that if you run off to the country."

Freddy straightened and wiped her cheeks. "Quite right. I'll be staying."

"That's my Ferocious Freddy."

Freddy grinned. "I quite like that."

Her sister winked at her. "I thought you might. Now, what do you think you'll do about Beckford?"

Freddy inhaled a long, deep breath, a sense of calm falling over her. "First, I'm going to fix a problem for him, which I hope might help matters, and then I'll continue to fight for him. For us."

"That sounds about right," Guinevere said.

Yes. Freddy smiled. *Yes, it does.*

Chapter Twenty-One

*G*etting out of the house and past Gabriel's guards went exactly as Freddy, Blythe, and Huntley had planned. Blythe and Huntley staged a row upon exiting the home while Freddy slipped out one of the windows. The three of them met on the corner of the street behind the house and then made their way together to the orphanage.

They were well ahead of the appointed hour that Hawk was to arrive, but they took care entering the dark orphanage. Huntley went in first, pistol raised, and crept from room to room to ensure no one was there waiting for them. Once he signaled all was clear, Blythe and Freddy entered. They went to the hiding spot by the window that Blythe had told Freddy about, which Blythe and Huntley had decided was the best option after visiting the orphanage several times. Huntley positioned himself belowstairs as Blythe and Freddy kept lookout.

Freddy's breath came out in white circles in the cold night air, and she shivered as she crouched by Blythe. To her left, something scampered and scratched, making her skin crawl, and to her right, water trickled from some unseen spot. She soothed herself by counting Blythe's inhalations, so when Blythe suddenly seemed to stop breathing, Freddy's heart stammered.

"He's here," Blythe whispered.

Freddy glanced out the window, and Hawk walked

through the heavy fog that had descended looking more like a ghost than a man. Blythe gave out a whistle to alert Huntley, and then she and Freddy rose and moved silently down the stairs to position themselves at the foot of the staircase deep in the shadows. If Huntley had any trouble overtaking Hawk, they would aid him.

Freddy clutched the pistol that Blythe had given her and Huntley had shown her how to use during several of their meetings. Blythe gripped one, as well. The half-rotted door they'd entered earlier screeched, and then a footstep thudded. Then another.

"Lady Frederica," called a voice that chilled Freddy.

She held her breath. At five paces, Huntley would spring on Hawk. Her brother should be directly behind the man by then. He and Blythe had counted the number of paces it took to fully enter the orphanage from every possible entrance, and they had determined it was the best time for Huntley to attack.

Three. Four. Five.

Noise shattered the silence as Huntley lunged at Hawk. Amid grunts, and the smack of fists against flesh, something clattered to the ground, then slid, scraping across the stone floor and stopping somewhere in the dark. Huntley delivered a solid blow to Hawk's chin, which sent the man reeling and thudding to the ground, which Freddy could just see through the shadows. Huntley came over Hawk, placing his foot on the man's chest and pointing his pistol at him. "I'll kill you, if you move."

"I'd be disappointed if you didn't try, Lord Huntley."

Freddy stilled, having already started to rise at Hawk's use of her brother's name. How did he know who her brother was?

Beside her, Blythe stood all the way up and strode toward Hawk and Huntley. Just as Blythe bent down and delivered her own hit to Hawk's nose, Freddy reached the trio. "That," Blythe said, "is for betraying me, Georgette, and Gabe so long ago. And this—" the woman punched him again, this time in the eye "—is for killing Georgette and the babe."

"I missed you, too, Blythe," Hawk said, eerie amusement in his voice.

"Blythe, go fetch Beckford," Huntley said. "Don't get distracted."

Blythe nodded. "You're certain you're good? I don't like that he knew your name."

"You always were a smart one, Blythe," Hawk said.

"Shut up," Huntley snarled. "Go, Blythe."

"I won't be but a moment," Blythe assured them, turning and fleeing to fetch Gabe as they'd planned.

"Point your pistol at him, Freddy," her brother urged gently.

Could he see how she trembled? Even still, she did as he'd said, her blood rushing in her ears. She glanced down at the man who'd taken Georgette from Gabe and who had wanted to take her, too.

Dark eyes sharpened on her, and a smile tugged up the corner of his lips. He was quite handsome aside from his crooked nose, which she knew was the result of a punch from Gabe years before.

"I've been watching Gabe teach you to defend yourself in the garden, Lady Frederica."

The news made Freddy shake so much that she almost dropped the pistol.

"Stop talking," Huntley growled and kicked out at Hawk.

In a blur, Hawk caught Huntley's ankle and jerked so

hard that Huntley flew backward, banging into Freddy as he
fell and knocking her pistol out of her hands. It clanked to
the ground out of her reach just as Huntley's weapon hit
the floor. Huntley rolled for it, but Hawk was faster. He
kicked the weapon with one foot, then pivoted and kicked
her brother square in the nose. Huntley groaned and blood
gushed as he attempted to gain his knees.

An arm slid around Freddy's neck from behind, and she
screamed but did as Gabe had taught her. She brought her
hands to the arm at the same moment she ducked and
stepped back, twisting under her assailant's hold and out of
his reach. But when she came up, she stilled at the sight of
her brother now kneeling with a pistol pointed to his head.
Her gaze darted from her brother to Hawk to her assailant—Lord Brooke.

"You bloody bastard," she said.

"I'll show you just what a bastard I can be." Lord
Brooke took a step toward her, and she scuffled backward.

"Enough," Hawk ordered. "Brooke get the weapon to
your right. Lady Frederica, go to Lord Brooke, or I'll end
your brother's life right now." She didn't hesitate. She
walked to Lord Brooke, and when she was almost to him,
Hawk said, "That's far enough. Turn around."

Her legs didn't want to comply, but she forced herself
to do as she'd been told and slowly turned toward Hawk.
The room around her seemed to tilt, and through the
rushing of her blood in her ears, she heard Hawk say, "Take
her out, Brooke." And then everything went dark.

⚜

Gabe rose from his seat opposite Carrington when his office
door burst open and Blythe raced into the room. She flicked

her gaze over Carrington and then speared Gabe with a smug look. "The wife you do not appreciate and I have lured Hawk out of hiding, and he's awaiting your dealing with him at the old orphanage."

The words took a moment to penetrate Gabe's brain, but when they did, he jerked up and was moving toward the door, kicking a chair out of his way rather than waste a second to go around it.

Behind him, Blythe yelled out, "You can thank me later. And you better thank Freddy when you get there. It was her idea and—"

"Fall in behind me, Blythe, before I turn around and ring your bloody neck. I need details."

Blythe immediately did as told as he strode through the hall of the club that led to the exit, trying to fight back the black wave threatening to drown him. Blythe never would have left Freddy in a dangerous situation. He knew that rationally, but he also knew that situations could change in an instant.

"I sent a message out weeks ago to men I hoped could get it to him letting him know Freddy was concerned for your safety and wanted to meet with him. It took him forever to answer, but I just knew he would." Blythe grinned, making Gabe truly want to shake her. "You know how smug he's always been. He would never have imagined a woman could plan his downfall."

He stopped abruptly and faced his sister, noting Carrington just behind them. "You don't really know him, Blythe. I kept the truth from you because Georgette begged me to do so. He forced himself on Georgette and got her with child. I didn't wed Georgette because I suddenly realized I loved her; I wed Georgette to protect her from Hawk and so her unborn child would not be a bastard. She thought she loved him. She gave herself to him, and then she saw him kill a man. She rejected him, and he ravished her."

Blythe gawked at him. "What?"

"Tell me she's not alone with him," he asked as he exited the club.

"Huntley's there."

Bloody Huntley. If anything happened to Freddy, he'd kill her brother for letting himself get talked into this. He didn't give a damn if the man was besotted with his sister. Gabe ran down the street, the cool air hitting him in the face, and his lungs burning. But he pushed himself faster until his lungs screamed, when he reached the abandoned orphanage, he withdrew the pistol tucked into his waistband, took the stairs three at a time, and flung open the door, immediately spotting Huntley lying on the floor struggling with ropes that bound his hands and legs, and what looked to be his cravat stuffed in his mouth.

Gabe's world flipped, and he went numb. He strode to Huntley, bent, jerked out the cravat, and demanded, "Where is she?"

"He took her. Lord Brooke was with him."

Hot liquid poured through Gabe's veins and curled his hands into fists. He should have killed Brooke when he'd had the chance. And Hawk. "Where?" was all Gabe could manage.

"I heard them say something about the Voltaire Club."

Gabe knew the place. It belonged to Hawk's old partner, a man known to profit in the sale of women. Gabe's worst nightmare, the thing he'd erected walls around himself to avoid, was knocking at his door. He opened up his mouth and roared. He could not lose her. He could not. He needed to save her, tell her he loved her, tell her she'd taken his damned heart when he hadn't given it, and then cherish her as she deserved to be cherished for the rest of her life. He wanted to raise their child and grow old together. He wanted to feel everything she made him feel, and if that meant worry and fear came along with it, he'd deal with it, with her by his side.

He stood and turned as Blythe and Carrington came into the room panting from the run here. "Free Huntley, Blythe. Carrington come with me."

He'd made a promise to Georgette, but he'd also made a promise to protect Freddy, and the latter trumped everything now.

Chapter Twenty-Two

*F*reddy woke with a start and a gasp. Her head pounded as her eyes adjusted to her surroundings and settled on Hawk, who sat across from her in a speeding carriage. "Where are you taking me?"

"To sell you." Hawk's lips curled back from his teeth, reminding her of a wolf. "There are lot of unsavory men, Lady Frederica, and not just in the rookeries. The worst I've ever met are the nobs like Lord Brooke."

She shivered with cold even as sweat trickled down her back. "How do you know Lord Brooke?"

Hawk leaned forward and set his hands on either side of her knees. Alarm raced through her, but she held perfectly still. "We go back years. He owed me more money than he could pay, and I let him live with a promise to keep an eye on Beckford and alert me the moment he found a lady he was interested in. And through these long four years, I've patiently waited to get my revenge, and I made sure to remind Brooke, by sending men loyal to me to beat him every so often, what would happen if he failed me."

She swallowed a lump in her throat.

Hawk leaned back into his seat and surveyed her with a look that made her skin crawl. "I was honestly shocked when I got to Town and learned he'd wed you so quickly after I'd been sent word of you. But then Brooke told me how Beckford had stood guard outside your parents' house some months before."

The news stole her breath. Why had Gabe done that? To ensure she didn't return to Covent Garden? To ensure she was safe?

"Brooke's an idiot, and I cracked him good for not sending me that information when it occurred. But it's turned out well enough. I got what I came for." He smirked at her.

It took all her will not to move her hands protectively over her stomach. "He'll never stop coming for you if you hurt me or make me disappear."

"Of course he won't. That's the point. He'll never find either of us, and it will destroy him to know he had the chance to kill me but didn't take it. And because of that, he lost you."

Noise buffeted her eardrums. The whoosh of the wind outside. The wheels turning over the road. The fast clops of the horses' hooves. They all joined the furious patter of her heart. She couldn't just sit idly by and let him do this. She licked her lips, expelling a painful breath as she flicked her gaze to his pistol, which had slipped to his side and now pointed downward. Gabriel may have made a promise not to kill Hawk, but she hadn't, and she would protect her unborn child at any cost.

She gritted her teeth and prayed for a moment when she could act. Not long later, Hawk closed his eyes on a yawn, the pistol dropping farther, and she didn't think, she just lunged for it.

Gabe's heart stopped at the sight of the abandoned carriage in the middle of the lane near the Voltaire Club. He motioned to Carrington to approach with caution as they descended from the carriage they'd come in, but caution wasn't needed. As he got near, the metallic smell of gunpower filled the air and stung his nose, and the carriage door was ajar. No one was inside, but there was something there—blood.

"Christ," Carrington muttered beside him.

He turned and speared Carrington with a look. "It is not her blood." He refused to allow the possibility even as a suffocating sensation tightened his throat.

"How do you want to approach the club?" Carrington asked.

It took several swallows before Gabe could open his mouth to answer, but before he got any words out, a scream rent the night. He moaned like a wild animal at the sound of Freddy's voice, and then a flood of energy fired though his body sending him racing toward her.

Footsteps pounded after him, but he was much faster than Carrington, whom he left behind. Years on the streets and in the ring dodging enemies had made him light of foot, despite his height and bulk.

Something flashed to his right. *Light-colored silk skirts maybe?*

He followed his gut, rounding the corner into a shadowy alley, and there she was, at the end, nothing more than a silhouette in the moonlight, but that silhouette was his whole heart. And at the site of her it thumped and expanded.

Hawk was stalking toward her. Gabe would know the man even in the darkest pits of Hell. He'd committed everything about him to memory—his stride, the sound his boots made when they hit the ground, the way he swung his arms and held his shoulders. He'd memorized that because if Hawk ever came to kill him, it had been the one exception to his vow that Gabe was willing to make, but now there were two more—Freddy and his child.

Gabe raised the pistol he'd readied when something clicked behind him. His blood froze in his veins.

Never leave your back unguarded when going into a dangerous situation.

Noise exploded, his ears rang, and a bullet tore a fiery path of pain through his left shoulder, shoving him forward and to his knees. Hawk turned, and Freddy lunged at him, only to be knocked backward when Hawk smacked her across the face.

Gabe reached down toward his second pistol, which he'd tucked into his boot. Just as his fingers grazed the cool metal of the weapon, someone grabbed him from behind. Roaring, he threw his right elbow back in a sharp, fast jab, hard bone cracking under the blow he delivered. Lord Brooke fell to the ground beside him, hands to his nose, writhing and grasping at his nose. For a breath, Gabe stared openmouthed at the man before he smashed his fist into his face once more. Brooke's body went prone.

Gabe glanced up to reach for his pistol, and as he did, Hawk aimed his weapon toward Gabe. *Too late.* Gabe was going to be too late to save her. Behind him, a gun exploded, making Gabe flinch and swivel around to see Carrington standing, legs spread, and his pistol raised. Gabe jerked back around to find Hawk staggering and clutching his leg. Gabe bent and grabbed his pistol, rising as Hawk turned toward Freddy.

Without hesitation, Gabe raised his weapon once more, blood singing through every part of his body, and he fired straight at Hawk's back. Gabe was running toward Freddy even as Hawk dropped his weapon, and fell beside her. Gabe scooped her up with his good arm and pulled her to his chest, her body shaking violently. A glance down at Hawk showed the man unmoving, eyes wide and unseeing, and his mouth open for words that would never be said.

"Freddy," he whispered, her name a balm for his soul. He fisted his right hand in her hair and brought her face to his to cover her mouth. He couldn't get her close enough, kiss her deep enough, hold her tight enough, and he wouldn't have pulled away, but she did.

"You're bleeding," she said, yanking his cravat off his neck and tying it around his shoulder. In the distance, Blythe and Huntley joined Carrington, and they started toward Gabe and Freddy.

He had so much he wanted to say to her. He cupped her face. "Freddy, I love you. I'm so damned in love with you."

"Good," she said, crying and laughing. He kissed away the tears trailing down her cheeks. "I'm bloody well good and in love with you, too." She kissed him again, then pulled back once more. "You watched my house. Why?"

He frowned. "How do you know—"

"Hawk. He had Brooke watching you, and Brooke reported it to him. Why did you do it?"

"I was afraid to give you my heart, Freddy, but damned if you didn't take it the very night I met you."

Much later that night, the door to Freddy's bedchamber creaked open. She rolled over in her bed to look, and her breath caught as Gabriel's profile appeared in the moonlight. He was shirtless and a bandage covered his left shoulder, which he'd assured her would be fine. He'd sent her home with Blythe from the scene in front of the Voltaire Club, and she had not argued, though she'd wanted to. In truth, she'd been shaken—she still was—but she had glimpsed in his eyes an urgent need to ensure she was safe, and she found she didn't mind that one bit.

He came to her silently, his boots thudding against the hardwood as he kicked them off, and then the bed dipped with his weight. His heat immediately enveloped her as the long length of his hard, solid body pressed against her. His hand came to her stomach, his fingers splaying there, as he rested his head on her pillow. He smelled of gunpowder and whiskey.

"How do you feel?" He'd asked her a dozen times right after the shooting, but she didn't mind that he wanted to ask her again. In fact, the concern and love in his voice filled her with a happy warmth.

"Tired, but good." She rested her hand on top of his on her stomach. "How is your shoulder?"

"Sore, but I'll live. I've endured worse."

"I want to hear all about what you've endured."

"All right, but first, did you eat when you arrived home as I suggested?" His concern made her smile at him in the dark.

"I ate a huge meal. I shall become very large."

"Good." He pressed a gentle kiss to her shoulder. "You're eating for two."

That truth still took her by surprise. "I'm sorry my plan ended as it did and that you had to break the vow you made to Georgette."

He removed his hand from her belly and said, "Look at me."

She turned over and met his gaze, just visible in the moonlight. "Listen, Freddy, there are some things I need to tell you."

She was sure it had to be about Georgette. She didn't want him to feel bad or as if he could no longer love

Georgette. "It's all right for you to still love her," she said. "I think there's room in your heart for the both of us."

"Good God, Freddy, you're a much better person than I am. I don't want you to love anyone but me *ever*." He brushed his lips to hers. "I did love Georgette, but not as you think. I understand why you thought it, and had I really considered what it might do to you, I would have set you straight sooner. I wed Georgette because she needed me to."

"What?" Freddy pressed up to look at him. "But Blythe said—"

"Blythe didn't know," he interrupted. "Georgette thought she might be in love with Hawk. She gave herself to him, and then shortly after, she saw him kill someone. She knew then, she couldn't be with him, and she told him so, and when she did, he forced himself on her, and got her with child. I didn't even know she thought she was in love with him until she lay dying. Nor did I know she'd given herself freely to him the first time until she confessed it in my arms as she was dying, but it would not have changed what I did for her.

She needed a protector, and she didn't want her baby to be a bastard, and she was my best friend, other than Hawk—who suddenly was no friend. She asked me to wed her, and to pretend we were in love. She was shaken and ashamed, and at the time, I couldn't imagine a future for me where it would matter, where someone like you might come into my life and I'd want to wed for love. So I married her, and Hawk twisted it in his mind. He convinced himself I stole Georgette from him, when in truth, he destroyed any possibility for them himself."

"But when you told me your honor was your downfall, you said I was nothing like Georgette."

"And you aren't." He hugged her tightly with his one

uninjured arm. "She came from the rookery but was soft. Fragile. You come from a pampered life but somehow are strong and resilient."

Freddy grinned into the darkness. "Yes, I'm quite different."

"You are perfectly different." He leaned in and gave her a kiss that made her want to rip off his clothes. "I was afraid to feel again, but you made me feel despite myself. I want to soak up everything you inspire in me and be damned the fear."

"What do I inspire?" she asked, her breath hitched for a confession she had hardly dared to dream of from this man she loved with all her heart.

"Humor." He kissed her cheeks. "Fulfillment." He rose up on his good arm and kissed her lips, then leaned over her belly and kissed it, too. "Deep love that feels like I could drown in it."

"You won't drown, Gabriel. We'll float together through calm waters and storms."

He straightened up and kissed her heart. "My Freddy. The wee lass that I love."

She smiled at that. She hoped to hear the part of himself he'd buried so long ago come out much more often now that he felt he could allow love once more. She placed a hand over his heart. "I've got your heart, you devil of a Scot, and I'm never letting it go."

"You better not," he whispered, and lying back, he brought her into crook of his arm where she settled with a smile, feeling more accepted, more cherished, and more at peace with who she was than ever before.

Thank you so very much for reading! I hope you enjoyed Freddy and Gabe's story!

Are you a fan of Scottish romances set in the medieval period? If so, I think you will love my *Highlander Vows: Entangled Hearts* series. You can read a bit about book 1 below.

Not even her careful preparations could prepare her for the barbarian who rescues her. Don't miss the USA Today bestselling *Highlander Vows: Entangled Hearts* series, starting with the critically acclaimed When a Laird Loves a Lady. Faking her death would be simple, it was escaping her home that would be difficult.

CLICK HERE TO READ WHEN A LAIRD LOVES A LADY, NOW >

I appreciate your help in spreading the word about my books, including letting your friends know. Reviews help other readers find my books. Please leave one on your favorite site!

Keep In Touch

Get Julie Johnstone's Newsletter
https://juliejohnstoneauthor.com

Join her Reading Group
facebook.com/groups/1500294650186536

Like her Facebook Page
facebook.com/authorjuliejohnstone

Stalk her Instagram
instagram.com/authorjuliejohnstone

Hang out with her on Goodreads
goodreads.com/author/show/2354638.Julie_Johnstone

Hear about her sales via Bookbub
bookbub.com/authors/julie-johnstone

Follow her Amazon Page
amazon.com/Julie-Johnstone/e/B0062AW98S

Excerpt of When a Laird Loves a Lady

One

England, 1357

Faking her death would be simple. It was escaping her home that would be difficult. Marion de Lacy stared hard into the slowly darkening sky, thinking about the plan she intended to put into action tomorrow—if all went well—but growing uneasiness tightened her belly. From where she stood in the bailey, she counted the guards up in the tower. It was not her imagination: Father had tripled the knights keeping guard at all times, as if he was expecting trouble.

Taking a deep breath of the damp air, she pulled her mother's cloak tighter around her to ward off the twilight chill. A lump lodged in her throat as the wool scratched her neck. In the many years since her mother had been gone, Marion had both hated and loved this cloak for the death and life it represented. Her mother's freesia scent had long since faded from the garment, yet simply calling up a memory of her mother wearing it gave Marion comfort.

She rubbed her fingers against the rough material. When she fled, she couldn't chance taking anything with her but the clothes on her body and this cloak. Her death had to appear accidental, and the cloak that everyone knew she prized would ensure her freedom. Finding it tangled in the branches at the edge of the sea cliff ought to be just the

thing to convince her father and William Froste that she'd
drowned. After all, neither man thought she could swim.
They didn't truly care about her anyway. Her marriage to
the blackhearted knight was only about what her hand
could give the two men. Her father, Baron de Lacy, wanted
more power, and Froste wanted her family's prized land. A
match made in Heaven, if only the match didn't involve
her...but it did.

Father would set the hounds of Hell themselves to track
her down if he had the slightest suspicion that she was still
alive. She was an inestimable possession to be given to
secure Froste's unwavering allegiance and, therefore, that of
the renowned ferocious knights who served him. Whatever
small sliver of hope she had that her father would grant her
mercy and not marry her to Froste had been destroyed by
the lashing she'd received when she'd pleaded for him to do
so.

The moon crested above the watchtower, reminding
her why she was out here so close to mealtime: to meet
Angus. The Scotsman may have been her father's stable
master, but he was *her* ally, and when he'd proposed she flee
England for Scotland, she'd readily consented.

Marion looked to the west, the direction from which
Angus would return from Newcastle. He should be back
any minute now from meeting his cousin and clansman
Neil, who was to escort her to Scotland. She prayed all was
set and that Angus's kin was ready to depart. With her
wedding to Froste to take place in six days, she wanted to be
far away before there was even the slightest chance he'd be
making his way here. And since he was set to arrive the
night before the wedding, leaving tomorrow promised
she'd not encounter him.

A sense of urgency enveloped her, and Marion forced

herself to stroll across the bailey toward the gatehouse that
led to the tunnel preceding the drawbridge. She couldn't
risk raising suspicion from the tower guards. At the
gatehouse, she nodded to Albert, one of the knights who
operated the drawbridge mechanism. He was young and
rarely questioned her excursions to pick flowers or find
herbs.

"Off to get some medicine?" he inquired.

"Yes," she lied with a smile and a little pang of guilt. But
this was survival, she reminded herself as she entered the
tunnel. When she exited the heavy wooden door that led to
freedom, she wasn't surprised to find Peter and Andrew not
yet up in the twin towers that flanked the entrance to the
drawbridge. It was, after all, time for the changing of the
guard.

They smiled at her as they put on their helmets and
demi-gauntlets. They were an imposing presence to any
who crossed the drawbridge and dared to approach the
castle gate. Both men were tall and looked particularly
daunting in their full armor, which Father insisted upon at
all times. The men were certainly a fortress in their own
right.

She nodded to them. "I'll not be long. I want to gather
some more flowers for the supper table." Her voice didn't
even wobble with the lie.

Peter grinned at her, his kind brown eyes crinkling at
the edges. "Will you pick me one of those pale winter
flowers for my wife again, Marion?"

She returned his smile. "It took away her anger as I said
it would, didn't it?"

"It did," he replied. "You always know just how to help
with her."

"I'll get a pink one if I can find it. The colors are becoming scarcer as the weather cools."

Andrew, the younger of the two knights, smiled, displaying a set of straight teeth. He held up his covered arm. "My cut is almost healed."

Marion nodded. "I told you! Now maybe you'll listen to me sooner next time you're wounded in training."

He gave a soft laugh. "I will. Should I put more of your paste on tonight?"

"Yes, keep using it. I'll have to gather some more yarrow, if I can find any, and mix up another batch of the medicine for you." And she'd have to do it before she escaped. "I better get going if I'm going to find those things." She knew she should not have agreed to search for the flowers and offered to find the yarrow when she still had to speak to Angus and return to the castle in time for supper, but both men had been kind to her when many had not. It was her way of thanking them.

After Peter lowered the bridge and opened the door, she departed the castle grounds, considering her plan once more. Had she forgotten anything? She didn't think so. She was simply going to walk straight out of her father's castle and never come back. Tomorrow, she'd announce she was going out to collect more winter blooms, and then, instead, she would go down to the edge of the cliff overlooking the sea. She would slip off her cloak and leave it for a search party to find. Her breath caught deep in her chest at the simple yet dangerous plot. The last detail to see to was Angus.

She stared down the long dirt path that led to the sea and stilled, listening for hoofbeats. A slight vibration of the ground tingled her feet, and her heart sped in hopeful anticipation that it was Angus coming down the dirt road on his horse. When the crafty stable master appeared with a grin spread across his face, the worry that was squeezing her heart loosened. For the first time since he had ridden out that morning, she took a proper breath. He stopped his stallion alongside her and dismounted.

She tilted her head back to look up at him as he towered over her. An errant thought struck. "Angus, are all Scots as tall as you?"

"Nay, but ye ken Scots are bigger than all the wee Englishmen." Suppressed laughter filled his deep voice. "So even the ones nae as tall as me are giants compared te the scrawny men here."

"You're teasing me," she replied, even as she arched her eyebrows in uncertainty.

"A wee bit," he agreed and tousled her hair. The laughter vanished from his eyes as he rubbed a hand over his square jaw and then stared down his bumpy nose at her, fixing what he called his "lecturing look" on her. "We've nae much time. Neil is in Newcastle just as he's supposed te be, but there's been a slight change."

She frowned. "For the last month, every time I wanted to simply make haste and flee, you refused my suggestion, and now you say there's a slight change?"

His ruddy complexion darkened. She'd pricked that MacLeod temper her mother had always said Angus's clan was known for throughout the Isle of Skye, where they lived in the farthest reaches of Scotland. Marion could remember her mother chuckling and teasing Angus about how no one knew the MacLeod temperament better than their neighboring clan, the MacDonalds of Sleat, to which her mother had been born. The two clans had a history of feuding.

Angus cleared his throat and recaptured Marion's attention. Without warning, his hand closed over her shoulder, and he squeezed gently. "I'm sorry te say it so plain, but ye must die at once."

Her eyes widened as dread settled in the pit of her stomach. "What? Why?" The sudden fear she felt was unreasonable. She knew he didn't mean she was really going to die, but her palms were sweating and her lungs had tightened all the same. She sucked in air and wiped her damp hands down the length of her cotton skirts. Suddenly, the idea of going to a foreign land and living with her mother's clan, people she'd never met, made her apprehensive.

She didn't even know if the MacDonalds—her uncle, in particular, who was now the laird—would accept her or not. She was half-English, after all, and Angus had told her that when a Scot considered her English bloodline and the fact that she'd been raised there, they would most likely brand her fully English, which was not a good thing in a Scottish mind. And if her uncle was anything like her grandfather had been, the man was not going to be very reasonable. But she didn't have any other family to turn to who would dare defy her father, and Angus hadn't offered for her to go to his clan, so she'd not asked. He likely didn't want to bring trouble to his clan's doorstep, and she didn't blame him.

Panic bubbled inside her. She needed more time, even if it was only the day she'd thought she had, to gather her courage.

"Why must I flee tonight? I was to teach Eustice how to dress a wound. She might serve as a maid, but then she will be able to help the knights when I'm gone. And her little brother, Bernard, needs a few more lessons before he's mastered writing his name and reading. And Eustice's youngest sister has begged me to speak to Father about allowing her to visit her mother next week."

"Ye kinnae watch out for everyone here anymore, Marion."

She placed her hand over his on her shoulder. "Neither can you."

Their gazes locked in understanding and disagreement.

He slipped his hand from her shoulder, and then crossed his arms over his chest in a gesture that screamed stubborn, unyielding protector. "If I leave at the same time ye feign yer death," he said, changing the subject, "it could stir yer father's suspicion and make him ask questions when none need te be asked. I'll be going home te Scotland soon after ye." Angus reached into a satchel attached to his horse and pulled out a dagger, which he slipped to her. "I had this made for ye."

Marion took the weapon and turned it over, her heart pounding. "It's beautiful." She held it by its black handle while withdrawing it from the sheath and examining it. "It's much sharper than the one I have."

"Aye," he said grimly. "It is. Dunnae forget that just because I taught ye te wield a dagger does nae mean ye can defend yerself from *all* harm. Listen te my cousin and do as he says. Follow his lead."

She gave a tight nod. "I will. But why must I leave now and not tomorrow?"

Concern filled Angus's eyes. "Because I ran into Froste's brother in town and he told me that Froste sent word that he would be arriving in two days."

Marion gasped. "That's earlier than expected."

"Aye," Angus said and took her arm with gentle authority. "So ye must go now. I'd rather be trying te trick only yer father than yer father, Froste, and his savage knights. I want ye long gone and yer death accepted when Froste arrives."

She shivered as her mind began to race with all that could go wrong.

"I see the worry darkening yer green eyes," Angus said, interrupting her thoughts. He whipped off his hat and his hair, still shockingly red in spite of his years, fell down around his shoulders. He only ever wore it that way when he was riding. He said the wind in his hair reminded him of riding his own horse when he was in Scotland. "I was going to talk to ye tonight, but now that I kinnae..." He shifted from foot to foot, as if uncomfortable. "I want te offer ye something. I'd have proposed it sooner, but I did nae want ye te feel ye had te take my offer so as nae te hurt me, but I kinnae hold my tongue, even so."

She furrowed her brow. "What is it?"

"I'd be proud if ye wanted te stay with the MacLeod clan instead of going te the MacDonalds. Then ye'd nae have te leave everyone ye ken behind. Ye'd have me."

A surge of relief filled her. She threw her arms around Angus, and he returned her hug quick and hard before setting her away. Her eyes misted at once. "I had hoped you would ask me," she admitted.

For a moment, he looked astonished, but then he spoke. "Yer mother risked her life te come into MacLeod territory at a time when we were fighting terrible with the MacDonalds, as ye well ken."

Marion nodded. She knew the story of how Angus had ended up here. He'd told her many times. Her mother had been somewhat of a renowned healer from a young age, and when Angus's wife had a hard birthing, her mother had gone to help. The knowledge that his wife and child had died anyway still made Marion want to cry.

"I pledged my life te keep yer mother safe for the kindness she'd done me, which brought me here, but, lass, long ago ye became like a daughter te me, and I pledge the rest of my miserable life te defending ye."

She gripped Angus's hand. "I wish you were my father."

He gave her a proud yet smug look, one she was used to seeing. She chortled to herself. The man did have a terrible streak of pride. She'd have to give Father John another coin for penance for Angus, since the Scot refused to take up the custom himself.

Angus hooked his thumb in his gray tunic. "Ye'll make a fine MacLeod because ye already ken we're the best clan in Scotland."

Mentally, she added another coin to her dues. "Do you think they'll let me become a MacLeod, though, since my mother was the daughter of the previous MacDonald laird and I've an English father?"

"They will," he answered without hesitation, but she heard the slight catch in his voice.

"Angus." She narrowed her eyes. "You said you would never lie to me."

His brows dipped together, and he gave her a long, disgruntled look. "They may be a bit wary," he finally admitted. "But I'll nae let them turn ye away. Dunnae worry," he finished, his Scottish brogue becoming thick with emotion.

She bit her lip. "Yes, but you won't be with me when I first get there. What should I do to make certain that they will let me stay?"

He quirked his mouth as he considered her question. "Ye must first get the laird te like ye. Tell Neil te take ye directly te the MacLeod te get his consent for ye te live there. I kinnae vouch for the man myself as I've never met him, but Neil says he's verra honorable, fierce in battle, patient, and reasonable." Angus cocked his head as if in thought. "Now that I think about it, I'm sure the MacLeod can get ye a husband, and then the clan will more readily accept ye. Aye." He nodded. "Get in the laird's good graces as soon as ye meet him and ask him te find ye a husband." A scowl twisted his lips. "Preferably one who will accept yer acting like a man sometimes."

She frowned at him. "*You* are the one who taught me how to ride bareback, wield a dagger, and shoot an arrow true."

"Aye." He nodded. "I did. But when I started teaching ye, I thought yer mama would be around te add her woman's touch. I did nae ken at the time that she'd pass when ye'd only seen eight summers in yer life."

"You're lying again," Marion said. "You continued those lessons long after Mama's death. You weren't a bit worried how I'd turn out."

"I sure was!" he objected, even as a guilty look crossed his face. "But what could I do? Ye insisted on hunting for the widows so they'd have food in the winter, and ye insisted on going out in the dark te help injured knights when I could nae go with ye. I had te teach ye te hunt and defend yerself. Plus, you were a sad, lonely thing, and I could nae verra well overlook ye when ye came te the stables and asked me te teach ye things."

"Oh, you could have," she replied. "Father overlooked me all the time, but your heart is too big to treat someone like that." She patted him on the chest. "I think you taught me the best things in the world, and it seems to me any man would want his woman to be able to defend herself."

"Shows how much ye ken about men," Angus muttered with a shake of his head. "Men like te think a woman needs *them*."

"I dunnae need a man," she said in her best Scottish accent.

He threw up his hands. "Ye do. Ye're just afeared."

The fear was true enough. Part of her longed for love, to feel as if she belonged to a family. For so long she'd wanted those things from her father, but she had never gotten them, no matter what she did. It was difficult to believe it would be any different in the future. She'd rather not be disappointed.

Angus tilted his head, looking at her uncertainly. "Ye want a wee bairn some day, dunnae ye?"

"Well, yes," she admitted and peered down at the ground, feeling foolish.

"Then ye need a man," he crowed.

She drew her gaze up to his. "Not just any man. I want a man who will truly love me."

He waved a hand dismissively. Marriages of convenience were a part of life, she knew, but she would not marry unless she was in love and her potential husband loved her in return. She would support herself if she needed to.

"The other big problem with a husband for ye," he continued, purposely avoiding, she suspected, her mention of the word *love*, "as I see it, is yer tender heart."

"What's wrong with a tender heart?" She raised her brow in question.

"'Tis more likely te get broken, aye?" His response was matter-of-fact.

"Nay. 'Tis more likely to have compassion," she replied with a grin.

"We're both right," he announced. "Yer mama had a tender heart like ye. 'Tis why yer father's black heart hurt her so. I dunnae care te watch the light dim in ye as it did yer mother."

"I don't wish for that fate, either," she replied, trying hard not to think about how sad and distant her mother had often seemed. "Which is why I will only marry for love. And why I need to get out of England."

"I ken that, lass, truly I do, but ye kinnae go through life alone."

"I don't wish to," she defended. "But if I have to, I have you, so I'll not be alone." With a shudder, her heart denied the possibility that she may never find love, but she squared her shoulders.

"'Tis nae the same as a husband," he said. "I'm old. Ye need a younger man who has the power te defend ye. And if Sir Frosty Pants ever comes after ye, you're going te need a strong man te go against him."

Marion snorted to cover the worry that was creeping in.

Angus moved his mouth to speak, but his reply was drowned by the sound of the supper horn blowing. "God's bones!" Angus muttered when the sound died. "I've flapped my jaw too long. Ye must go now. I'll head te the stables and start the fire as we intended. It'll draw Andrew and Peter away if they are watching ye too closely."

Marion looked over her shoulder at the knights, her stomach turning. She had known the plan since the day they had formed it, but now the reality of it scared her into a cold sweat. She turned back to Angus and gripped her dagger hard. "I'm afraid."

Determination filled his expression, as if his will for her to stay out of harm would make it so. "Ye will stay safe," he commanded. "Make yer way through the path in the woods that I showed ye, straight te Newcastle. I left ye a bag of coins under the first tree ye come te, the one with the rope tied te it. Neil will be waiting for ye by Pilgrim Gate on Pilgrim Street. The two of ye will depart from there."

She worried her lip but nodded all the same.

"Neil has become friends with a friar who can get the two of ye out," Angus went on. "Dunnae talk te anyone, especially any men. Ye should go unnoticed, as ye've never been there and won't likely see anyone ye've ever come in contact with here."

Fear tightened her lungs, but she swallowed. "I didn't even bid anyone farewell." Not that she really could have, nor did she think anyone would miss her other than Angus, and she would be seeing him again. Peter and Andrew *had* been kind to her, but they were her father's men, and she knew it well. She had been taken to the dungeon by the knights several times for punishment for transgressions that ranged from her tone not pleasing her father to his thinking she gave him a disrespectful look. Other times, they'd carried out the duty of tying her to the post for a thrashing when she'd angered her father. They had begged her forgiveness profusely but done their duties all the same. They would likely be somewhat glad they did not have to contend with such things anymore.

Eustice was both kind *and* thankful for Marion teaching her brother how to read, but Eustice lost all color any time someone mentioned the maid going with Marion to Froste's home after Marion was married. She suspected the woman was afraid to go to the home of the infamous "Merciless Knight." Eustice would likely be relieved when Marion disappeared. Not that Marion blamed her.

A small lump lodged in her throat. Would her father even mourn her loss? It wasn't likely, and her stomach knotted at the thought.

"You'll come as soon as you can?" she asked Angus.

"Aye. Dunnae fash yerself."

She forced a smile. "You are already sounding like

you're back in Scotland. Don't forget to curb that when speaking with Father."

"I'll remember. Now, make haste te the cliff te leave yer cloak, then head straight for Newcastle."

"I don't want to leave you," she said, ashamed at the sudden rise of cowardliness in her chest and at the way her eyes stung with unshed tears.

"Gather yer courage, lass. I'll be seeing ye soon, and Neil will keep ye safe."

She sniffed. "I'll do the same for Neil."

"I've nay doubt ye'll try," Angus said, sounding proud and wary at the same time.

"I'm not afraid for myself," she told him in a shaky voice. "You're taking a great risk for me. How will I ever make it up to you?"

"Ye already have," Angus said hastily, glancing around and directing a worried look toward the drawbridge. "Ye want te live with my clan, which means I can go te my dying day treating ye as my daughter. Now, dunnae cry when I walk away. I ken how sorely ye'll miss me," he boasted with a wink. "I'll miss ye just as much."

With that, he swung up onto his mount. He had just given the signal for his beast to go when Marion realized she didn't know what Neil looked like.

"Angus!"

He pulled back on the reins and turned toward her. "Aye?"

"I need Neil's description."

Angus's eyes widened. "I'm getting old," he grumbled. "I dunnae believe I forgot such a detail. He's got hair redder than mine, and wears it tied back always. Oh, and he's missing his right ear, thanks te Froste. Took it when Neil came through these parts te see me last year."

"What?" She gaped at him. "You never told me that!"

"I did nae because I knew ye would try te go after Neil and patch him up, and that surely would have cost ye another beating if ye were caught." His gaze bore into her. "Ye're verra courageous. I reckon I had a hand in that 'cause I knew ye needed te be strong te withstand yer father. But dunnae be mindless. Courageous men and women who are mindless get killed. Ye ken?"

She nodded.

"Tread carefully," he warned.

"You too." She said the words to his back, for he was already turned and headed toward the drawbridge.

She made her way slowly to the edge of the steep embankment as tears filled her eyes. She wasn't upset because she was leaving her father—she'd certainly need to say a prayer of forgiveness for that sin tonight—but she couldn't shake the feeling that she'd never see Angus again. It was silly; everything would go as they had planned. Before she could fret further, the blast of the fire horn jerked her into motion. There was no time for any thoughts but those of escape.

About the Author

Julie Johnstone is a *USA Today* and #1 Amazon bestselling author. Scottish historical romance, Regency historical romance, and historical time travel romance featuring highlanders, aristocrats, and modern-day bad billionaire bad boys are her love, and she enjoys creating both with a hefty dose of twists, plenty of heartstring tugs, and a guaranteed happily ever after.

Her books have been dubbed "fabulously entertaining and engaging," making readers cry, laugh, and swoon. Johnstone lives in Alabama with her very own lowlander husband, her two children – the heir and the spare, her snobby cat, and her perpetually happy dog. In her spare time she enjoys way too much coffee balanced by hot yoga, reading, and traveling.

Made in the USA
Monee, IL
18 June 2021

71685296R00148